SILENT THREAT

OTHER TITLES BY DANA MARTON

Personal Recovery

Forced Disappearance
Flash Fire
Girl in the Water

Broslin Creek

Deathwatch
Deathscape
Deathtrap
Deathblow
Broslin Bride
Deathwish

Agents Under Fire

Guardian Agent
Avenging Agent
Warrior Agent

Mission Redemption

Secret Contract
Ironclad Cover
My Bodyguard
Intimate Details

Hardstorm Saga

Reluctant Concubine
Accidental Sorceress

Other Titles

Shadow Soldier
Secret Soldier
The Sheik's Safety
Camouflage Heart
Rogue Soldier
Protective Measures
Bridal Op
Undercover Sheik
Sheik Seduction
72 Hours
Sheik Protector
Talk, Dark and Lethal
Desert Ice Daddy
Saved by the Monarch
Royal Protocol
The Socialite and the Bodyguard
Stranded with the Prince
Royal Captive
The Spy Who Saved Christmas
The Black Sheep Sheik
Last Spy Standing
Spy Hard
The Spy Wore Spurs
Most Eligible Spy
My Spy
Spy in the Saddle

SILENT THREAT

DANA MARTON

Montlake
Romance

Text copyright © 2018 by Dana Marton

Published by Montlake Romance, Seattle

www.apub.com

Amazon, the Amazon logo, and Montlake Romance are trademarks of Amazon.com, Inc., or its affiliates.

ISBN-13: 9781542047982
ISBN-10: 1542047986

Cover design by Letitia Hasser

Printed in the United States of America

*I'd like to dedicate this book to the deaf community,
and my heroes among them.*

Chapter One

Sunday

AN HOUR BEFORE HIS DEATH, MITCH MORITZ WAS IN AS GOOD A MOOD AS HE'D ever been. He couldn't wait to get home. The rehab center in Broslin, Pennsylvania, had been great, everything a recovering army vet needed, but he missed his wife and kids too much.

The weeks spent in rehab were worth it, sure. He'd come in a mess—nightmares, rage, depression, anxiety—and left feeling like a man again. Still, this was definitely the best part: zipping up his suitcase and leaving.

He picked up the remote to turn off the TV, then paused to let the bald little man on the screen finish his spiel. The weatherman was hopping and beaming, trying to sound superhyped about news that was anything but sensational.

"A tropical depression in the western Caribbean was just updated to Tropical Storm Rupert. We're going to keep a close eye on that for you folks. You know how these things go. Anything could happen."

Mitch flicked off the TV before the guy could spin a barely there storm into the meteorological end of the world.

He gazed around the room one last time, then pulled his suitcase out into the hallway.

"Hey, good luck!" The greeting came as he turned the corner.

"Thanks."

The man walking toward him carried two cups of coffee and a pastry bag. He gave a rueful smile. "Can never resist loading up at the cafeteria." He held out one of the cups to Mitch. "Here. Take it. I shouldn't drink this much coffee anyway."

"You sure?" Mitch had a long drive ahead of him, down I-95, all the way to Florida. He hated flying. The two-day drive didn't bother him. The weather was supposed to be clear all the way. He'd still be home for his daughter's second birthday. "If you really don't want it, I'd be happy to have it."

"How about a couple of carrot muffins?" the man asked.

"My carrot-muffin days are over." Mitch grinned. He couldn't wait to be back on his wife's cooking.

Thirty minutes later, he was on the six-lane highway, crossing into Maryland as he finished the last of his coffee. The brew tasted off, but he'd drunk it anyway, even if he wasn't a fan of artificial sweeteners.

His eyes blurred. He blinked. His vision cleared.

Fifteen minutes later, a flashback slammed into him. In the car one second, inside a burning tank the next. The hallucination came in full color, complete with the smell and pain of burning flesh.

Mitch scrambled to escape, but before he could even unlatch the hatch, the tank exploded.

Then, nothing.

Then, a couple of seconds until Mitch realized he hadn't been in an exploding tank. He'd hit a tractor trailer head-on, on the highway. His bones were broken. His entire body was wet. *Blood*. People were yelling around him, but he couldn't make sense of the words.

Five minutes later—long before the ambulance reached him—Mitch Moritz was dead.

Monday

Do not confront your stalker.

That sounded like a smart rule, the kind of advice the cops—or any sane person—would give.

Annie Murray pivoted on her heels in line inside the gas station and looked her stalker straight in the eyes.

"You can't keep doing this, Joey."

She didn't mean to sound harsh. She didn't think she did. But Joey Franco's eyes widened with hurt to the size of portholes through which she could see all the way to where his heart bled.

"Twenty-two fifty," said Mac from behind the counter. "Hey, Annie."

Robbie MacMillan and Joey were buddies, going way back, so Mac kept a studiously neutral expression, messing with the cash register and pretending he hadn't heard Annie call Joey on his shit.

Annie swiped her credit card. Her gaze flicked to the TV on the wall behind Mac and the weatherman waxing poetic about a tropical storm named Rupert gaining strength and slowly moving toward the Greater Antilles.

Her transaction was approved. She signed the receipt. "Could I have the key to the bathroom, please?"

She didn't look at Joey again as she walked out into the gray-skied September morning. He managed to bump into her nearly every day, always with those lost-puppy-dog eyes and that hurt expression. *Look what you've done to me.* And, of course, Annie specialized in lost puppies.

"Could we talk?" The question hooked into the back of her shirt as she was about to turn the corner.

She stopped at the mouth of the narrow alley. The ten-foot strip of concrete between the gas station and a windowless warehouse on the other side was a desiccated wasteland. *They should clean up this place and put a couple of potted plants back here,* she thought. And then: *Shouldn't have had that second cup of tea with breakfast.* If she didn't have to use the bathroom, she'd be out of there by now.

She *needed* to be out of there. She had a new patient today, a former Navy SEAL.

Behind her, Joey stepped closer, his boots scuffing on the concrete.

"Please stop following me," Annie said. "It's making me uncomfortable."

He had not been violent with her, but he *had* been violent with others—drunken brawls, mostly. Mostly started by his cousin, Big Jim, who could talk Joey into anything, but chose to talk him into only the immoral and illegal. Big guy, big talker, the oldest of the cousins, Big Jim always had the best stories and the worst ideas.

Actually, the whole family was pretty messy.

"I need to tell you something." Joey kept coming. "I'm your man. You know I am. Meant to be."

He was about five feet eleven inches, the beginnings of a beer belly giving him some girth, a country boy who wore Timberlands and Levi's with a plaid shirt and a red Phillies baseball hat. He was like a puppy who hadn't taken to training, then grown big and just wanted to do what he wanted.

"I can't be late for work," she said.

"You care more about your patients than you care about me."

She had no intention of justifying herself. Again.

"Listen, when I came back to Broslin last year, I was in love with the idea of coming home. A return to childhood and innocence and a safe place, you know? You were my best friend back in elementary school. So you kind of represented all that for me. But that's not enough for a romantic relationship."

Misery drew grooves around Joey's eyes, a whole set all at once, like drawing in sand with a garden rake. "Can I come over tonight?" He moved forward again, caught himself, stopped. "Just to talk."

"No. I'm sorry. Goodbye, Joey." Bathroom key in hand, Annie hurried into the alleyway.

When she finished in the bathroom and turned on the tap, she looked into the cracked mirror over the sink. "Joey is moving on. The new patient will commit to therapy and make amazing progress. I'm going to have a great day today."

She'd already said her affirmations while combing her hair this morning, but repetition wouldn't hurt.

She washed her hands, grabbed a paper towel, and kept it in hand as she reached for the doorknob.

OK, Joey, please don't be waiting.

He wasn't. But the man not two feet from the door, whirling around with a feral growl, was infinitely worse. Insanely huge. Wide shoulders. Corded muscles. Shaved head. Barbed-wire tattoos above his ears.

The man's skin was a shade or two darker than Annie's, his nearly black gaze hard and merciless. He wore army boots and fatigues with an olive T-shirt that covered neither the scars nor the ink on his massive arms and neck.

His half-raised hand promised death.

All that took Annie a split second to register as her heart broke into a panicked rush to punch its way out of her chest.

"Don't." She braced for impact, the paper towel dropping from her fingers.

She was stuck in the narrow doorway, the door half-closed behind her. She couldn't make any moves, her self-defense training useless. She had no room to maneuver.

But instead of letting the punch fly, the man stepped back, dropping his frying-pan-size hand. "You startled me."

His rusty voice gave the impression of a hermit who rarely left his mountain hideaway. The look he gave her was in that vein too—a hard look from a hard man unused to human interaction. Maybe not a hermit, no, nothing that harmless. *A bear.* A grizzly coming out of hibernation: slow for now, considering, a lethal predator awakening.

Oh, for heaven's sake. Get a grip.

He had some Pacific Islander heritage: wide jaw, flat nose. He was thirtyish. Not that much older than she. *Just a man, not a homicidal maniac.* This was Broslin, small-town Pennsylvania. They had maybe one murder a year, and this year's box had already been checked. Broslin was nothing like the seriously dodgy Philly neighborhoods Annie had lived in during the past decade.

She drew a steadying breath. As the mad banging in her chest quieted, her gaze dropped to the massive hand the man had lowered—the skin battered and bloody, his knuckles busted.

He must be in pain was her first thought, the second being that he might not mean to kill her, but he *had* killed someone. Recently. With his size, if he'd pummeled anyone hard enough to cause that much damage to his own hand, the other guy had to be dead. Broslin's murder rate had just doubled.

Where was the victim? Her gaze darted to the deserted alley behind him on reflex.

The sky hung low, a heavy dark-gray—a metal coffin lid, trapping the world. The giant billboards that lined the top of the warehouse next door blocked what little light there was, leaving the alley a dim space.

No bodies—dead or alive.

Never mind. The most important question was, could Annie jump back into the single-stall bathroom fast enough to close the door in the killer's face and lock herself in while she called the police?

As if the man could hear the panicked rush of blood in her veins, he took another step back. "Don't be scared." His tone dipped and grew another notch gruffer. "I'm leaving now. All right?"

He grunted with frustration and pulled his neck into his shoulders, hunching, hiding the bloody hand behind him, trying to appear less menacing. His downcast expression said he was used to people being afraid of him. He'd come to expect it.

Annie's first impression of him had been that of a man who could take a person apart without breaking a sweat—and not be particularly bothered by it either. But he *was* bothered that he'd scared her.

He half turned to walk away.

"Wait," she blurted.

Oh cripes. She hadn't meant to say that. But when his dark eyebrows twitched with surprise, she continued, "You should clean that hand."

She held the bathroom door open, the sink and paper towels behind her.

He didn't move toward her, but he didn't walk away either. He took her measure once again, more carefully this time, like a person who'd opened a box and found something other than what he'd expected.

She squirmed under his scrutiny. *Should have let him walk away.*

"Who did you fight with?" Again she had spoken without thinking. Thinking people didn't chat up violent men in abandoned alleys and invite them to incriminate themselves.

A shadow passed over his broad face. *Embarrassment? Unlikely.* He didn't seem like a guy who'd be easily embarrassed.

"I punched the bricks." He jerked his shaved head toward the wall. "Got frustrated."

"Ever tried meditation?" There she went with the blurting again.

Are you for real? his dark eyes asked. But he withdrew his damaged hand from behind his back, as if deciding that she could handle the sight after all. "I guess washing the blood off wouldn't hurt."

Oh God. Blood. Right. Now that she wasn't in imminent fear for her life, the whole blood thing hit Annie full on the chin and knocked her back.

Don't throw up. Don't pass out. She kept her eyes on his face.

She stood aside as he went into the bathroom. She didn't offer to help with cleaning his wounds. The sight of blood filled her with the acute need to run the other way.

She hurried over to her car and grabbed the first-aid kit from the trunk. Running away did feel great. But then she made herself return to the bathroom with the red plastic box.

He had washed off the blood already—thank God—and was now dabbing his busted knuckles with a paper towel. He showed no sign of pain, as if he were made out of the same bricks he had punched earlier.

She stepped closer. "Let me see that."

"It's no big deal." The way he pulled back said he was equally uncomfortable with their proximity.

She balanced the box on the edge of the sink and popped it open, then pulled out the minuscule brown bottle of hydrogen peroxide.

After a moment, the man held out his hand—twice the size of hers—knuckles up. She poured the peroxide, let it fizz, poured more. Then she picked up the first Band-Aid to begin covering up the worst of the damage.

For this, she had to touch him.

His chest was silent, as if he'd stopped breathing. Or maybe she couldn't hear him because the blood was once again roaring in her ears—a normal response to being in that small space with an enormous man. Who, a minute ago, had been *bleeding*.

Don't think about that.

She focused on how fast she could cover his injuries. "You know, there are less self-destructive ways to deal with frustration."

When he didn't so much as grunt in acknowledgment, she glanced up. *Too big. Too close.* Her throat constricted. Swallowing hurt.

The bathroom was tiny and airless. She needed air. But before she could scramble back out, he was past her and outside in a blur, without ever once touching her, which didn't seem possible.

"Thanks." That rough voice, a single word. Then he strode away, as fast as if he had a date with another brick wall and he was late.

She stared after him.

"Hey, what's your name?"

His broad shoulders didn't turn. He kept walking. Looked like he'd had enough of her.

Annie watched him for a few more seconds before she caught herself. She closed her first-aid kit, then picked up the paper towel she'd dropped earlier. As she tossed it into the overflowing garbage can, along with the little white Band-Aid tabs, her fingers trembled.

She shook the tension out of her hands, then tucked the kit under her arm and hurried off to return the bathroom key to Mac inside the gas station.

Joey was nowhere in sight. Yet, as Annie slid behind the wheel, an uncomfortable sensation washed over her, an odd prickling she'd been feeling a lot lately. Had Joey stuck around? Was he watching her from somewhere? Was he developing an unhealthy obsession that she was mistaking for temporary disappointment?

Not a good mistake to make.

She *would* have to talk to Joey again. And she would have to be firmer next time. She would have to tell him that if he didn't stop stalking her, she was going to get a restraining order.

First things first. She had to get to work and her new patient.

Annie Murray smiled into the morning. No matter what else was skidding off the rails in her life, her job was great. She loved every single aspect of it. She got to help people. She made a difference.

She pushed everything else out of her mind. Her day was full of possibilities, and she would make the best of them.

Annie looked into the rearview mirror and beamed. She infused her words with the power of belief. "I'm going to have a wonderful day."

Chapter Two

ON HER WAY TO WORK, ANNIE PASSED THE BUSTED-KNUCKLED STRANGER walking on the shoulder, going in her direction. Her foot moved from the gas pedal and hovered over the brake for a second before moving back to its original position.

There was helpful, and then there was reckless.

The man was in shape to walk, his stride determined, his long legs carrying him fast. She had no doubt that wherever he was going, he'd get there. Unlikely that anyone would give him any trouble.

After she passed him, she glanced into the rearview mirror. He was looking straight ahead, his face expressionless, his mind clearly a million miles away. She silently wished him luck and returned her attention to the road.

Leaves and other debris littered the blacktop. A nasty windstorm had blown through overnight. The ominous sky promised more violence, which did not bode well for her outdoor sessions today.

She could be in a rush for nothing.

Her cell phone rang in the cup holder. She glanced at the display. *Kelly*. Her cousin.

Annie tapped the Bluetooth, but not without a flash of reluctance. "Hey."

"Are you ready for your big day tomorrow? You didn't call this morning. We were supposed to have that last-second powwow."

Annie pulled into the parking lot at Hope Hill, an alternative-therapy rehab center. "Sorry. Meant to call after I stopped for gas. Got distracted."

She jumped out and headed across the parking lot toward the cluster of buildings.

Kelly—two years older, a real estate agent with dreams of world domination—was saying, "I can't wait to be in front of those cameras. The whole town will be watching. I've been telling everyone that we'll be on the morning show. Sylvia will be taping it for Gramps. Are you excited?"

Sylvia was their grandfather's housekeeper.

Kelly's enthusiasm was flooding through the phone, impossible to resist. Annie had to give her something. "I'm cautiously optimistic."

"Good. I'm wildly excited for the both of us. This is going to put me on the map. Broslin's top real estate investment consultant. Everybody wants to rehab and flip these days. Now, when someone local thinks about it, I'll be the first person they'll think of. And a complete home makeover is exactly what you need. Win-win."

Annie wasn't sure what she needed, but she was almost certain that having her house demolished on live TV wasn't it.

She walked through the rehab center's front door and headed to her small office. "I have to go. I'm at work. I'll call you tonight."

They said goodbye, and Annie clicked off her phone, then dropped it on her desk, feeling guilty because Kelly was genuinely excited while Annie was . . . partially still mired in the past. Not something she'd ever show, and yet, she would never be as comfortable with her cousin as her cousin was with her.

She turned on her laptop, went through today's schedule, and read the patient files. She gave special attention to her new patient, Cole Makani Hunter, former Navy SEAL.

Depression, PTSD, multiple surgeries, loss of hearing, loss of mobility in right arm. Added notes: POW, torture. Under family history, one thing jumped out: father—suicide.

She read the more detailed patient report, none of it pretty.

She nodded at the file on the screen. "OK. Let's do this."

Laptop turned off, she went off to meet the man. Their first appointment was set for nine o'clock at the trailhead. At least he was cleared for all physical activity.

She cut through the courtyard that belonged in an antique Chinese woodcut, the layout as well designed as the Frank Lloyd Wright–style buildings that surrounded it. A picturesque weeping willow dominated the space, accented with artistically placed rocks.

The handful of patients she passed greeted her. She wished them a good morning, but didn't stop to chat.

The morning clouds were clearing out—no storm after all. Good. The sun finally decided to bathe everything in warmth and golden light, the temperature rising. Would be nice if the weather stayed this way for another couple of weeks.

Past the courtyard, Annie cut through the exercise yard and its basketball court, then walked straight to the edge of the woods. Here, she stopped to wait, kicking off her Keds, letting the soft grass tickle her bare toes.

Since she had another minute or two, she closed her eyes and breathed in nature. She inhaled peace, filling herself with serenity.

Comfort smelled like the green leaves, underscored by the crisp tone of pines and the rich scent of earth. She drank in the sounds of the birds in the trees and the bugs in the fallen leaves—life's steady, unstoppable music at its purest.

She breathed and listened until she found her center, until her thoughts and emotions settled. She didn't want to bring any of her own baggage into therapy. Her patients deserved better.

She let the tension of the morning melt off her until her shoulders relaxed. She opened her eyes.

On the other side of the yard, men moved between the buildings, going to their appointments. A few of them waved at her. She waved back. She watched for an unfamiliar face without knowing what to look for in particular. The patient files didn't include photographs.

Her new patient's injuries were . . . *challenging*. The good news was, physical disability had no relation to mental recovery. That came from attitude, for the most part. Physical strength had little to do with the kind of therapy Annie practiced. The patient simply had to open up to what she was offering.

Across the exercise yard, a large, bulky shape separated from the others.

Oh. Annie's mouth slackened with recognition.

A heavy, dark gaze pinned her through the distance as if marking her for . . . *demolition*. Her brain kicked up the word.

Don't be stupid.

Yet that newly familiar shape barreled toward her, the ground shaking from the impact of his combat boots as he crossed the yard. His mood had clearly slipped several notches since she'd last seen him.

A tremor ran up Annie's spine, but she held her ground, and she held his hard gaze. He wasn't the first disgruntled bear she'd run into in the woods.

The man moved as if he meant to run her down, as if he was angry to find her here, as if she had somehow tricked him earlier at the gas station.

He pulled to an abrupt halt about two feet from her. Resentment radiated off him. This time he didn't back off, didn't give her space, didn't reassure her that he meant no harm.

You flinch, you lose. Annie didn't flinch. She couldn't allow him to knock her off center again.

Remain positive and cheerful.

"Cole?"

He gave a sharp nod.

"Hi again." She thought about also signing the greeting, since his file said he was deaf. But then, he hadn't needed signing at the gas station. "You're pretty good at reading lips."

He jabbed the piece of paper he'd been carrying toward her, her Band-Aids flashing on his knuckles. "How about you just initial the damn thing so I can get out of here?"

Don't let them see you scared. He might have spooked her back in the alley, but this was her turf. He was her patient, her responsibility.

Annie accepted the treatment log from him and tucked it into her back pocket. She flashed him her best professional smile to let him see she wasn't rattled. "Let's just follow Hope Hill protocol."

His dark gaze pinned her in place.

According to his paperwork, he'd been a sniper, and he looked at her like one, as if he was noticing every little detail about her. As if he was evaluating a target: noting distance to the last inch, and maybe the wind speed and direction, calculating how best to eliminate the *problem* he had to deal with.

His assessment required only seconds. "Shit Hill can shove their protocols up their—"

"I'm Annie Murray, your ecotherapist at Hope Hill. How are you this morning?" She held out her hand, drawing comfort and strength from the trees behind her. "Nice to meet you, Cole. I'm looking forward to working with you."

He didn't even look at her hand, let alone take it. Suddenly he was watching her as if she were something he thought about eating for breakfast and he was wondering if he should bother with a knife and fork or just grab the damn thing.

She ignored the urge to step back and instead rolled into her spiel. "We have a two-hour introductory session today. I'd like to walk the full five-mile track."

"Do the inmates ever get a choice?"

"I think the word you're looking for is *inpatient*. A wonderful program, isn't it? The intensive therapy you'll receive here will make a huge difference."

Disdain oozed from his pores.

"But back to your question." She smiled. "You do get a choice. All therapy is voluntary here. We will have our introductory session today, and then you can decide if nature therapy is something you'd like to add to your schedule."

He watched her.

"OK," she said. "That's an impressive don't-mess-with-me look."

"Smart people usually heed it."

The words *those who don't are dead* hung unsaid in the air between them.

She shook off her sudden sense of doom and said, "The sooner we start, the sooner you'll feel better." She poured all the cheer and optimism she had into her voice, even as her gaze dipped to his combat boots.

"Actually, let's start with this," she amended. "I know the boots are obviously sending a message." And so did the camo cargo pants and faded military T-shirt he wore. Street clothes were strongly encouraged at Hope Hill, both for the patients and the staff. Civilian readjustment was one of the program's goals.

"But for now," she continued, "I'm going to ignore that. Your reluctance for civilian wear should be discussed in your counseling session with your psychiatrist, Dr. Ambrose. I'm sure he'll bring it up, if he hasn't already. My objective for today is to explain ecotherapy and lay out a treatment plan for the month that you'll be spending at Hope Hill. If you choose to work with me, over the next weeks, we'll work that plan. Then, toward the end, we'll focus on continuation, providing you with a list of things you can do once you leave here."

He frowned so hard, she was pretty sure that if she squinted she'd see the wrinkles on his forehead spell out *no way in hell.*

She kept on smiling. "You don't have to wear boots." She wiggled her toes on the dirt path. "Barefoot feels pretty great."

He said nothing.

She smiled wider. "To start with, I'd like to introduce you to *earthing.* Easy peasy. We'll walk around barefoot in nature. It's a relaxing and healing practice. Our bodies absorb negative electrons—which are actually good for us—from the earth through the soles of our feet."

The birdsong fell silent for a moment, as if nature were asking, *Did she say* easy peasy *to a murderous-looking Navy SEAL?*

Yep, she did. And the look on his face said she'd be super smart not to say it again. But she'd gone too far now to go back, so she forged ahead.

"Also, walking around barefoot on an uneven surface massages the pressure points in your soles. I can tell you more about it, if you'd like, or you can ask Libby, our reflexologist."

His angry-bear grunt stopped her.

He stepped forward and then around her. "The sooner we start, the sooner we finish. How about we walk in silence?"

She reached after him to touch his elbow so he'd turn back to her. "Actually, this session requires removal of footwear."

He looked at her as if he'd seen smarter dandelions. "Military people protect their feet. A sliver can become an infection. Slow soldiers are dead soldiers."

"You're not in the military. You're at Hope Hill. We are not heading into combat. Take off your boots, please."

He set his feet apart and brought his hands to his hips. He let his gaze slide over her with deliberate slowness, not assessing this time, but going for a blatantly male vibe. He clearly couldn't believe he hadn't shut her up yet, and he was now switching to a different tactic.

"What else do you want me to take off?" His voice turned richer, smoother, suggestive. "Are we going to run through the woods naked?"

"No." If he thought he was going to rattle her with *that*, he had another think coming. "But if you'd like to do it privately, on your own time, it might be beneficial. You have twenty acres at your disposal. The property is posted, so there should be no trespassers."

He blinked. "Have you ever run naked through the woods?"

"Certainly." She allowed a moment to enjoy the way his eyes flared.

"Why?" His voice roughened, deepened, back to that just-awakened grizzly-bear tone.

"To be one with nature, without barriers. To feel the wind and the moonlight on my skin."

Several seconds passed before he responded. "You can't feel moonlight."

She smiled at him mysteriously. He'd come here with a set of expectations about how this session would go—with him firmly in charge. Anything that knocked him off that rail and made him think was good.

"Is this a progression kind of thing?" His energy grew more intense with every word. "Today no shoes, tomorrow no shirt." His gaze slid to her chest. "Then the next session, no pants, and we'll be running through the woods naked by Friday?"

"We are not going to run through the woods naked together at any time. What we have here is a therapist-patient relationship."

When his gaze dipped back to her chest, she added, "Which also means that you should stop checking me out, and you should probably stop flirting with me."

He frowned. "I don't flirt."

At least he didn't deny checking her out. She shoved her thumbs through the belt loops of her cargo shorts. "I'm pretty sure you talking about us getting naked together is flirting."

A lot of the guys Annie had sessions with flirted. She often went along with it as long as they didn't cross any lines. They were here because they were injured; some were missing limbs or had other disabilities. For these alpha-male warriors, the need to reassert their masculinity was pretty strong.

Annie didn't take it personally. She redirected their focus, exactly the way she was going to do right now.

She pointed at a verdant young pine on the side of the path. "Over millions of years, humans evolved in nature. For most of our human history, we lived in harmony with nature. We were made for nature, both our bodies and psyches." She looked at Cole. "What would happen if we dug this tree up right now, put it in a pot, and took it inside a house? How would it grow?"

The word she was looking for was *stunted*, or *sickly*, or any version of the concept. But Cole said nothing, unimpressed with her teaching skills.

"A lot of people are reluctant and wary of new experiences," she said. "Let's just do this."

His mouth tightened. "Cut the BS. Don't manipulate me by telling me not to be scared. I'm not going to jump when you tell me, just to prove I'm not scared."

Definitely not going to be an easy case.

Yet she would make the session work. She had to succeed with this patient and all the others. She needed to be upgraded to a full-time employee. She needed those paychecks for the small animal sanctuary she was running out of her home. She needed to fix her house. She was at the sink-or-swim point in her life, so she was going to swim like a salmon on steroids, and she wasn't going to let anyone block her way.

Cole towered over her, waiting for her to give up and tell him they were finished.

Annie held his dark, contemptuous gaze. If this was a staring contest, she wouldn't be the one to look away first.

Sure, he could be an obstacle to her goals, *if* she let him. But if he was a boulder, she would be water. She would run over him and around him. She would wear him down, until his resistance was nothing but a manageable little pebble that she could put in her pocket.

OK, she might have crossed from positive thinking straight to fantasyland there, but she didn't let that discourage her. She unhooked her thumbs from the belt loops and rocked back on her bare heels.

"Fine." She replaced her professional smile with an equally professional listen-to-me-buddy look. "Let's cut the bullshit, then, on both sides and save ourselves a lot of time. You are here for a reason. Pretending that you don't need any of this is poppycock. So how about you suck it up and do the work?"

The corner of his mouth looked like it was struggling to twitch, but she couldn't be sure, because the next second he bent to unlace his boots at last.

She felt as if she'd moved a mountain. *Better not get overconfident.*

She waited until he straightened, kicked off his boots, and looked at her once again. Then she said, "Ecotherapy is basically ecopsychology. We use nature to connect to our inner nature."

There. I'm the boss, and you're going to have to get with the program. "About seventy percent of people report improvement in their depression after a green walk. We start by paying attention to the energies that connect us to the land and all other living things—"

He turned and strode forward on the path in front of her, effectively shutting her down, like turning off the TV.

Fine. She could use a breather from his intensity. She needed a moment to process her first impressions of him. Like that massive wall inside him that she sensed hid scary things. Dead things. Things she wasn't sure she wanted to know about. Surface Cole was all she could handle this morning.

However, she did have to prove in this first session that she *could* handle the ill-tempered SEAL. So Annie hurried after him.

Inside the main building of the Hope Hill facilities, a man stood by the window. He stared absently at the trail where the big Hawaiian had disappeared minutes ago with Annie.

The man at the window had a plastic bag of pills in his pocket, and he worried them through his fingers, as if praying the rosary. He finally had enough pills to put even a large man to sleep. *Permanently.*

He had sent Mitch Moritz to his rest. He was ready to send another.

He didn't think of it as murder. They were all troubled souls here. He would simply give another one the rest that the man desperately needed anyway.

He liked taking care of people. He took care of his mother. He was a good son.

He kept fingering the pills. The thought of finally using them was giving him an erection.

That was where pretty little Annie Murray came in.

Annie with her carefully kept distance. That wasn't polite, now, was it? Soon she'd learn that trying to keep him at arm's length was a poor decision on her part.

Poor decisions had consequences. Women were to be protected. But only women who knew their place.

He would teach Annie.

He liked helping people.

He only wished that they were smart enough to understand that he was the good guy here.

Chapter Three

COLE MAKANI HUNTER WANTED NOTHING TO DO WITH THE WOODS, OR THE ecotherapist.

At least he got to choose if he wanted to look at her, had a way to turn her off.

Or maybe he didn't.

She skipped ahead of him and began walking backward.

She was tall, neither lean nor overweight, but full of soft curves. She wore khaki cargo shorts that reached her knees and a soft, flowing, short-sleeved, greenish cotton shirt. Her camo colors blended into the trees. She had plain, symmetrical features. Her reddish-brown hair—it looked like her natural color—cascaded to the middle of her back, uncurled, unironed, and frizzy from the humidity. No makeup. The cosmetic industry wasn't getting rich off her.

She wore an old-fashioned wind-up watch on her wrist. No electronics—so no cell phone. The instruction sheet had been clear that none of that would be allowed during ecotherapy sessions.

She smelled faintly of lavender. Cole knew the scent only because his mother grew lavender on her windowsills.

"Tell me about your tattoos." Annie wasn't shouting at him, which he appreciated. She made sure to talk only when he was looking at her. "What do they mean?"

He had a feeling that if he didn't respond, she'd just push harder. The woman was way too earnest, and she had an overabundance of enthusiasm for her subject.

He pointed at the flower on his arm. "The hibiscus is for Hawaii. My father was from Maui."

"Is that where you were born?"

"Never been to Hawaii. Born in Chicago. My mother's family's been in Chicago since it was a one-horse town."

"How did your parents meet?"

"My grandfather was in the navy. My mother's father. He served with my father, took him under his wing. My father had no family, so my grandfather invited him home now and then when on leave to make sure the kid got a home-cooked meal."

"How about your other tattoos?"

"The trident is for the SEALs."

"And the rest?"

More difficult to say, but Cole said it anyway. "The names are the friends who didn't come back. The barbed wire is one barb for every month of bloody torture."

The smile disappeared from her face. "When you were held captive."

He nodded.

"I'm sorry."

He appreciated the sentiment. He would have appreciated it more if being sorry kept her quiet. It didn't.

"How did you learn to read lips so well?" she asked next.

"Grandmother was a smoker. When she got cancer, they had to take out her larynx." She'd lived with Cole and her parents at the time, and when the artificial larynx hadn't worked for her, they all learned to read her lips. Cole, a kid, thought it a fun game. Then later, when he became a sniper, his ability to lip-read became an invaluable skill.

"Can you sign?" Annie both signed and asked the question.

He signed back. "I can, but ninety percent of everybody else can't, so what's the point?"

"ASL is the fourth-most-studied language in college now. And it'll grow your brain. Studies documented an eight- to thirteen-point rise in IQ in kids who study ASL."

He didn't respond. What was there to say? She had everything tied up in a nice, optimistic bow. They lived in different worlds.

A minute passed as they walked.

"So this is it?" He nodded toward the trees with his head. "The whole therapy is just walking through the woods?"

"This and other things," she said. "In one-on-one therapy, we'll do our green walks. Then, in group therapy, we'll clear new trails. We'll also be planting a fruit orchard. And we'll spend some time picking trash out of the creek. Ecotherapy is about healing both people and their environment."

"In other words, free labor." Cole didn't bother to keep the snark out of his voice.

"In the process of healing others, we heal ourselves."

He snagged that thought. There was something there. "Is that why you're a therapist? Trying to heal yourself while messing with others?" He scrutinized her. "What's wrong with you?"

He meant it as a gibe, because he was in a piss-poor mood this morning. And because she was pushing him into places he didn't want to go, so he needed to push back.

Her root beer–colored eyes widened, opening a window to a deep darkness that looked uncomfortably similar to his own cave of horrors. Pain flashed through her gaze. For a second, her serene expression turned . . . *stricken.*

Cole felt as if he'd opened the door to a room he wasn't prepared to enter. There was something deep and raw here, something that maybe scared him a little and scared her a lot. So he slammed the door shut and backed away. He didn't know her. He didn't want to know her.

"There's nothing wrong with me," she said at last. "And there's nothing wrong with you." She paused before asking, "Do you think there is something wrong with you?"

He shot her a warning look. "You can tell me about your trees, but stay out of my head."

He went back to studying her. She was less complicated on the outside than on the inside.

Her only jewelry was a leather string tied around her slim ankle, decorated with seven golden brown beads that matched her eyes. If she was going for the earth-mother look, she'd nailed it. *A born tree hugger.* Cole was surprised her T-shirt didn't say MAKE LOVE NOT WAR.

If she brought up the subject, he was willing to do his part. His right arm and his ears might have quit, but his dick still worked. Even, apparently, when the woman was delusional.

The nonsense she could say straight-faced . . . *Our bodies absorb negative electrons from the earth through the bottoms of our feet.* If she thought he was going to buy any of the smoke she was blowing up his ass, she was going to be tragically disappointed.

"I'm not here to mess with you," she said. "Nobody at Hope Hill is. We're here to help."

"You got a time machine?"

Because the path narrowed, she pushed branches carefully out of the way so they wouldn't break. "You're being uncooperative."

You haven't seen uncooperative *yet,* he thought. *I'm here, aren't I? I'd much rather be in my room, staring at the ceiling.* "And you're careless."

He kept going, past the narrowing out onto a wider trail again, following her as she walked backward, all the while expecting her to fall on her curvy ass.

"How am I careless?" She didn't as much as stumble. She could walk backward better than a crab, and she probably knew every inch of the trail.

"Being alone in the woods with me." Cole gave his voice a deliberately dark edge. "Don't you know all of us PTSD fucks are monsters? Barrels of gunpowder waiting for a spark. You never know what'll set one of us off."

"I'd appreciate it if you didn't curse."

He quirked an eyebrow. "It hurts the trees' ears?"

He wasn't a fan of the woods. *No more than twenty feet of visibility.* As an ex-sniper, he wanted wide-open places. The woods made him uncomfortable, and his senses had been tingling already, a strong feeling that they were being watched as they stood at the edge of the trees a few minutes ago. The odd sensation had been the only reason he'd agreed to go on her damn walk with her.

She held his gaze, her eyes clear and peaceful now, soothing like the surface of a hidden mountain lake.

Cole nearly stumbled over his own feet. Had he just thought that? *No way.*

The whole ecotherapy bullshit made him feel stupid and awkward. So he turned his demeanor menacing even as he knew he was being a jerk. "You shouldn't be out here with me alone. I could do anything to you."

She kept her gaze level. "Try it."

"I don't want to." Or did he?

Sex was becoming a distant memory. The first batch of drugs the doctors prescribed had messed with his body. He'd switched to different pills but . . . He'd never been into meaningless hookups to start with, and he couldn't imagine spending enough time with a woman now to get to know her. Not to mention, who would want to spend time with him when he was like this?

But, *hey*, he had her invitation.

Maybe he'd get lucky and get kicked out of ecotherapy, which was a colossal waste of his time—made-up mumbo-jumbo science no sane person could take seriously. So he reached for Annie, not entirely clear what he meant to do with her once he had her. He wanted to put hands on her, he supposed, to prove that he could.

Next thing he knew, he was looking up at the sky, lying at her feet.

He blinked. Then blinked again.

In what universe . . .

He was beginning to get used to not being able to recognize his life, but this took the cake.

He stayed down, staring at her bare calves for a second before raising his gaze to her face. "How did you do that?"

"A couple of things," she said with admirably restrained smugness, and counted them out on her fingers. "One: I grabbed your injured arm, then used twice as much force as I thought I'd need, deliberately overestimating you to be on the safe side. It almost wasn't enough."

Huh.

"Two: You think I'm a tree-hugging hippie, so you underestimated me. Probably figured your therapist isn't going to beat you up during a session. I think you were lulled into a false sense of safety."

He definitely had been. Not too smart.

"Three: You are drugged. Your reflexes aren't what they should be."

Which was exactly why he was doing all this, because the main shrink, Dr. Ambrose, had told him that if he participated in other therapies, he might be able to cut back on the drugs.

"Four: Back at the gas station, you took me by surprise. Here I was prepared and ready, expecting you to make that move.

"Last but not least"—more smug crept into her voice—"you're a gentleman. I think you didn't fully resist because you didn't want to hurt a woman."

Was that a self-satisfied smirk at the corner of her soft lips? He didn't mind the smug, but he had to do something about the smirk. "Yeah. Don't count on the gentleman thing."

He scissored his legs, pulled hers out from under her, and brought her to the ground. Then, on some stupid impulse, he rolled on top of her to immobilize her, like he would have with an enemy combatant.

She stared up at him, wide-eyed, her long hair spread over the carpet of autumn leaves. She was soft against all his hard places.

Swaying branches crowded his peripheral vision. He didn't mind them so much, suddenly. All his attention was focused on the woman under him.

Her eyes were lighter than he'd first thought, not the color of root beer but amber. They were too wide for her face, as if she wanted to gobble up all the light in the world.

"Maybe I could get into this one-with-nature business." But really, he only said the words to get under her skin.

She'd be the worst possible woman for him to get involved with, even beyond the fact that he was her patient and she was his therapist, beyond his secrets. If they met under different circumstances, somewhere far away, they still wouldn't make it a week. Her earth-power mumbo jumbo would either drive him to suicide or to strangle her.

"Not my type," she said, breathless from having the air knocked out of her.

"Yeah. Same here. Bad idea all over. Sanity," he said as he straddled her ankles like they were sit-up buddies, "ought to be at the top of the list of qualities everyone should be looking for in a partner. And, let's face it, neither of us has it."

She came up on her elbows. "You think I'm insane?"

"Not certifiable, but definitely on the spectrum. You hug trees."

She wasn't what he'd first thought of her. He felt as if she'd tricked him, and that angered him.

He had his guard up against the therapists and other quacks. But back at the gas station, he hadn't known she was a therapist at Hope Hill. He'd let his guard down.

She'd been brave enough to talk to him. She'd been open-minded enough to see past his scowl, his tattoos, and the generally intimidating way he tended to appear to strangers. Even though blood obviously made her queasy, she'd been kind enough to help him. It'd been that reckless, uncalculated kindness that had gotten to him.

Back at the gas station, he had liked her. Back at the gas station, he hadn't known she was just another person who'd want to poke around in his head so she could tell him what was wrong with him. Back at the gas station, he hadn't known that she was the enemy.

Frustration made him clench his teeth.

"I'm a freaking cripple, all right? I'm dealing with that. I don't need people looking into my head. I don't need anyone to tell me that I'm a crazy cripple."

"I don't think you're crazy."

"Then what am I?"

"A diagnosis after five minutes? That's a lot of pressure."

"You had another five at the gas station. That makes it ten."

She watched him, her gaze open and curious. He didn't know many people who could stay as unruffled as that when he was in this kind of a mood.

She said, "I think you are . . . off balance."

Off balance.

That came closer to how he felt than anything anyone else had told him so far, after a lot longer acquaintance. So, all right, maybe he'd give Miss Murray half a chance.

Half because he still wasn't sure about any of this.

And also because he figured half a chance was all she needed. Given half a chance, Annie Murray would run with it like a rabbit with her tail on fire.

Chapter Four

ANNIE LOOKED UP INTO COLE'S DARK, ASSESSING GAZE AND TRIED TO DECIDE what to do with him. She couldn't complain that he'd brought her down. She'd started the fight. She'd put him on his ass first. She hadn't worried about the fall hurting him, not on the spongy groundcover of old leaves and mulch spread on the path.

She couldn't believe she'd been able to knock him down. OK, she hadn't knocked him off his feet—she'd knocked him off center, and then his own weight pulled him to the ground. He hadn't resisted for fear of damaging her. Even when he'd had her fully restrained, he'd been careful not to put his full weight on her.

He *was* a gentleman, despite his protests. But he was rough and gruff too. A wounded warrior.

Her patient.

She sat up and pushed against his shoulder.

He held her for another second, because this *was* a power play, and the whole point had been to show her that he was the top predator in these woods.

His point made, he rolled smoothly to his feet and extended a large Band-Aid–decorated hand to help her up.

She ignored the hand and came to her feet on her own power. "If you hate being here this much, why did you enter the program?"

He began walking again, and she figured he wouldn't answer, but he said, "I promised my mother." He glanced back at her.

When she said nothing, he asked, "What? I don't look like I have a mother?"

"Now that you mention it"—she dragged her gaze across the span of his shoulders—"you definitely look like you could be the love child of a grizzly bear and a navy destroyer."

The joke was for herself, to regain her equilibrium, but for the first time, his face lightened an infinitesimal measure. Not anything as drastic as a smile, but as if he'd passed a billboard with a smiling person this morning and he was remembering that. The lighter look didn't make him handsome, but a maybe a little less mountain-of-doomy.

Since he looked almost approachable for once, she asked, "Where do your parents live?"

The light look disappeared. He stilled, as if having a silent debate with himself. Then he answered, his tone reluctant, as if every word cost him, as if he had to put a dollar into an imaginary jar for every syllable. "My mother lives in Illinois. My father is gone."

Father—suicide. How could she forget, even for a second? He'd thrown her off-kilter when he'd rolled her under him. He'd thrown her off-kilter by being the guy from the gas station. He'd taken her by surprise.

She needed to get her act together. "Would you like to talk about your father?"

A couple of seconds ticked by as Cole looked up the path. "He got sick from the chemicals in the First Gulf War. Became too much for him in the end."

She touched his hand so he would turn to her. "I'm sorry."

He shrugged. "Makes my mother worry."

Annie could see why it would. According to the notes in his file, he'd spent a month refusing to leave his apartment—holed up with a cache of loaded weapons.

Chances of suicide for a person who had a close family member who'd committed suicide were two to three times that of the general population—a risk factor therapists took seriously.

"Are you now considering, or have you ever considered, suicide?"

"No." His tone was sure, his gaze straight.

"Good."

He walked forward, too fast, but she didn't tell him to slow down. She matched her steps to his and waited for him to look at her before she asked, "Where did you get the scar on your arm?"

"RPG. Rocket-propelled grenade." He kept going. "Freak accident. The insurgents didn't know our position. They were shooting blindly at the hillside. A one-in-a-million chance that they'd hit us. I made it. My spotter didn't."

"Spotter?"

"Ryan watched my back. We'd split surveillance. A sniper can't be looking through the scope all day. You don't want eye fatigue just when the target pops up behind a window and you have a second to take the shot. A sniper and his spotter are like two halves of a whole."

"I'm sorry you lost Ryan."

He turned from her. "I picked the spot."

She touched his hand again. And when he looked at her, she said, "It's not your fault."

"The regular shrink already said that. Your job is to tell me about trees and . . . I don't know, bushes?" From the bottom of his troubled soul, he looked unhappy with the prospect, but at least his tone was no longer combative.

She would take from him what she could get. Progress was a beautiful thing, even when it came in drips and dribbles.

She eased her pace. "We should start by slowing down."

After a moment, he matched her speed, so they stayed side by side.

Next step. "Notice the way the dirt feels under your feet, how great the air smells, how beautiful the trees are, how calm and majestic."

He snorted, and she could tell he was fighting not to roll his eyes as he asked, "Calm as opposed to what? All the other trees that run around like headless chickens?"

She bit back a smile. He might be gruff, but he wasn't without a sense of humor.

For long minutes, they walked in silence. The peace of nature seeped into her body. The woods always had this effect on her. Hopefully, Cole would feel the same in time, but for right now, he was a bundle of pain and raw nerve endings. All his bluster was nothing but a coping mechanism.

As they walked around a bend, passing under majestic oaks, she touched his hand. And when he looked at her, she asked, "How much of the birdsong can you hear?"

"The high notes."

His voice vibrated with tension—his demeanor alert, his gaze constantly scanning the forest when she wasn't talking. She hadn't fully understood until now how his being deaf would affect his experience . . . how the sounds of the forest—the soothing rustling of the leaves, the birds, and the bugs serenading them—would be lost to him.

They were approaching her favorite clearing, a spot she'd come to think of as her meadow. She liked lying down in the open space, closing her eyes and listening to the primal, unspoiled song of life. The earth's music filled her up, cleansed her, wrapped her up in peace.

The idea that Cole couldn't have that tightened her throat. He didn't have the worst disability among her patients—some of the men were missing multiple limbs—but deafness or blindness could be incredibly isolating. Definitely an extra challenge for ecotherapy. She'd read about it during her studies, but she hadn't had a patient before with either problem. She would have to feel her way forward here.

For Cole, the loss of therapeutic sound probably wasn't even the most difficult part. He was a soldier. He'd been trained to watch and listen for danger. A soldier who didn't hear someone sneak up on him was a dead soldier. How *could* he let his guard down, knowing he was, without a crucial sense, vulnerable? How on earth was she going to make him relax?

No wonder he was so ready to fight, ready to strike first. The way he'd whirled on her, ready to attack, in the alley by the gas station made sense now. He'd been standing there with his back to the bathroom door and hadn't heard her turn the lock, only caught the sudden movement behind him.

You startled me, he'd said.

He'd sure startled her right back.

"I don't think you holed up in your apartment with those weapons because you were thinking about suicide," she told him.

"Didn't I just say that?"

"I think you did it to feel safe. Back to the wall, gun in hand. That way nobody could creep up on you."

He didn't respond.

"I'm glad you were able to move past that phase. You could have just as easily developed debilitating anxiety and tipped over into agoraphobia."

Again, he looked at her with that peculiar expression, as if reassessing her.

She would love to know the result of his assessment, but she didn't ask. They walked in silence for a while.

When they reached her meadow, Annie meant to walk past. The practice of quiet listening would have to be skipped for Cole. But then she changed her mind, strode into the calf-high grass, and turned to him. "I usually stop here."

"Is this when we hug a damn tree?" he grumbled. "Forget it. I'm drawing the line."

"We'll work up to tree hugging." She put some mock censure in her gaze. "You can't just walk up to a stand of unsuspecting oaks and start touching. They'd think you're getting fresh with them."

He was . . . not exactly smiling, not even thinking about smiling. But he was maybe thinking about someone he'd seen smiling at breakfast in the cafeteria.

Annie decided to count it as another tiny drop of success.

The grassy clearing was around a fifth of an acre. If she lay down in the middle, she would still be able to see a ring of treetops in her peripheral vision. She was happy anytime she could see, hear, or touch her natural surroundings. All three at once was perfect.

She walked to the trampled spot where she usually communed with nature. "Why don't you lie down, be still with the world for a while, and then tell me what you think."

He lay down on his back, feet apart, arms open to the side, spread-eagle. He looked up at the sky. Then at her. "Are you going to lie down?"

"No." She had an idea. "I'm going to step back and stand guard. You can close your eyes. Stay as long as you want. Breathe in the forest. You pay attention to that. I'll pay attention to everything else."

His eyes narrowed. "You think you can lull me into some false sense of safety and sneak in some ecotherapy unnoticed. I know what you're trying to do."

She wouldn't fight him. "Good. I like smart people. Makes conversation so much more stimulating."

When he ignored her comment, she said, "We're going to relax."

"I can't relax." He looked as if he was maybe swallowing a curse. "I stayed alive for six months as a POW by never, ever relaxing. Never, ever letting my guard down. If they caught me unprepared, if I gave them a single second to do that, they would have broken me. I wouldn't have made it back."

The stark truth lay between them like a hand grenade with its pin pulled.

For a moment, she let herself imagine his life in captivity. The images in her head were unbearable. She wanted to cry for him, but tears weren't what he needed.

"You're not a POW anymore. That's what you're here to learn." When the tension in the air refused to thin, she added, "I'm going to go to the end of the clearing and sit on a stump."

The turbulence in his eyes held her in place. Slowly, slowly, the tension ebbed. She could fill her lungs at last. Then she lost her breath all over again when he gestured to the ground at her feet. "Sit here."

His voice was studiously neutral. Too studiously. Which meant that for some reason this was important to him.

Annie sat, cross-legged.

He left his hand stretched out, moving an inch so the back of his hand touched her bare knee. She waited. If he put his hand on her, she'd turn it into a teaching moment about what was and wasn't appropriate between them. But he didn't make another move.

He asked, "What do you hear?"

"A bee buzzing around your toes. Birds are calling out overhead. I can hear Broslin Creek, faintly, in the distance."

The music of the earth filled her heart with joy and peace, and her chest ached at the thought that Cole couldn't fully experience this sacred moment.

"I like thinking," she added, "that the forest sounds the same as it did millions of years ago, and it will sound the same millions of years from now. I find the endlessness comforting. It puts my small problems into perspective. Like looking at the stars at night and real-izing that everything I worried about all day is utterly insignificant compared to the vastness of the universe."

He closed his eyes. A couple of ants crawled up his arm. She leaned forward to brush them off.

Without opening his eyes, he said, "Leave them."

So she did.

Sensory perception. He was missing one sense. Maybe the ants tickling his skin made up—in some small way—for the silence in his ears.

If he was one of her other patients, she would be talking now, explaining the science behind ecotherapy. But with his eyes closed, she couldn't do that. She let him rest, watching as the lines on his face smoothed out, as his breathing evened.

His face relaxed, still not handsome, but no longer harsh either. Cole Makani Hunter had strong, tough-set features. He had a scar under his jaw she hadn't noticed before. His nose wasn't just a little flat, it'd been broken.

He was several notches rougher and tougher than the average guy she usually saw around town. Annie couldn't imagine herself walking into Broslin Diner with someone who had barbed wire tattooed on his shaved head.

The softest thing about his face was his eyelashes, nearly black and slightly curled.

Her gaze slid to his lips. Now that they weren't pressed together in disapproval . . . *Quit looking.*

Annie turned her attention to the meadow and the forest around them. She breathed in the peace of the forest and let all distractions float away from her.

Minutes ticked by. Half an hour passed. She shifted in place, rolled her neck and shoulders, careful not to break the connection between them.

She settled into this new experience of being physically connected to someone while being connected to the earth. She normally didn't touch her patients, but with Cole she had no other way of getting his attention when he wasn't looking right at her. She was going to have to get used to that.

Of course, she wasn't trying to get his attention now. He was asleep. Yet she stayed where she was. She felt as if some kind of sacred circle had formed, something unfamiliar but powerful and important. So she decided to be still and give herself to the experience.

She thought about lying in the grass next to him, but she'd promised to stay on guard.

Fifteen minutes before their session was over, she woke him with a gentle nudge of her knee to his hand, so they'd have time to get back.

His bottomless dark eyes blinked open. He looked straight at her. "How much longer do we have to do this?"

"Done for today." She smiled, pretending that her breath hadn't hitched at that sleepy, half-hooded look. "You fell asleep."

"I was resting my eyes. Can't sleep without drugs."

"You just did."

"Might have blinked out for a minute, but that's it." He sat up and brushed strands of dried grass from his shoulders. "Sounds like your watch is broken."

Instead of arguing with him, she pushed to her feet and stretched her legs.

They headed back to the path side by side.

She turned so he would be able to see her lips. "How do you feel?"

He gave an exaggerated groan and a flat look. "Thinking about hugging a tree and getting it over with. It'd save you the effort of trying to manipulate me into it next time."

"Does that mean you'll be giving ecotherapy a try?"

"Might as well, or the program coordinator will push me into art therapy. Believe me, nobody wants to see that."

She bit back a smile. "There's music therapy too."

He didn't credit her comment with an answer. But then he said, "So, tomorrow, same time, same place?"

"Not tomorrow." She pushed back the unease that tried to settle on her. "I'll be off for the rest of the week."

She expected him to leap with joy, but instead, his forehead pulled into a frown. "What for?"

"Worried about missing me too much?"

"I like a regular schedule. You going on vacation?"

"Going on a TV show." She tried not to think about everything that could go wrong in the next couple of days.

"Making people roll in dirt in front of cameras, on national TV? Don't look at me if you're asking for volunteers."

"Only the local channel, thank God. But it'll be live." She swallowed. "My cousin is a Realtor. I'm helping her out with something."

She didn't mind helping. She just wished Kelly hadn't asked *this*.

Cole stopped walking. "Yeah?"

Annie tried not to appear as unhappy as she felt. The key was to look at the show as an opportunity.

Losing all her savings to Xane, her boyfriend before Joey, back in Philly, had been a major hit. Xane had serious rock-star delusions. He'd cleaned out her bank account to upgrade the band with new equipment, informing her after the fact with, *I'll pay you back when we make it big, babe.*

And then Annie had gotten laid off. Lost the apartment.

Kelly had helped. She'd told Annie about the new rehab facility in Broslin, the small town where they'd both grown up. The position paid enough to qualify for a mortgage on a small fixer-upper. Annie was in.

"My cousin is branching out from real estate agent to real estate adviser. She's remarketing herself as someone who helps people find good investments for rent or flipping. I'll be on the show with her."

"Doing what?" Cole asked.

"Returning a favor. She found my house for me. I need to reno-vate it. She's kind of managing the reno and got the local TV to cover the transformation. She'll be giving tips on how to increase home value for a sale or flip."

"Establishing herself as the local expert."

Annie nodded. She didn't want to go into the topic any deeper, hadn't meant to go into it at all. But maybe sharing something per-sonal would set Cole at ease. Establishing a more open relationship between them could only benefit his therapy.

His gaze didn't leave her face. "You're not excited. My mother would be dancing down the street in a hula skirt. She's hooked on those house-makeover shows on TV."

"I'm excited," Annie said, working hard at it. "I need to move. With a makeover, I might actually be able to sell."

He stopped. "Moving away?"

"Just to a house with a bigger property. We've outgrown the back-yard a lot faster than I expected. I have animals." She had a dream for her life, and she was determined to make that dream a reality. This was going to be her lucky year.

She was *not* going to do anything to mess up her dream, or the job that made it all possible. Which meant she would make things work with Cole, find a way to ensure that ecotherapy helped him.

She'd gotten off on the wrong foot with him somehow during this intro session. Should she have kept more of a distance between them? She couldn't, not when she had to touch him to make him look at her every time she needed to tell him something.

At least she had the rest of the week off. By the time she returned to work, today's odd vibe would be forgotten. She would hit the reset button and start over with him. Would not let her heart flutter because he slept his first drug-free sleep in months next to her, the back of his hand touching her knee.

Attraction toward a patient was the kind of forest fire that could burn down her life and career before she had a chance to blink. She'd made enough bad decisions already to last her a lifetime. She was starting over here.

"Got a boyfriend to help you with all that work?"

"God forbid," she said before she could catch herself.

He raised a dark eyebrow as they began walking again. "That bad?"

"A genetic, pathological inclination to be attracted to the wrong guy."

Cole's expression turned lighter than it had been so far. Apparently, the thought of her failings cheered him up. "How bad can it be?"

"One of them is still stalking me."

The hint of amusement disappeared from Cole's gaze. As if someone had turned a switch, in a blink, he was all badass killing machine, laser focused and ready for anything. "Are you in danger?"

"Forget I said that. Joey is harmless. Just part of the family curse."

"He's cursed?"

"I am."

Cole didn't look sold on the concept. Which just showed how little he knew.

"The women in my family," she told him, "have a long history of ending up with the wrong men. My grandmother married a cold-hearted jerk who drove her to an early grave. My mother chose a series of men who were increasingly large disasters."

"And you?"

The first man Annie had ever lived with was Xane Ebner in Philly; he was a mellow guy who used to sing in an Earth, Wind & Fire–type band called Green Leaf. They'd met at a concert the band gave to benefit the environment. Xane had been her soul mate for nearly a full year before he'd decided to morph into a self-proclaimed rock-and-roll god who'd gotten into drugs, other women, *and* her bank account. Last she'd heard of him, he was flirting with pop. *Gotta go where the money is, babe.*

Annie had moved back to Broslin and run into Joey.

When Joey had asked her out, she'd said yes, without first figuring out what kind of man he'd grown into. She didn't realize until too late that the adult Joey wasn't anything like the kind and funny kid-Joey she remembered.

His life had gone off track when he'd been studying for a pharmacy degree, and his cousin, Big Jim, had talked him into mishandling some drugs. That had ended Joey's career before it could begin. He'd slipped into a series of part-time jobs and more shenanigans with Big Jim. Joey wasn't stupid; he was just entirely without motivation.

But both Xane's and Joey's bad-boy quotient paled next to Cole Makani Hunter's. The man lived and breathed danger. Cole might not be criminally inclined—that Annie knew of—but if she were smart, she would buy him a T-shirt that said WRONG MAN and make him wear it to their sessions.

"I don't think my love life is a proper topic in a session," she said when she realized that Cole was still waiting for her answer to his question.

"What were you doing at the gas station earlier?" she asked him to change the subject.

"Walked down for some cigarettes."

"You shouldn't smoke."

"I don't. Thinking about starting."

She fixed him with her stern-therapist look. "I find out you do, and I'll write *self-destructive tendencies* in your file."

His face remained expressionless. "Now you're scaring me."

"You'll be scared when they disable the lock on your door and you get hourly checkups."

He quirked an eyebrow. "What do you get for blackmail and intimidation?"

She tried not to smile at his wry, understated humor or acknowledge that she liked it. "I'm just worried about you."

"I don't have self-destructive tendencies."

"You punched a brick wall so hard you almost broke your hand." She let that sink in. "Want to tell me what that was about?"

She was surprised when, after giving her a moment of consideration, he actually did.

"Car almost ran me over. Didn't hear it coming. Then the guy behind the wheel yelled something at me, but he was half-turned so I couldn't read his lips. I didn't know whether to yell back, *Don't worry about it*, or *Fuck you too*." He gave a one-shouldered shrug. "So you can stop worrying about the self-destructive thing. Chances are, something I can't hear coming is going to destroy me. If this place doesn't drive me crazy first."

Her heart twisted. But she couldn't drop the subject. She was one of his therapists. "I bet those tattoos hurt. Some of them look new. Are you punishing yourself with pain? Maybe because you feel like your body is failing you?"

"No." He didn't hide his exasperation. "Everybody has tattoos."

"Not everybody."

He looked her over leisurely, with an insolent expression she now knew meant he was going on the offensive.

He didn't disappoint. "You want me to take your word for that? How about you prove it?"

She *knew* he was trying to rattle her, but his dark gaze still got to her and sent a faint tingle up her spine. Of course it did. Because he was easily the most inappropriate guy for her in a hundred-mile radius.

Good thing Annie was breaking with her genetic destiny. She wasn't even going to think about being attracted to Cole Makani Hunter. She was not going to be another misguided Murray woman in a long line of misguided Murray women.

You make a mistake once, it's a mistake. You make a mistake twice, you're a slow learner. You make a mistake three times, and it's a habit. Maybe it's who you are.

Cole was her patient. Annie was going to help him. Then, when he left Hope Hill in a few weeks' time, she was going to forget about him.

Chapter Five

Tuesday

"READY?" KELLY SMILED. SHE WAS DRESSED IN A PURPLE SATEEN SHEATH SHE'D called urban aubergine, and silver stilettos, as if she were heading to a cocktail party instead of hanging out in a construction zone. Her hair and makeup soared to new heights of overdone, but maybe that kind of thing played best for the cameras. "Is this the most exciting thing we've ever done or what? Everybody we know is watching."

Annie could have done without being reminded. She was tricked out too, so over-the-top she could be an announcer at the Hunger Games. She had barely recognized herself in the mirror when the stylist—one of Kelly's friends—was done with her. She wore a tight, black strapless bodice, a red ballet skirt and, of course, heels—because nothing said house renovation like broken ankles.

You don't have to enjoy this. You just have to survive it.

And hopefully not go bald in the process. Her hair had enough product in it to grout the kitchen backsplash. Her outraged eyebrows were plucked within an inch of their lives. And her makeup was exaggerated enough to scare a teenager out of her goth phase. Almost as overdone as Xane's the last time Annie had seen him in concert.

"Ready," Annie said carefully so as not to crack the thick layer of lipstick on her lips.

All right, fine. She was a little excited. She glanced around. *God, let this work.*

David Durenne, the producer, was watching Kelly with rapt interest, but Kelly didn't notice. Which probably meant he was a nice guy.

The family love curse was pretty widespread. Kelly was expanding her Realtor business because her loser ex had successfully sued her for alimony. Ricky had cheated on her then left her, and now Kelly had to support him financially while he frolicked around with his cliché twenty-year-old hairdresser.

If there was a loser jerk within a hundred miles, one of the Murray women found him. Guaranteed.

The producer held up a finger, his eyes going unfocused as he listened to the bud in his ear.

"Hold on," he said. "We have a thirty-second delay. Weather update. Tropical Storm Rupert was just upgraded to a hurricane. It's making landfall in Kingston, Jamaica." He frowned as he listened. "Might come up the Eastern Seaboard."

Before Annie could worry too much about it, the man began counting back on his fingers.

"Five, four, three, two, one."

The cameras began rolling.

"Good morning," Kelly cooed. "I am Kelly Murray, and this is my cousin, Annie. Two savvy single ladies doing business. We're going to show you today how to double the value of your real estate property for sale."

Annie barely flinched at the word *single*. Totally expected it. She held on to her pleasant, neutral expression as her cousin went on about the importance of picking the right location when thinking about flipping.

"So tell us about how you created a sanctuary for those poor darling animals." Kelly held her smile for the count of three, then turned it all off.

"They're cutting in the footage we shot of the llamas earlier." She grabbed her compact from her back pocket to pat more powder on her face. "People want a personalized story."

Done with the compact, she stashed it away and pulled out a travel-size can of glitter hairspray. She fluffed Annie's hair with one hand and sprayed with the other.

While Annie tried to choke as quietly as possible, her cousin flashed a look of approval. "There. You look like a lady. You never know who might watch this thing. Maybe we'll catch the eye of a hot doctor or a sexy lawyer. You have to look like the kind of wife a professional man would want."

"Coming back in five, four, three, two, one," the producer called out as the hairspray disappeared.

Kelly turned on again, flipping the beauty-contestant switch that Annie decidedly didn't have. They had very different upbringings. Not Kelly's fault. Resenting her for it would be stupid, and Annie didn't. Yet she was aware of an emotional gap between them.

"Unfortunately, as you can see, the house is in rough shape," Kelly said.

The cameras panned around.

Kelly had actually made the mess on purpose. The place looked like a dump. Annie tried not to wince at the thought of the whole town seeing her like a slob, a borderline hoarder.

"Especially the kitchen." Kelly led the way. "And your dream is one big open space, right?"

No. Annie wanted to leave the walls where they were. But her cousin insisted that the show would work best if the difference between *before* and *after* was dramatic.

Since Annie had agreed to let Kelly do what she wanted with the house as long as the end result was a substantial increase in equity, she said, "That would be great."

"All right, then, guys," Kelly called to the crew, "let's knock this wall out of the way!"

Six stud muffins in ripped jeans and tool belts sprang up to obey, swinging giant hammers. They weren't as big as Cole Makani Hunter, nor as mean-looking. These guys were the smiley, friendly handy-man types who played well on TV—ridiculously handsome to the last man, picked for the camera, probably straight from the YMCA where Kelly went for yoga classes.

Not that Annie was going to start comparing every guy she met to Cole. She pushed the SEAL from her mind while her cousin retreated from the room to escape the dust.

The camera filmed the men. Right until they cut to commercial break.

Everybody hurried to the bathroom to take their places for the next segment.

"Five," the producer said, flashing Kelly a smile, "four, three, two, one."

Kelly whispered to Annie, "Look like a lady." Then she said into the camera, "Welcome back. Now here, we are turning this tiny hole of a dark bathroom into a sumptuous spa bath."

A spa bath being another thing that Annie hadn't wanted, but Kelly said luxury was the latest rage.

Kelly gave the signal for Rob, the guy who'd been waiting with the jackhammer. The twenty-two-year-old college student from West Chester University had gym muscles on top of his gym muscles.

Annie had talked to him for a few minutes earlier. His goal was to graduate without debt. He'd been on the cover of a couple of romance novels written by a local author before he'd snagged this gig. He knew jackhammers because he worked construction during the summers.

He was nearly as tall as Cole, but not as wide in the shoulders . . .

Not thinking it!

Annie made sure to keep the smile on her face. Kelly was right—they did need to look professional. Annie had patients watching at Hope Hill.

The jackhammer went wild in the tiled shower stall, the noise deafening, debris flying. Then a different kind of noise. And then the shower stall caved. The next second, the outer wall of the bathroom fell away with a crash that shook the floor under them.

The jackhammer stopped.

As the dust slowly settled, Annie could see the backyard and the fence on the far side of the yard. For a moment, she thought she saw a dark figure at the edge of the cornfield that began past her fence. Then the figure disappeared—probably Joey—and Annie refocused on the giant hole in front of her. She'd lost a wall. An *entire* fricking wall. An *outside* wall!

That was not supposed to happen.

The words tumbled from her lips before she could call them back. "Fucking spa bath."

Which, as she later found out, was the last thing she said on live TV.

The camera guy immediately cut the feed, while the producer shouted, "Out. Out. Out. Get out to safety!"

They all ran for the back door, the closest exit. When Kelly stumbled in her high heels, the producer picked her up and carried her.

Annie came to a stop in her backyard, barely hearing the team's shocked exclamations over the blood pounding in her ears.

Her phone pinged. On reflex, she pulled it from her pocket. Text message from Joey. The eighth one today.

She'd been determined to have a good week, but as she stood there staring at the hole in the wall, her stomach churning, she had to admit defeat.

Her job still hadn't been made full-time.

Her ex would not give up stalking her.

Her new patient was difficult. *An understatement.*

And her house stood open to the elements.

With a hurricane coming.

"It's not that bad, right?" Kelly's eyes swam in guilt. She was standing on her own feet once again, although the producer hovered nearby. "You can find the positive in anything. Say something."

Annie tried. She really did. But she ended up shaking her head. There weren't enough affirmations in the world.

Chapter Six

BY THE TIME COLE WATCHED ANNIE DRIVE UP THE LONG DRIVEWAY AT HOPE Hill, everyone there knew what had happened to her house. She was going to stay in one of the empty rooms tonight because her place had to be inspected for structural damage. Cole sat on the front porch of the main building in an Adirondack chair one of the inmates had built. *Patients,* Annie would correct, but she wasn't fooling him.

A calico cat slept in the next chair. Cole had seen about half a dozen cats around the facilities so far. They came and went as they pleased. He ignored the cat and focused on the woman.

Annie drove a green Prius. *Naturally.* The only way she could be truer to herself would be to ride a bicycle. Maybe she did that too. Cole wouldn't be surprised if she only drove the car once a week.

He didn't go to greet her or offer to carry her luggage. He hadn't been waiting for her. He was taking a break. He only watched her because there wasn't much to look at out here.

She didn't appear hurt. She appeared . . . admired. A dozen guys crowded around her, some staff, some inmates.

Since the parking lot was well lit and they were heading his way, Cole could read a couple of lips.

"Are you OK?"

"Let me take that."

"Man, that's terrible."

"I'm glad you weren't hurt."

If they could, the men would have picked her up and carried her in their arms.

One of the guys wore a T-shirt that said MAY THE TREES BE WITH YOU.

Sucking up much?

Not that Cole cared. The patients and staff at Hope Hill could do whatever they wanted as long as they left him alone. And as long as they didn't figure out his real reason for being here.

Annie smiled at the numb-nuts, laughed at something T-shirt guy said, asked how they've been. They wanted to take care of her, but she would have none of it and pulled her own suitcase. They followed her like eager puppies.

She was no sex kitten. She had to be close to thirty. Some of the guys were a good five years younger than she was. What did they see in her? Weren't they bothered by all the woo-woo? *Absorb negative electrons from the earth through the bottoms of your feet.*

Cole stood from his chair and left her to her groupies. Might as well head off to the cafeteria and grab dinner. He had work to do tonight, but not until later.

After a bean burger and sweet potato fries—a miracle that nobody had choked the cook yet—he went to the gym. He couldn't do weights with his injured arm, but he could run on the treadmill. Since most people were still at dinner, he had the place to himself. He liked it that way.

He ran until sweat poured down his body, until he pounded everything out of his brain, until nothing remained but his burning lungs and muscles. He was still running when Trevor Turner came in, a twentysomething former marine.

The kid made a beeline for the treadmill in the corner.

At a normal gym, the equipment faced the wall mirrors. Here, the equipment faced the room, because everybody here preferred having their backs to the wall. They didn't like people behind them. Military habits die hard. As in never.

Another guy came in and went straight to the weights section, straight to bench-pressing. Alejandro Ramirez. Every time he lowered the weights and the bar dropped into place, Trevor startled. He sped up his treadmill, maybe to block out the clanging Cole couldn't hear.

As Cole's boots slapped on the rubber, he knew he had to be making noise too. *Thump. Thump. Thump.* He was no lightweight. Each step rattled the machine.

Trevor's eyes jumped from Cole to Alejandro, then back. As both men kept up a steady pace with their own efforts, Trevor's face became a mask of misery.

Did the noise bother him?

Cole shut off his machine and went over to the water fountain next to Trevor for a drink.

Trevor slowed his own treadmill but didn't stop completely. "How long are you in for?"

Cole appreciated the wording. "As long as they deem it necessary. Initial sentence is four weeks."

"You think any of this works?" The kid's gaze held an edge of desperation.

"I know it does." Cole said what the kid needed to hear. "I had a nap yesterday without pills."

"Oh, man."

The longing that brimmed in Trevor's eyes twisted Cole's cold, hard heart. He took another drink. "You should see the ecotherapist."

Never thought he'd say those words in million years. Maybe the cafeteria had seasoned the bean burgers with brainwashing powder.

Trevor's expression lit up. "I've been seeing Annie. Isn't she great? Reminds me of my mom. Soft and strong at the same time, you know?"

Cole did know. Although, when he looked at Annie, he certainly wasn't thinking about his mother.

Trevor said, "I have to do some concentrated psychotherapy right now. I do that in the mornings, then PT in the afternoons. I only have Annie once a week. I wish I could have her every day. I think she could make me better."

"You'll get there."

"You think?"

What did Cole know? He'd only been here two days. "You bet."

The aura of distress around Trevor faded. His eyes lost some of their jitteriness.

"I like the food here," he said when Cole moved to walk away. "You think they'll have cupcakes again tomorrow?"

"If they do, they'll probably be gluten-free. Made from carrots or zucchini or, what was it the other day? Aubergine."

Trevor rolled his eyes. "Total bait and switch, man. Sounds like French pastry. Turns out it's freaking eggplant. Seriously." He shook his head. "Still, better than MREs."

"Not saying much, is it?" Dried dog turd was better than Meals Ready to Eat, the standard freeze-dried food packets used in the military.

"Where were you stationed?" Trev asked. "First I was assigned to JTF-Bravo in Honduras, then in Afghanistan."

"All around. Little bit of this, little bit of that."

Because the kid clearly needed the conversation to ground him, Cole lingered a few minutes to talk. He only left when more people came in. One of them, Marco, a tall black guy, acknowledged Trevor with a chin lift before limping across the big room to take the tread-mill next to the kid.

Shane, a wiry Texan, headed to the weights. He checked his phone. He did that every couple of minutes. His mother had bone cancer, and he liked to keep in touch with her. He put the phone down, then stepped over to the TV in the corner and turned off CNN, which had been showing a Senate session on health-care reform.

"Love my country, hate the damn government," he said, in case anyone needed explanation.

Cole thought about that while heading back to his room. As he cut through the courtyard, he caught sight of a small shadow under the great willow tree in the middle.

A civilian would have missed it. The branches of the weeping willow nearly touched the ground, making it difficult to see in there. But Cole's sniper eyes had been trained to pick up the smallest movement.

He grabbed for his nonexistent weapon on instinct. Pain shot up his useless right arm. Then his brain caught up. *Rehab. Safe.* The tree was unlikely to hide insurgents.

If he were a betting man, he'd bet Annie Murray was in there, communing with nature in the middle of the night. Probably upset over her house.

None of Cole's business.

They weren't best friends. Or even friends, loosely speaking. He needed to get back to his room. He needed a shower, then he had a new thriller he wanted to read. And yet he couldn't help himself. He swept the branches aside and stepped inside the dark cocoon of the tree.

Annie Murray sat with her slim legs crossed, her back against the trunk. She turned her face into the single sliver of moonlight so he could read her lips. "Hey."

"Hey."

Now what?

Should have gone to the room. Cole shifted on his feet, then silently cursed himself. *She* was the weird one. So why was he the one feeling strange?

Backing out now without another word would make him look like an even bigger idiot, so he sat down facing her. "Can't sleep?"

"Can't stop thinking about the hole in my house."

Cole nodded. Sitting under the tree with her in the dark felt disorienting. He wasn't sure what he was doing here.

Chasing the peace of the meadow.

He still didn't understand what had happened there. Maybe she'd hypnotized him. Only one thing wrong with that theory: he didn't believe in hypnosis.

"The contractor will fix it." Tree hugger or not, he didn't like seeing her upset. He didn't like seeing anyone taken advantage of. "Want me to come over tomorrow and have a talk with him?"

A tired smile stretched her full lips as she sat slumped against the tree. "Thanks. I should be able to handle it."

She probably could. She was competent enough, and definitely the Zen type, not one to fly off the handle. Even now, peace hung around her like mist around mountain peaks.

That nap he'd taken with her at the clearing the day before had been a gift, and he wished he could return the favor.

"If you need help, let me know," Cole said. "You should go to bed and get some rest."

"You too."

He nodded as he pushed to his feet. "Just came in to say hi."

"You didn't earlier. I thought maybe you'd had enough of me yesterday."

Had she seen him on the front porch when she'd pulled up? He hadn't thought so. He'd been in the deep shadows, and she'd been under the parking-lot lights.

Before he could comment, she said, "I saw you standing outside the branches. Your boots sound different on the gravel than sneakers."

"Not me." Cole shook his head.

She blinked at him, then murmured something that looked like "Oh Jesus, Joey," before dropping her head into her hands.

The name rang a bell. "Would that be the stalker boyfriend?"

She looked up. "Ex-boyfriend slash stalker. He really is harmless. He thinks if he keeps reminding me how much he's suffering, I'll take him back." She picked at her pants. "He's a part-time driver for the laundry service that picks up the linen from the rehab center. But today is not one of his days. I didn't expect to see him here."

She stood and brushed off her jeans. "I have to go home to feed my animals. They're in the garage. I'm allowed in there. Only the house was damaged."

"What needs feeding at midnight?"

"Babies."

Cole pictured a basket of orphaned puppies. During their session the day before, she'd mentioned something about needing a bigger backyard.

"I'll go with you."

"I'm all right."

"Gives me something to do other than stare at the ceiling. Can't sleep anyway." He shrugged. "Not hearing anything . . . That only works when I have my eyes open. At night, when I close my eyes, I hear the explosions. Over and over."

He was telling her the truth, but he was also manipulating her sympathies. He didn't like the idea of her going out in the middle of the night. Not with a stalker ex-boyfriend on the loose. Whose ass Cole was going to kick, free of charge, gratis, if they ran into him tonight. It'd help him work off some of his frustrations. A little ass kicking might be more therapeutic than any of the treatment he'd received so far at Hope Hill.

Annie stopped to make sure he could read her lips. "You don't take the sleeping pills?"

"Only every couple of days. Hate feeling groggy the next day."

Her eyes narrowed for a second, as if she might object, but instead she nodded, then walked through the supple willow branches.

He followed her, the leaves feeling like a caress on his shaved head, like a fond goodbye from the tree.

He bit back a disgusted groan at the thought. *One* ecotherapy session, and he was getting as batty as she was. He needed to watch himself around Annie Murray.

He caught up with her as she left the facilities and headed to her car.

When he popped in on the passenger side, her hand hesitated on the key in the ignition.

"While I try to develop a friendship with my patients, I don't normally take them home with me."

"Is there a rule against it?"

"Not officially." The dome light revealed that her eyes were red-rimmed. She'd had a rough week so far.

Cole had been part of it, no doubt. He'd given her plenty of grief yesterday. He bit back a disgusted grunt. He wasn't fit for human company, dammit. But he wasn't going to let her go out alone, in the middle of the night.

"I'll be on my best behavior. I swear. Consider it therapy. Animals are supposed to help with PTSD. Right?"

She turned the key in the ignition. The dome light went out. She reached up to turn it back on. Presumably so he could see if she said something, but she drove out of the parking lot in silence.

"When can you go back home for good?" Cole asked when they were on the road.

She turned slightly, enough so he could read her lips. "I'll find out tomorrow if the house is structurally sound. Apparently, the bathroom studs rotted away from water that's been leaking behind the shower tiles for decades."

Her slim fingers tightened on the wheel. "I seriously want to strangle the home inspector who missed that when I bought the place. I paid him to catch problems like this."

Lips pressed together, she looked like she might be growling.

What would that sound like?

Cole batted the thought away. "I doubt a woman who wouldn't break a tree branch in the woods would kill a man. I don't think you're the type for cold-blooded murder."

"Nobody said anything about cold-blooded. Believe me, I feel pretty passionate about him right now."

Her full lips forming the word *passionate* made him focus on them more carefully than necessary. She had great lips, fuller on the bottom than on top, almost to the point of looking swollen.

Generous lips. He'd heard the expression before but hadn't thought about what that might look like, until now. Annie Murray had generous lips. No hardship looking at them at all. And he had carte blanche for staring.

He had to force himself back to the conversation. "Still couldn't do it."

She raised an eyebrow. "You know a lot about killers?"

"Takes one to know one," he said noncommittally.

She paled, which was a pretty good trick since she'd been plenty pale already. Her gaze darted to his. "Sorry. I didn't mean it like that."

"Don't worry about it. I spent a decade overseas with the navy. We both know I wasn't baking cupcakes."

One hundred twenty-five confirmed kills.

They sat in silence as the car rolled through the night, down quaint small-town streets dotted with flower shops and bakeries. The Pennsylvania small town was a lot like Annie: too good to be true, too innocent and untouched.

Cole didn't trust this kind of purity. It didn't mesh up with all he'd seen and done in the service. He couldn't picture belonging in a place like this.

She pulled over on an average-looking residential street, in front of a rancher that looked the same as all the others, except for the construction dumpster that sat by the curb. A yellow Do Not Cross tape had been wrapped around white porch columns, and it flitted in the night breeze.

The front yard was the size of a helicopter landing pad. The mailbox looked like it'd met some idiot high school kids with baseball bats. Actually, that last bit made the town feel more real for some reason.

When Annie headed to the two-car garage that stood separate from her yellow house, on the opposite side of the worn driveway, Cole loped after her.

"What's going to happen to the house?"

"My cousin's crew tarped the hole, in case it rains," she said. "Anything more will have to come from a real contractor. Kelly's guys could remove an interior, non-load-bearing wall or do cosmetic fixes. This is structural. Too big for them. I have a pro coming in the morning."

She stepped into the garage through the side door, and Cole followed. When she flipped on the light, he stared straight ahead, dumbfounded.

He'd been prepared for orphaned puppies her bleeding heart couldn't leave at the pound, but reality was so much worse.

"You run a skunk sanctuary?" He stood still on the fresh hay that covered the floor. He barely breathed. He couldn't have been less inclined to move if he'd suddenly found himself in the middle of a minefield.

"I take in injured animals." A touch of defensiveness crept into her expression, probably in response to his are-you-freaking-crazy tone.

"Cats and dogs are easy to adopt out once they recover. The cats at Hope Hill came from here. Wild animals go back into the woods, if they can be self-supporting. I find homes for those with permanent injuries." Her shoulders lifted then fell—probably a sigh. "Nobody wants the skunks."

Because most people aren't completely nuts.

He didn't say that out loud. Maybe he was regaining some of his social skills. Since that was one of the stated goals of his treatment plan at Shit Hill—hey, good going.

"I'd prefer not to get sprayed."

"They only spray if they feel threatened."

She moved to the minifridge—shuffling so she wouldn't step on anyone—warmed milk in the microwave on top of the fridge, and made two bottles. Then she sat on a folded comforter in the corner, and the half dozen juvenile skunks ran over.

She said something that looked like "Come here you little stink muffins," which made Cole's lips twitch.

She gently pushed the first few off her lap. "Babies first." She waited until another half dozen smaller ones made their way to her.

"Two abandoned litters." She helped them on her lap, one by one. "The mothers were run over on the highway."

She rotated the bottles among the babies and murmured to them. He didn't see what, since her face was angled downward. He imagined she was making cooing mama-skunk noises.

Since all the skunks were crowding around her, Cole figured he might be safe now. He looked farther into the garage.

Boxes and baby gates blocked off the area. The light of the single bulb by the door barely reached to the far end. Pens and crates filled the entire place. He'd been so startled by the skunks, he hadn't noticed them immediately.

Damn drugs. The sleeping pills kept his mind in a haze even on the days he didn't take them. All the chemicals were piling up in his system. In what universe did he not have complete situational awareness at all times?

In this one, apparently—a whole new world for him. He despised feeling this freaking helpless and useless. Every single day, he knew he was only alive because nobody had tried to kill him.

His shrink, Dr. Ambrose, kept telling him he needed to learn to relax, needed to learn that he didn't have to be on his guard around the clock anymore. Cole was a civilian now—danger no longer waited for him around every corner. But being a Navy SEAL had been indelibly written into every cell of his body. Telling him to relax was like tossing a fish in the air and expecting it to fly away.

He peered into the darkness where other animals moved, probably making noise he couldn't hear.

When he looked back at Annie, she said, "They've already been fed. They just want to party."

He gestured toward them with his head and quirked an eyebrow. She responded with, "Go ahead."

He didn't turn on the overhead light, didn't want to rile up everyone in the middle of the night. Instead, he stepped over a baby gate and waited until his eyes adjusted to the semidarkness.

A tabby cat with a splint blinked at him from a pillow. A black potbellied pig with a newly healed gash in its side rooted around inside a pen. A raven watched him from the rafters, one wing bandaged. Three blue eggs slept in a nest in a cage, under a heating lamp.

Another divider came next. Past that, five emaciated llamas and a one-eyed donkey turned their heads to stare at him. He stared right back for a couple of startled seconds before scanning the rest of the space.

Bags of food for various animals stood piled against the wall. Running the menagerie must cost a pretty penny just in feed.

The llamas and the donkey stuck to their corners and showed no inclination to get to know Cole better. He reached in with his good hand and scratched the pig behind the ears. If there were delighted squeals, he didn't hear them. He went to pet the cat, but the cat swiped at him.

The raven gave him a squinty-eyed look that said *Don't even try.* He couldn't reach the bird anyway. He went back to Annie.

He found her half-asleep.

"What's up with the llamas?"

She blinked at him. "People moved and left them behind."

He glanced back, but that end of the garage was too dark to see the animals. She had saved them in the nick of time. They looked like they were still pretty close to starvation.

"What was the worst you ever had?"

"A tarantula that lost a leg." A delicate shiver ran through her. "I hate spiders."

"Did you save it?"

A tragic look came over her face. "A goat ate him."

A strangled laugh escaped him. "What happened to the goat?"

"Adopted."

"Do you ever turn anything away?"

She rubbed the head of one of the baby skunks with the back of her crooked index finger. "Not anything, not ever."

That people like her lived in the world scared Cole a little. Too softhearted, too easy to take advantage of, too vulnerable. Annie Murray needed a keeper. Not that he was volunteering.

He watched as she slid down into the hay, flat on her back, her head on the folded comforter. The skunks were all over her instantly, like love-smitten kittens, snuggled into every nook, a different baby tucked against every curve.

She closed her eyes, the picture of peaceful bliss.

Cole stood against a nearly irresistible pull to lie next to her and be part of the magic she was weaving.

He never thought he'd be jealous of a skunk, but he wanted to be tucked against her breast. She had generous breasts to go with her generous mouth. She was murmuring something to her little charges that he didn't catch, a soft half smile on her lips.

He wanted to sink into Annie Murray's earth-mother goodness, dissolve in her peace.

She was the most wholesome person he'd ever known.

He was the opposite—too damaged in too many ways. He was deaf, and his right arm might never fully function again. He had nightmares . . .

He wouldn't wish waking up next to him on his worst enemy.

In his dreams, either he was killing someone, or someone was killing him.

He *was* a killer. He'd been a damn good sniper before his right arm had been rendered useless. Maybe as punishment for his sins.

He didn't care about the arm. He didn't care about his lost hearing. He would gladly give more, give anything, if it brought back Ryan, his spotter, his best friend.

Since Ryan and the others had died, screaming in pain, Cole hadn't been the same.

So *no*, he could not have the peace Annie Murray was offering.

She could barely keep her eyes open. She must have realized she was falling asleep, because she shook it off and came to her feet.

"I can drive back to Shit Hill," Cole offered as they walked out to her car.

She glanced at his bad arm.

He saved her the trouble of having to ask. "I'm getting pretty good at driving with my left. We're not on a racecourse. Small town, past midnight. The roads are empty."

She nodded, handed him the keys, got in on the passenger side, and promptly fell asleep.

Who slept like that? At the drop of a hat?

Probably people with a clear conscience.

Although, he too had been like that while in the service. Soldiers slept when the opportunity presented itself. Once upon a time, he'd been able to nod off without a problem.

He drove her through town, stealing glances at her. She didn't wake until he parked the car. She looked even softer and warmer, all sleep-mussed. She blinked at him and then looked around, processing that they were at Hope Hill. "Thanks."

He opened his mouth to say *No big deal*, but from the corner of his eye he caught a dark shadow moving between buildings. He turned to catch more, but the shadow disappeared.

"What is it?" Annie yawned.

"Someone's out there."

She blinked out the window. "Maybe deer. It's pretty late. They come out of the woods at night."

"Could be." But Cole didn't think so. He knew a man's shape when he saw it. "You don't think it could be your ex?"

After a second of consideration, she shook her head. "Joey works the night shift at the gas station on Tuesdays. Even if he was here earlier, he'd be at work by now."

Just another patient, then. Maybe even Trevor. Maybe the kid couldn't sleep.

Cole could certainly relate.

He got out and tossed the keys to Annie, and then they headed to their rooms. They were in the same building: Annie on the first floor, Cole on the second.

He made sure she got to her door safely before he went up the stairs. But he didn't go to bed.

At three o'clock, he eased out into the dark hallway. Everyone knew he was an insomniac. If he got caught, he had a ready-made cover.

He headed toward the main office.

When he'd told Annie his mother had been concerned about how he was handling his injuries, he hadn't been lying. But his mother's concern wasn't the reason that Cole was at Shit Hill. He'd come because his former commanding officer had asked him to do some undercover work.

Two weeks ago, a brief, coded message had been texted from the rehab center to a known enemy agent in Yemen. According to his CO, a dozen more messages had been sent since, one nearly every day. Each contained military information at various levels of confidentiality— mostly troop movements and troop locations. Cole's job was to find out who was sending the messages. He was tasked with quietly catching the end of a loose thread so that intelligence services could unravel the organization the traitor was feeding.

Thirty-six vets were currently being treated at the facility—all men. A coincidence, the others had told him. Sometimes they had female vets here too.

The staff numbered nineteen.

Step one was to narrow down the field of suspects. Cole had been working on that for the past two days.

The patients—some of them still active-duty—were the ones with military information, and Cole suspected the traitor had to be one of them. His CO was running detailed background checks, working the case from that end.

So far Cole had crossed off Trevor and Alejandro, then Dale, a grumbling marine. Trevor was too emotionally brittle to pull off being a spy. Alejandro and Dale had never been stationed in some of the regions the clandestine messages had mentioned.

Cole had talked to as many guys as he could. He'd had plenty of opportunity: in the cafeteria, in group therapy, in the gym. But he wasn't going to overlook the staff either.

From the staff list, he'd crossed off Annie Murray. That left him with fifty-one more names on the combined list. He needed to cross off fifty names to find the traitor.

He stopped in front of the main door that led to the admin offices.

The hallway stood deserted. Next to the door, a little red light blinked on the magnetic card reader. Only staff could enter.

Cole reached into his pocket and pulled out the card he'd lifted from Annie's bag while she slept on their way back from her house.

For the breadth of a second, he thought about the trust she'd put in him: letting him go home with her, then sleeping next to him as he drove her back.

If she found out that he was using her like this, their budding friendship would end in a hurry. Cole ignored a twinge of regret. He wasn't at Hope Hill to make friends.

The man sat in his car two houses down from Annie's house. She'd brought a patient home with her. *Cole Makani Hunter.*

The man in the car slammed his fist in the steering wheel.

He didn't follow them when they left, after they'd spent a full hour in that damned garage. Alone. Together.

He knew where they were going. Hope Hill.

He needed time to calm the rage that flowed in his veins. He pictured Annie Murray, on her knees in front of him, offering a tearful apology. He pictured himself slapping her. Hard enough to make that smart little brain of hers rattle.

That would shock her, wouldn't it? She thought he was all kind and soft and mild—as if he were half a man. He was a good guy, but that didn't mean he was a wimp. One of these days, he was going to introduce her to the real him.

He found the thought arousing. He finally turned the key in the ignition and pulled into the street. He took the scenic route by the reservoir, the road deserted this time of night.

He saw one car, a white pickup, coming from the opposite direction.

Then the flash of a fox trotting out onto the road.

The pickup braked, but the back tire hit the fox with a glancing blow.

As the pickup moved on, the fox flopped on the road, stunned but alive—a large, beautiful beast.

The man angled his steering wheel and crossed into the opposite lane. *Thump.*

He stopped the car and looked into the rearview mirror.

One leg was still twitching.

The man put the car in reverse and backed over the stupid animal for good measure.

Then he pulled over and got out to inspect his kill.

Perfect.

Chapter Seven

Wednesday

ANNIE WOKE DISORIENTED, IN A STRANGE BED. A CONFUSED MOMENT PASSED before the events of the previous day came back to her in a staggering rush. She groaned into her pillow. *Oh God, the house.*

Her house was missing a *wall*.

The temptation to stay in bed and in complete denial was overwhelming. Except, the contractor was coming this morning. With another groan, Annie threw off the covers.

She grabbed her phone from the nightstand to check the weather. Local weather—clear all day. Rupert, however, had been upgraded to a category 2 hurricane, heading north to Cuba.

Annie said a prayer for the people affected by Rupert, then pushed herself out of bed and opened the window that faced the courtyard and the weeping willow. She did a few stretches and breathing exercises. She kept her eyes on the tree, determined to put herself into a positive frame of mind to start her day.

"The hurricane is turning away. There is no structural damage to the house. It's going to be an easy fix. I'm going to have a great day."

Some days her morning affirmations were more elaborate, but this was all she had in her today. She cleaned up, dressed, then hurried down the hallway.

Her stomach growled. Too bad she'd overslept. She had an appointment with Dr. Ambrose, the psychiatrist on staff, at eight.

Could she cancel?

Normally, she would have fed her animals by now and let the llamas and the donkey out to graze. She had a ton of stuff to do today.

Or was that just an excuse to cancel because she didn't want to see Dan? She had conflicted feelings that she wanted to unconflict first.

All the therapists and counselors were in therapy themselves. They took on various emotional burdens from patients that needed to be dealt with. Trouble happened when problems were allowed to pile up and be internalized.

Annie had gone to some dark places with her patients. She had to cleanse herself on a regular basis to wash away that darkness, to be ready for the next session and the next. So, fine, Dan wasn't optional.

"Here she comes." Dan Ambrose had his door open and waved her in.

The staff psychiatrist was forty-two and kept in shape, although he didn't have that warrior body most of the patients at Hope Hill did. He didn't look military; he looked like an academic. Which he was. He gave classes at West Chester University now and then, a class or two every couple of semesters—Psych 101 and Abnormal Psychology. When he'd had the flu this past summer, Annie had helped him grade papers. He was handsome in a soft, good-looking professor kind of way, with dark-blond hair, brown eyes, and a pleasant face.

He reached for the bulky, knitted sweater on the back of his chair and pulled it on. "I sit too much," he said on a sigh. "My circulation isn't what it used to be. I'm always cold lately. Shouldn't I be too young for this?" He gave a self-depreciating chuckle.

Annie closed the door behind her and slid into the large leather armchair that faced the desk. The chair had been bought with well-built soldiers in mind. She felt like Alice in Wonderland after taking the pill that made her shrink.

"I hear you had a rough day yesterday," Dan said.

"Not as rough as it could have been. I got a room here."

"Good." Dan flashed a warm smile.

They'd gone out together a few times. Actually, she'd thought they were consulting over dinner. Right up until Dan had tried to kiss her. Could have knocked her over with a feather. She'd extricated herself, but things had been awkward for a week or so after that. She had no idea what he'd been thinking. Dating a coworker was as big a taboo as dating a patient. Technically, she *was* his patient. They had sessions.

Maybe Dan liked her because they had psychology in common, and other things too. She'd been raised by a single mother; he'd been raised by a single father. They often talked about that. But their similar pasts and interests wouldn't be enough basis for a romantic relationship, even under different circumstances. She'd never felt any attraction toward him.

"So how is the house?" he asked.

"I'll let you know after I talk with the contractor."

"If there's anything you need, just let me know."

"Thanks."

Dan held her gaze for a moment to make sure that she really was all right, and then he glanced at his notebook. "You started with a new patient this week. How is that going?"

How long do you have?

Annie didn't want to talk to Dan about Cole, but she had to. She felt an unexpected attraction to him that wasn't entirely patient-appropriate. Normally, when she looked at a patient, she didn't allow attraction as an option. But when she'd first met Cole, she hadn't known that she would soon be working with him.

She settled back in her chair and gave the abridged version of their initial meeting, then talked about Cole going with her to the midnight feeding.

With any other patient, she wouldn't have done it. But Cole did have that possible tendency to self-harm, which still worried her. And he had a marked resistance to therapy. Spending extra time with him could work. Being away from the facility might help him let his guard down. If she could build credibility with him, that would increase the chances for a successful treatment outcome exponentially.

Dan kept his voice carefully neutral when he asked, "Do you think it's smart to see him outside of therapy?"

"I think he needs normalcy. They all do. And I think being around animals is therapeutic."

"We have the cats for that."

She bit back a smile. "The skunks did alarm him."

He watched her as he steepled his hands. "Are you getting attached to this man?"

"No." A slight attraction did not equal attachment. "I like him." She could admit that much. "I don't know why." She slumped in the chair. "He's not a fan of ecotherapy. Only signed up for more sessions because he liked the idea of art therapy even less." And he needed the minimum required therapy hours to be able to stay at Hope Hill.

Dan tapped his steepled fingers together as he evaluated her revelations. But instead of warning her to be careful with Cole, he moved on. "How are you doing with Trevor?"

Trev. Annie switched gears. "I wish I could see him more."

"Maybe soon. I do think you and I will have to do the lion's share. No offense to Milo, but Trevor isn't going to improve from having needles stuck in his ass." He waved his hand as if trying to erase that last word. "Sorry. I'm tired. I've been working too much."

Dan was somewhat of a professional snob. Out of all the people at Hope Hill, he considered only Annie as his *almost* equal, because she had a degree in psychology. He was unfailingly polite to the other staff members and supported their therapies, but he believed them to be the icing on the cake. Annie was pretty sure that Dan thought he did all the real work.

"What are you working on? Another article?" she asked, because she didn't want to argue about Milo, who was an excellent acupuncturist.

"The History of Medieval Medical Practices." Dan was proud, to the point of vanity, of his publication record.

He cleared his throat. "Back to Trevor. He's not making much progress with me. I'm worried about him."

That put Annie on alert. Dan wasn't prone to worry. "I'll pay extra attention to him at our next session."

They talked about Trevor for another few minutes, then about her other patients, and then, at the end, about her continued troubles with Joey.

After the session, Annie grabbed a granola bar and a cup of tea from the cafeteria before heading out. Time for the morning feeding, finally. Time to let the grazing animals loose in the backyard. Esmeralda the donkey, especially, didn't like to be cooped up in the garage.

Her phone rang. Annie took the call as she walked.

"How are you?" Kelly asked. "I'm so sorry for what happened. I'm going to help you pay for it. Want me to come over to help clean up?"

"Let's wait with that until I find out if it's safe to go in. Thanks for offering. I'm not mad at you. I swear."

"I'm mad at myself. Home reno looks a lot easier on TV." Kelly did sound miserable. "Listen, I just listed a house for a client. When it sells and I get the commission, I'm going to give you the money."

"You have your own mortgage. You have alimony to pay."

"Loser exes. What's wrong with them? Has Joey stopped stalking you?"

Annie glanced at her phone. "No texts so far today."

"It's early yet." Kelly called out a greeting that came through the line faintly, as if she'd put the phone down for a second. Then she said, "I'm at the agency. People just came in. I have to hang up. Are you going to be OK?"

"I will be one hundred percent better than OK." Annie raised her voice a notch so the universe could hear her.

"Let me know when you find out more about the damage," Kelly said before they hung up.

Cole was leaning against Annie's car in the parking lot, as if he'd been waiting for a while. And maybe thinking about bench-pressing the Prius out of boredom. Seriously, he probably could have. One-handed.

He pushed away from the trunk as she reached him. "I thought I'd go with you and help. I have a couple of hours." He jerked his head toward the silver pickup next to the Prius. "We could take my ride today."

"If you have a car, why were you walking to the gas station the other day?"

"Just rented it this morning. When I came here, I flew into Philly from Chicago and had the shuttle bring me out here from the airport. I didn't want to drive through Philly one-handed. Out here, it's no big deal. There's no real traffic."

She eyed the pickup. The truck definitely fit him better than her Prius.

"Ram 1500 HFE," he said, as if the words actually had meaning. "Highest gas mileage in its class. I figured I couldn't get you into it otherwise. EcoDiesel three-point-zero liter, V-6, two hundred forty horsepower, intercooled turbo engine."

He looked so pleased with himself that she didn't have the heart to say no. He was reaching out to another person. He was venturing out into the civilian world. He was taking interest in something other than his dark memories. All of that supported recovery.

So she said, "I only understood half of that, but OK. Maybe we could pick up a couple of bales of hay."

He didn't exactly smile at her. But the way he looked at that moment, she could almost imagine him having a twin brother who might have smiled. Once. She could almost imagine what a smile might look like on Cole's face.

He opened the passenger side door for her, glancing at the Prius. "How do you usually bring home all the hay and feed?"

"They deliver. But as long as you have this monster, I wouldn't mind skipping the delivery fee."

As she stepped between his car and hers, she caught sight of her employee ID card on her driver's seat, so she grabbed that and put it back into her purse. *Must have fallen out last night.* Then she climbed up into the pickup.

"Big, right?" His voice dripped with manly satisfaction.

"As far as environmental impact goes? Might as well set the Redwood National Park on fire."

"I don't think the National Park Service would agree." He sniffed toward her cup. "That doesn't smell like coffee."

"Herbal tea. Hibiscus pomegranate."

He shook his head as he started the engine. "That's not normal. You know that, right?"

"Considering the effect caffeine has on the nervous system, everyone should—"

He raised his index finger between them. "If you bad-mouth coffee, I don't think we can be friends."

She watched him as he drove out of the parking lot.

Friends. Is that what they were becoming?

Not really.

He was her patient. In a few weeks, he would be gone. He shouldn't need a lot more time in intensive therapy than that. What the staff did at Hope Hill worked.

Annie liked seeing patients getting better and stretching their wings, flying away. And she'd be happy for Cole when he did the same. If she felt a pang of something else at the thought of him leaving, she shoved the knowledge away.

"Might as well stop by the feed store on the way over." She gave him directions. Best to just focus on the work.

At the store, she picked out what she needed and asked for help with loading the truck. While she was chatting with Maddie at the counter, the woman's eyes rounded as she openly ogled Cole through the window. She was forty, newly single, and definitely enjoying the freedom to look.

Annie turned, her gaze snared by the sight of Cole tossing fifty-pound feedbags into the back of the truck one-handed. And when Maddie sighed, Annie might have echoed her.

Then she snapped out of it and ran. If he hurt himself, the physical therapist was going to strangle her.

"Cole!" But because she was behind him, he couldn't hear her, so she had to tap his shoulder.

"What?" he turned, his gaze immediately snapping to her mouth. He wasn't even breathing hard.

"Don't hurt yourself." As soon as the words were out, she knew she shouldn't have said them.

A hard look came into his eyes. "I'm not useless."

"That's not what I meant. Obviously, you're stronger one-handed than I am with two. But you're still recovering."

"No."

"No what?"

"I'm not recovering." The words came out clipped. "I'll never be *recovered*. My right arm will never regain full movement."

Her heart fluttered and maybe bled a little. But the last thing he'd want was her pity.

So she said, "Let's not pretend you can't do twice what normal men can, with one arm tied behind your back. Honestly. To be frank, this kind of petty whining is completely unappealing. Also unbecoming a Navy SEAL."

She passed him and put the milk for the skunks into the cab. When, from the corner of her eye, she saw him shaking his head and going back to work, she got into the cab without offering to help.

A couple of minutes passed before he slid behind the wheel next to her. "Don't think I don't know you're trying to manipulate my emotions with some kind of therapist ninja tricks."

She rolled her eyes. "I'm an ecotherapist. Ninja therapy is a completely different branch. I could never do that. I don't even like wearing black."

The tight set of his mouth softened again. He didn't look quite as lighthearted as earlier, but he wasn't back to full resistance either. Annie relaxed into her seat.

Recovery had two components: physical and psychological. As far as she was concerned, the latter was more important. She was always fully conscious of that during a therapy session. In a session, she would never tell anyone they couldn't do something, like she had just done to Cole. She'd slipped. Cole was out here, in her real life, and it threw her off.

The patients at Hope Hill weren't locked up. Annie ran into them in town all the time, chatted, even had coffee with a few. But they hadn't hung around her like Cole, hadn't gone home with her.

He was more intense, more take-charge than the others. He didn't exactly ask. He went ahead and did what he wanted. Maybe the need to dominate was a Navy SEAL thing. Would those qualities help or hinder him in his recovery? She hoped for the former.

"Did you always live in Broslin?" he asked.

"Lived here as a kid, moved away, then moved back recently."

"Big family?"

"One grandfather and one cousin."

"How do they feel about the nature-therapy thing?"

She grinned. "You make it sound like I'm a pole dancer."

His gaze sharpened. A hungry-bear look came into his eyes, and it sent a shiver of awareness down her spine.

"Ecotherapy is a legitimate branch of therapy, based on scientific study," she rushed to say as they stopped at a red light. "Paoli Hospital is not that far from here, up on Route 30. They did one of the early studies there. The ward where their gallbladder patients recover has an odd arrangement. Half the rooms have windows that look at a brick wall, and the other half look at a courtyard with trees. The patients in the rooms that look to the courtyard were able to go home a day early, on average. They needed one dose of heavy drugs postsurgery to deal with pain. The brick-wall patients needed four."

He didn't say anything. Looked thoughtful. At least he was no longer laughing at the concept.

"Japan and Germany have done a bunch of similar studies," she added. "Nature therapy has been long accepted and used there. In Japan, they call it *shinrin-yoku*, forest bathing." And because Cole didn't stop her, she kept going.

By the time they reached her house, the contractor's truck waited by the curb, next to the dumpster. As Cole pulled into the driveway, Ed Sanders came around the back.

The contractor was in his midfifties, in good shape, hair that sexy salt-and-pepper gray. He wore his trademark overalls stamped with the red company logo designed by his wife. He lifted a calloused hand in greeting. "Hey there."

After Annie introduced the two men, Ed fitted her with a hardhat from the back of his truck and took her around back, leaving Cole to unload the feed bags. Nothing she could say to him would stop him anyway.

"How bad is it?" She eyed the blue tarp tacked to where the bathroom wall used to be.

"Not good." Ed looked upset on her behalf. "You ought to look up whoever inspected this house when you bought it and ask for your money back."

"The thought had crossed my mind. The house isn't going to collapse, is it?"

"Not from this damage, but let me look inside before I give you a definitive answer."

She had the keys, so she let him in the back door, into the kitchen that also stood in shambles.

He walked through, making sympathetic noises. "Natalie saw the show. She said it was something."

Natalie, his wife, was a soft-spoken, lanky black woman who ran the Broslin Ballet School. She was about five years older than Annie, always impeccably put together, graceful, and kind. She donated free dance lessons to foster kids.

Back in July, Natalie had Annie bring two orphaned baby goats over to the dance school so the girls could copy the goat kids' frolicking for two hours as a movement lesson. Annie had never laughed so hard in her life. She had a feeling neither had some of the girls. She had the video on her animal-sanctuary website. That single video had received twice as many clicks as all her other posts put together.

Ed thought Natalie hung the moon and the stars. That Annie still believed in true love was at least half due to the two of them.

Ed scratched his neck. "So I take it Kelly's crew ain't coming back to fix this mess?"

Annie winced. "They aren't really a crew. They were picked more for decoration. Kelly pulled them together for the show."

"Were they insured and bonded?"

Annie looked down at her shoes. "I feel pretty stupid."

Ed patted her arm in a fatherly gesture. "You were helping your cousin."

"She was helping me too. Can't blame her for not knowing the bathroom studs were rotten. I live here, and I didn't know it either."

They walked back to the bathroom, to the worst of the damage. Every time she looked at that blue tarp, she wanted to cry.

Ed tapped around and shone his flashlight into the walls and partially open ceiling. He hemmed and hawed, but then finally said the words Annie most wanted to hear. "Good news is, the house definitely isn't gonna collapse."

But before Annie could sink into sweet relief, Ed added, "Bad news is, I'm booked a couple of months out. I'll ask the crew and see how many guys can come over after the regular hours." He frowned.

"But?"

"They can still only put in an hour or two a day. Construction's hard work. They're pretty tired by the time I'm done with them. *And* they'll want overtime."

While that sounded reasonable, it also sounded expensive. And slow. So much for a quick fix.

She must have looked as discouraged as she felt, because Ed said, "You could ask someone else. I won't be offended."

"I'd rather wait for you." She wanted someone she trusted.

"I'll send out someone with some plywood, tomorrow the latest. He'll seal up the hole, so at least the house will be secure. Then I'll make sure someone comes by to clean up the construction rubble inside. I saw you have a construction container already, so at least we don't have to wait for that."

"You have a roundabout estimate?"

"I'll work one up by tomorrow. Then I'll see if I can squeeze you in the schedule somehow. If you're sure Kelly's crew won't come back."

"I'm sure. Her guys looked traumatized." Rob, the one who'd knocked out the wall, had called twice to apologize. "And I think Kelly lost confidence."

"She'll bounce back. That girl always does. Shame about her husband."

Annie couldn't deny Kelly's resilience. She wanted their relationship to be less strained, but she wasn't sure how to overwrite the past.

"I called the insurance company yesterday," she told Ed. "They're sending a claims adjuster next week."

"We shouldn't do anything until they see everything and take pictures." Ed began walking out. "Give me a call after they leave. Think about how you want to fix up things, how much budget you can get together. See how much the insurance gives you, then call the TV station and Kelly. They should take responsibility."

"I'll contact the TV station." Although, as far as she knew, the tiny local station was always strapped financially. And Annie definitely wasn't going to sue her own cousin.

Ed left with an encouraging smile and a friendly wave. Annie headed to the garage, not surprised to see Cole's shiny new truck in the driveway already unloaded.

She went in search of him.

He wasn't in the garage. Weird. He hadn't been in the house, so where was he?

Finally, as she went around the front, she saw him by the road. She could see the tight set of his mouth even from thirty feet away. Now what? Then she saw what he was looking at, and her breath caught.

Could I, please, catch a break?

A ten-foot section of her fence was down past the garage, posts and wire fencing lying on the ground, demolished.

Cole must have seen her from the corner of his eye, because he turned toward her.

"When did this happen?" she asked.

He raised an eyebrow.

She was moving too fast, nearly running, so he couldn't read her lips. She slowed down as she neared. "When did this happen?"

"Sometime after we left last night." He ran a hand over his bald head, his wide shoulders stiff as he considered the mess. "I would have seen this kind of damage as we drove away. It's a big fricking hole."

She didn't grind her teeth, but only because she couldn't afford the dentist. "Someone went off the road. Did they leave a note?"

"Not here."

She checked her phone. Nobody had sent her a text or left a message while she'd been talking with Ed. If a neighbor had done this, they might have. "I'm going to check the mailbox."

Whoever had run over her fence had better step up to the plate and accept responsibility—pay for the repairs. She had to have the fence fixed. The llamas, along with Esmeralda the donkey, and sometimes even Dorothy the pig, spent most of their day outside. It would be bad enough when the weather turned cold and they had to be cooped up inside.

She searched through her mailbox and groaned when she found nothing but junk mail and bills. She put them in Cole's pickup. She'd look through them at Hope Hill.

By the time she returned to Cole, he was standing on the shoulder of the road, among her small field of colorful whirligigs. His expression was closed, his body even tenser than when she'd left him.

Then she saw the small lump in the grass next to him, and she tensed too.

Not again. She moved forward with dread.

The fully grown fox lay motionless, eyes glazed over, limbs frozen in death. His beautiful autumn-red fur ruffled in the slight breeze.

Annie's throat tightened. Her heart clenched. She *hated* seeing an animal hurt. She hated seeing one dead. What people felt for the loss of a beloved pet, she felt for every deer, woodchuck, and raccoon she saw by the side of the road. She'd always been that way. She couldn't even stand it when people ran over the worms on the asphalt after a rain.

"I hate this stupid curve in the road." Misery and frustration thickened her voice. "You have no idea how many animals get hit here."

"Is that why you have all these?" Cole jerked his head toward the slowly clattering whirligigs.

"Yes. To scare animals away from crossing the road here where people can't see them as they drive around the curve."

Cole watched her with that expressionless gaze of his, probably thinking she was a nutjob for being this upset over a stray fox and for trying to stop animals from getting run over. But when he opened his mouth, he didn't bring up her weirdness.

Instead, he said, "Whoever hit your fence didn't lose control of their car. They hit the fence on purpose."

She glanced between him and the fence as she processed his words.

"No skid marks on the road," he pointed out. "No skid marks on the shoulder. No skid marks on the grass." He watched her. "Your stalker ex?"

Her mind, too, immediately jumped to Joey, but she rejected the idea just as fast. "Joey wouldn't do this. Nobody would do something like this on purpose. Why would they?"

She wanted agreement from Cole, but Cole wasn't done yet.

"The fox wasn't hit here." He toed the animal with his boot and turned the stiff body, making Annie's stomach lurch. "No blood on the ground. No blood on the road. No blood on the shoulder. Somebody hit this fox somewhere else, or found the carcass on the side of the road, and brought it here."

She blinked at him and shivered. She rubbed her arms, frowning in her effort to understand. Someone brought her a dead animal? *For what possible purpose?*

"You say this happens a lot," Cole said in a careful tone. "How often?"

She had to think. "Once a week? Sometimes more than once."

"Since when?"

"It started a couple of months ago. Around the time when they broke ground on that new development on Victoria Circle. I figured the noise was scaring animals this way. I started finding—" She flinched. "When I come out in the morning."

"Do they do construction at night?"

What? "No."

Then she caught his meaning. *Oh.* She always found the broken little bodies in the morning. The animals were hit at night. But they wouldn't be running from the construction noises at night.

She felt stupid for not having thought of that before. Yet she still wasn't ready to concede. "That doesn't mean someone is bringing them here."

The maliciousness of the idea raised goose bumps on her arms. She had a hard time believing anyone would do that. There had to be another explanation.

Cole kept watching her. "You drive around town an average amount?"

She nodded.

"Do you see roadkill always in the same spot, this often?"

She thought about it. "Roadkill yes, but here and there, not concentrated like this. It's the country. We have animals all over. You see roadkill every day. But not in the same place."

She had trouble comprehending what that meant. After all the grief and worry and heartbreak she'd felt because she hadn't been able to save these animals . . . someone had done that to her on purpose.

Who would do something like this?

She still didn't want to accept the possibility. "I don't think—"

Irritation flashed across Cole's face as he took her by the shoulders. A shoulder and an elbow, actually, since his injured arm didn't have full range of motion and couldn't reach all the way up.

He fairly towered over her, and her breath caught. He really was as big as a bear.

He flashed a dark scowl. He was standing too close, his gaze too heated, his tone clipped when he said, "You can't brush this off."

She tried to shrug his hands off, but he was unmovable. "Stop trying to scare me."

"Stop pretending, dammit! Denial can be as lethal as a hand grenade." He growled the words.

Chapter Eight

COLD FURY COURSED THROUGH COLE AT WHOEVER WAS THREATENING ANNIE. Close on fury's heels came frustration. He couldn't stand seeing her so crestfallen.

His fingers tightened on her as he drew in a rough breath. "You're too damned determined to assume the best of everybody."

She needed to grow up, and in a hurry.

"You're the most softhearted person I've ever known, you know that?" Pure light. Hopelessly unfit for living in a harsh world. He wanted to shake her and snap her into reality. He wanted to protect her.

Maybe if he stopped acting like a Neanderthal, she'd let him.

He dropped his hands.

"I'll see what I can do about the fence." He pivoted while she still stood there, wide-eyed at his outburst. He stalked toward the collapsed section, calling over his shoulder, "You call the cops."

Whoever was messing with her like this had to be a sick and evil man. A sick and evil man Cole meant to hunt down and deal with before he left Broslin.

He glanced back. Annie had wrapped her arms around her midsection. Her gaze cut to the fox, then back to Cole. She looked as if someone had punched her in the gut. "I don't think the police will care about someone moving roadkill around."

He turned and took a step back toward her, then decided to stay where he was so he wouldn't put his hands on her again. "You've been stalked. Then dead animals were left for you to find." He gestured at the fence behind him. "And now destruction of property."

Because she still wasn't reaching for her phone, he added. "It's called *escalation*. Whoever wants to terrify you is escalating. Do you understand? Next step could be to harm you physically."

A shudder ran through her.

Damn if the thought of someone trying to harm her didn't make Cole's blood boil. He didn't enjoy scaring her, but he would hate it even more if she got hurt. "Call the police."

When she pulled out her cell phone at last, he resumed walking toward the fence, but he kept an eye on her.

She made the call while heading back to her garage, probably to feed her animals.

When she passed out of sight, Cole assessed the damage—more than he could fix here and now. He noted the supplies he'd need: a hole digger, two posts, a ten-foot section of chain link. The rest, he could probably reuse from what lay on the grass. He began separating what he could salvage from what would have to go to the dumpster.

He kept going until he saw a police car pull up. Had to give credit to the cops; even though it wasn't an emergency call, the cruiser was there in less than ten minutes. Cole left the fence and went to join Annie.

Detective Harper Finnegan was in his midthirties, built and sharp-eyed, but with plenty of small-town friendliness. Smart too. He took Annie seriously on the first try, without Cole intervening.

Then the detective turned his attention to Cole, dropping a few degrees on the friendliness meter. "And how are you involved in all this, Mr. Hunter?"

His expression wasn't accusatory, but Cole could see where Finnegan was going. Cole was handy. If the whole trail of nastiness could be pinned on him, the detective could be home for lunch. Nobody wanted to do things the hard way if an easy way was readily available.

Cole shot Finnegan a look that let him know Cole and *easy* didn't live in the same area code, in case the man was prone to delusions. "I am helping Annie with her animals."

Annie said, at the same time, "He's from Hope Hill."

They began walking back to the fox.

"How long have you been in Broslin?" the detective asked, clearly not intimidated by the fact that Cole probably had thirty pounds of muscle on him.

"Five days. Came up from Chicago." Cole watched as Finnegan mentally matched that fact against the months-long harassment and made the decision that Cole likely wasn't involved in the mystery of the roadside carcasses.

But because he was apparently a decent detective, he didn't drop the issue quite that fast. "Is that your truck in the driveway?"

"Rented it this morning." Best to give the man whatever he needed. No need to start a pissing contest. The sooner they were done here, the sooner Finnegan could go after the real perpetrator.

"When I first got here," Cole said, "I wasn't sure if I wanted a car, how much I'd leave the facilities. But it's a pretty nice little town. They keep telling us to interact with the local community. Civilians and civilian life and whatnot."

Not that any of that had been on his mind when he'd decided to stop by the car-rental place. He'd been thinking along the lines of wanting to help Annie.

The detective nodded. "Let me grab a bag."

As he strode off toward his cruiser, Annie turned to Cole. "Do you think he'll figure out who did this?"

"Probably not." Cole silently swore. "Whoever hit the fence wouldn't have gotten out, so there wouldn't be fingerprints. The ground is grassy, so the cops can't take a tire mold. And even if the guy grabbed the roadkill with his bare hands, you can't take fingerprints off fur."

He watched the detective check out the front of the rented pickup for damage. He was thorough. That gave Cole some hope.

Finnegan grabbed a black garbage bag and gloves from the trunk of his cruiser.

Annie's full lips turned down at the corners. "Why are we going through all this, then? I don't want to waste Harper's time."

Harper. They're on a first-name basis. Cole hadn't caught that when the detective first showed up. He'd still been back by the fence.

So Annie and Finnegan knew each other. Cole set that thought aside for later. For now, he focused on the fact that Finnegan might work harder for a friend.

"I wanted you to call so there's a record." Cole watched the man approach. "So if you need help in an emergency, they'll know you're being stalked and threatened. I want them to take you seriously and haul ass."

"I've been threatened?" She turned from Finnegan as he bagged the fox. And before Cole could answer, she said, looking at him at last, "Yes, I feel threatened. I haven't thought of it like that. Nobody left me a threatening message on my phone or anything."

Cole gestured toward the bagged fox as Finnegan carried the carcass back to his cruiser. "There's your message."

When she shivered—a heartbroken, devastated look on her face—he had this crazy impulse to put his arm around her, but he was pretty sure she wouldn't want that. She'd flinched earlier when he'd grabbed her. He was a big-ass guy, they barely knew each other, and they weren't exactly friends. And she was on his right. He couldn't raise his right arm as high as her shoulders.

He kicked at a rock, sending it flying through the tall grass.

When she began walking toward the driveway and Harper Finnegan—who stashed the fox in his trunk—Cole followed her.

"Are you staying here?" the detective asked Annie as he slammed the trunk closed, glancing toward the yellow Do Not Cross tape. "Leila saw the show. Sounds like it was a mess."

"I'm staying at Hope Hill until Ed Sanders can fix things up."

"Good idea." The detective stepped around the back of his cruiser as his radio went off, the lights flashing red on the unit. "If you see anything suspicious, or if you feel like something's off, making you nervous, call the station. Trust your instincts."

He waited until Annie nodded before getting into the car and responding to the call. Since he had his back to them, Cole couldn't read what he said.

After Finnegan left, Cole turned to Annie. "Is this a small-town thing? Everyone knowing everyone?"

"I don't really."

"You knew Ed."

"Everybody knows Ed."

"You know Leila."

"Leila is the dispatcher at the police station. I met her at the Christmas bazaar last year. We both volunteered."

Of course they did.

"You knew Harper Finnegan."

"I know most of the cops. Murphy Dolan, my boss, used to be a cop at the PD. Then he and Kate, his girlfriend, moved away. When they moved back, they decided to build the rehab center. She's a therapist too. She won some kind of a grant, and they started with one building. The town did most of the other fund-raising, I think. All that happened before I came back. But since Murph used to be a cop, the guys in the PD helped out a lot. They still stop by sometimes to talk with Murph."

"Is Finnegan one of your exes? He responded to the call pretty fast."

"What? No. We just have a good police department."

The shoulder tension Cole hadn't been aware of relaxed. He chose not to examine the reasons behind that.

"Esmeralda wants to go out," Annie said. At his raised eyebrow she added, "She's rattling the garage door."

He stilled. Listened. Couldn't hear a damn thing.

She kept talking. "They all need to get out. They usually spend the day outside. But the donkey is the troublemaker."

She had a one-eyed donkey, named Esmeralda, who was a troublemaker. For some reason that made Cole want to smile. For the last couple of months, his default mood had been teeth-grinding frustration. Annie Murray was definitely softening him.

In some ways. Certainly not in others.

She might look all innocent, but he was beginning to think she was as dangerous as naval combat.

He stepped toward his truck. "Let's go get what you need for the fence."

She tilted her head, exposing her graceful neck. He made himself look at her lips so he could read when she said, "Don't you have any appointments?"

Looking at her full lips made him want to—

Patient—therapist. Keep your head straight, Sailor. "Not until after lunch."

She still hesitated. "You don't have to do this."

Abandoning someone in trouble went against everything he was. "True. I could be lying on my bed, staring at the ceiling, thinking dark thoughts. Or I could be outside, with another person, being social, enjoying some physical exercise. And restoring something, which, as we know, also restores one's soul. As my therapist, which one would you say is better?"

She got into the truck without another word.

At the farm store, Maddie behind the counter looked like she'd been expecting them. "Harper was here." She stopped to fan herself. "We had a shoplifter. He said . . . I mean Harper, not that good-for-nothing Miller kid . . . that your fence was down. We have everything in the back."

"Thanks, Maddie." Annie headed that way like a woman on a mission, focusing on the fix instead of on her problems.

Maddie stopped her and said, "If you don't mind used . . . Harry Ormuz was here for nails when Harper came in. Anyway, Harry said he'd just pulled out a perfectly good split-rail fence at a job over on Ridge Road. They're putting in a pool, so they need a full four-foot fence. He hated throwing out all that good wood. It's all in his backyard. He said he won't be home, but you can swing by and take as much as you want. You know where he lives."

So they ended up buying only a roll of chain link and renting the hole digger. Annie spent only half of what Cole figured she would.

She gave him instructions to Harry Ormuz's place, a few blocks away. Cole felt weird walking onto private property and taking the fence posts. Maybe that too was a small-town thing.

They weren't halfway across the front lawn when a giant black dog raced around the house and charged straight at them.

Cole reached for Annie to shove her behind him, but she was already running forward. His heart stopped when she dropped to her knees and let the dog jump and slobber all over her.

"Hey," he called after her, his hands on his hips, "are therapists supposed to give patients heart attacks?"

She grinned back at him, hugging the behemoth dog for all she was worth.

"Could have warned me." Cole came up next to them, holding his hand out for the dog to sniff. Good-looking dog, he noticed, once his heart wasn't jumping out of his chest.

Annie kissed the beast on the top of its head. "This is Mouse. Tossed from a car when he was a puppy. He had a broken leg when I found him. Harry adopted him from me."

Why Cole hadn't expected this, he had no idea. Of course the dog was one of Annie's. Cole patted the massive head that reached above his waist. "Mouse?"

"He was tiny when I found him. He fit in my cupped hands. You should have seen him. He was the sweetest thing ever."

Looking at the dog the size of an elephant calf, Cole had trouble believing he'd ever been that small.

Mouse jumped circles around them, his tongue lolling like a big doofus. He practically sighed in pleasure when Cole scratched him behind his ears.

They spent more time with Mouse than they should have before they finally loaded up the fencing, the dog underfoot the whole time. He barked at the truck as Annie waved at him through the window when they left.

"A big dog like that would provide more security at your place than the llamas," Cole said as he pulled away from the curb. "A pig and a one-eyed donkey aren't going to do much for you, no offense."

A wistful look came into her eyes as she turned to him. "It'd be nice to have a dog. But they're adopted out so easily. If I keep one, every bag of food, every vet bill . . . I'd have to take that money from the animals nobody wants."

"You mean you might not be able to take in another litter of skunks."

She was hopeless. Yet there was something in her stubborn dedication to all things living that touched his hardened soldier's heart. Her company was like a feather drawn over an old, puckered scar that had only a little feeling left, just enough to appreciate the soft caress of that single feather.

There. He'd *never* had thoughts like that before he'd met her. Her weirdness was definitely contagious. She softened him and made him think about things he wouldn't normally think about. Being with her was like . . . reading poetry. And why he would think of that, he couldn't fathom. He hadn't read poetry since high school, dammit.

The two of them couldn't be more opposite. She'd saved countless lives, and he'd taken them. They had nothing in common.

Then a strange little thought unfurled in his mind: Maybe a world that had people like him in it needed people like her. Maybe they balanced out the cosmic scales.

He found the thought reassuring. He also discovered that the twin boulders of anger and regret that usually sat on his shoulders felt lighter when he was with her. Annie Murray threw light into all his dark places.

Another damn stupid thought he couldn't believe he was thinking. Yet he couldn't deny that he liked spending time with her. He enjoyed her company more than he'd enjoyed anyone else's in a long time. She did make him feel better.

He wanted to return the favor, help her if he could, with whatever he could.

He would start by fixing her fence.

Of course, he ended up needing her assistance.

Since the accident, every time Cole forgot that he was now a cripple and was confronted with his limitations, he'd flown into a dark rage. But the hours with Annie, having her by his side, didn't feel like a bad thing.

She'd had a rough morning, but she was all right. She was smiling, working without complaint, talking about the birds and the trees and her animals. She filled up the space around her with sunshine. She was an oddity, a curiosity. Which was why Cole kept watching her. He *had* to watch her to read her lips.

Keep telling yourself that.

When they finished with the fence, the job not half-bad, she let out her animals. The one-eyed donkey, Esmeralda, brayed her fool head off in delight, kicking her feet in the air.

Annie laughed. Cole strained to hear the sound. He couldn't, not a single note.

A strange feeling spread through his chest. Someone else might have called it longing, but Navy SEALs didn't long. *Jesus.*

As she caught his gaze, her expression switched from amusement to concern. "What's wrong?"

"Hungry." He said the first thing that came into his mind. "Want to grab a sandwich before we head back?"

"Depends. Is it tofu? Because—" He bit off the rest. When was the last time he'd teased anyone? He couldn't remember.

Before he could think too much about it, she asked, "How about organic ham and local cheese on rye bread with some greens?"

His stomach growled in answer.

He followed her inside the house through the back door. "Since we're in here, I take it Ed found no structural damage?"

He took two more steps before he stopped in his tracks. The wall between the kitchen and the living room had been knocked down and left there. Drywall and broken two-by-fours sat in dusty piles.

She turned from the rubble as if it hurt to look at the mess. Hell, it hurt *him,* and he had nothing to do with the place.

"No structural damage," she said. "Let's eat outside anyway. I'll grab the food from the fridge."

Her backyard was pretty simple, about a quarter of an acre, all fenced in, all grass, unmowed. She probably left it like that for her animals. She also had half a bale of hay tossed out there in the middle, and a lone picnic table with attached benches on the gravel patio.

"Won't the ham upset the pig?" he asked as he helped her carry out the packages.

"If she asks, we'll say it's tofu." She gave a soft sigh. "Dorothy belonged to an old couple. Some neighborhood boys stole her one night. They had the brilliant idea of cutting a rack of bacon out of her."

"She squealed like a pig and escaped?"

"Something like that. I talked with Edna and Al and offered to keep Dorothy while she was healing since they both walk with walkers. Catching her to disinfect the wound and change bandages wasn't going to happen. By the time she had healed, Al was in the hospital with a stroke. Edna asked me if I could keep Dorothy permanently."

Maybe the pig sensed the true origins of the lunch platter on the picnic table, because she stayed away.

The llamas and the donkey came over to investigate. The llamas moved on after a few seconds, but Annie had to shoo Esmeralda away from the bread.

The back fence stood about fifty yards from her back door. Right behind it, a massive cornfield began. The corn was still green, seven or eight feet tall in places.

Cole didn't like the lack of visibility. Someone could be skulking fifty yards from Annie's house, and she'd never know. Someone could hide in that corn and watch her. While Annie sat at her weatherworn picnic table, Cole strode to the fence and walked the perimeter.

The menagerie followed him, as if they were going for a walk together. When he stopped, Esmeralda tried to nip his butt.

"Hey."

The donkey blinked her one eye at him, the picture of innocence.

Cole pointed a warning finger at Esmeralda, then turned toward the house. The tarp would do little to keep someone out. The four windows had curtains, but none were drawn. At night, with the lights on, if someone was standing where Cole was right now, he could see right in.

One window belonged to the kitchen, over the sink. He wasn't sure about the others. Was her bedroom window on this side of the house?

He turned toward the cornfield. He didn't know much about farming. When did they cut corn? *The sooner the better.*

His gaze snagged on a spot where the weeds were trampled.

A faint path led into the corn. *Deer trail?*

Maybe deer regularly cut through the corn and jumped Annie's fence here, then cut through the property. Maybe they helped themselves to some of the hay she put out for the llamas and the donkey.

On Cole's side of the fence, he couldn't see if the track continued, since Annie's animals walked all over the backyard, trampling every square inch.

Annie waved at him from the picnic table, her expression warm, her movements graceful. Her lips moved, but he couldn't read them from this distance. He didn't need to. The body language was enough. She was telling him to come and eat.

"I'll be back in a minute," he called back to her. Then he jumped the fence.

He hurried forward on the narrow path that cut through the corn in a fairly straight line. He came out at the side of a country road a couple of minutes later. Could be the deer crossed the road here.

Or this could be where a stalker got into his car after watching Annie. Cole's muscles tensed. His instincts were sounding the alarm, but he had been trained to see danger everywhere. Dr. Ambrose had been talking to him about tuning down those instincts, adjusting to a civilian environment.

Cole was no longer at war. He was no longer a POW. He no longer had to be vigilant 24-7. He could sleep, and nobody was going to drag him from bed in the middle of the night to pull out his fingernails.

He turned and hurried back to Annie, hating the fact that not only could he no longer trust his body and his hearing, he couldn't even trust his instincts. In captivity, his instincts had kept him alive. Now, back home, among normal people, those hair-trigger instincts made him paranoid and antisocial—according to his shrink.

By the time he jumped the fence again, the food was all laid out, and Annie waited for him with an expectant smile.

God, what a picture—a painting of domestic bliss.

To live like this—uncomplicated, a picnic in the backyard with a smiling woman, without sounds and images from hell playing in his mind on an endless loop . . . That some people had this on a daily basis boggled the mind. Cole had never envied others, but just now, just for a second . . .

"How good is your self-defense training?" he asked, to give his thoughts a new direction.

"Spotty." She handed him a plate. "The police department gives classes for free every couple of months. Officer Flores does it. Gabriella. She teaches good stuff, but I don't practice enough. The guys at Hope Hill taught me a couple of pretty neat tricks too," she added. "Sometimes I work out at the gym. It's an employee benefit. But I'm pretty much a one-trick pony. The move I used on you on the walking trail is the only move I can do well."

"I think you could be good at it, if you put in the time."

"It's not my thing."

No. She wasn't a fighter.

"Who owns the cornfield?"

A subtle change washed over her features. Wariness came into her eyes, and some other emotions he didn't recognize.

"My grandfather. He's got about forty acres. Gramps can't work the land anymore, so he rents it to another farmer."

"Your grandfather lives around here?"

"The farmhouse is on the other side of all the corn."

"Must be nice to have family close by."

"You'd think so." Her smile strained. "How about a drink? I have peach iced tea."

He had no right prying into her family business, so he didn't. "Iced tea would be great."

She brought him a bottle and sat.

He picked up his sandwich. "Do you know there's a trail through the corn?"

"Sure. Deer. I use it too sometimes to cut through, if I don't feel like driving around."

He chewed. *There. A reasonable explanation.* One of those cases where he saw danger when he shouldn't have.

"Thanks for all the heavy lifting," she said.

"Not bad for a broken man?"

She put her sandwich down and put on her serious-therapist look. "We don't use terminology like that at Hope Hill. It's not helpful. Nobody is broken. Broken is a machine term."

He raised an eyebrow.

She winced. "Sorry. Can't turn it off. I'll stop lecturing now."

"Go ahead. I don't want you to bust something by holding it in."

She grinned. But then, too soon, she grew serious again. "Do you view yourself as a killing machine?"

"I was a sniper."

"So here's the thing." She pushed her plate away, gearing up. "Back when machines were first invented, they replaced a lot of workers.

Machines were just plain better, faster, and more efficient. The whole machine terminology—output, optimum performance, downtime, and all that—was soon applied to people. Especially in business. And then the military. A machine does what it's told without asking questions. Produce, produce, produce. Or fight, fight, fight."

"Sounds familiar so far."

"But people are not machines." Her gaze held sincere compassion that touched a cold spot inside his chest and warmed it. "You have an arm that doesn't work the same as your other arm. You have trouble with hearing. You are still you. There is nothing wrong with you, even if you can't *produce* like someone else can right now. You can do other things. You are not measured in terms of output. You are an incredibly complex, unique, creative, and curious human being with a soul. Your value to the world cannot be measured in machine terms like units of production."

Something inside him shifted. For the first time, he truly caught a glimpse of the world as Annie Murray saw it. And damn if he didn't want to live in that world. She drew him. When her face lit up like this, she had a kind of ethereal beauty that made it impossible to look away from her.

"I'm guessing," he said, "that ecotherapy principles are the opposite of the machine view?"

Her responding smile was radiant.

Cole didn't have the heart to add any snarky remarks. For the first time, he actually *didn't have* any snarky remarks.

"I'm willing to consider there might be something to all this," he said, wanting to keep that smile on her face.

"Does that mean you're willing to go into our sessions with a completely open mind?"

"I'll think about it. But I'm still not hugging a tree."

Chapter Nine

COLE BROUGHT ANNIE BACK TO HOPE HILL AFTER THEY'D BOTTLE-FED THE BABY skunks their lunch. He went for his session with Dr. Ambrose, then for a full hour of therapeutic massage. Back in his room, he tried to get into the thriller on his nightstand, but he gave up after a few minutes. The restlessness that filled him wouldn't let him sit still, let alone read.

Ten minutes later he was running around the track at the rehab center, appreciating the even ground. Now that one of his arms couldn't move as it should, balance was an issue. People constantly pumped their arms as they walked and ran, balancing their bodies. But with his right arm hanging uselessly at his side, Cole was slightly less sure on his feet. Especially when he was running.

In the gym, he held on to the treadmill's handlebar with his left. Out here, he had slightly more difficulty. Which was why he was out here. He needed to retrain himself, rewire his brain, and regain mastery over his body.

Annie was right. He wasn't a machine. But he still abhorred weakness.

Trevor was the only other person on the track, working hard to catch up with Cole. Cole cut back on his speed.

The kid nodded a greeting with an expression that was half gratitude and half relief, as if he wasn't sure whether Cole would want to talk to him again.

"Gonna rain any minute." Trevor was gasping for air, so his lips were more difficult to read than usual.

Cole caught enough to respond. "A little rain never hurt anyone."

Trevor flashed the kind of grin a kid would give an older brother he idolized. "I guess Navy SEALs aren't much bothered by water."

The comment didn't require a response, so Cole didn't give any.

"Ever done any high-profile missions?" Trev asked. "Like the Bin Laden thing?"

"Just average stuff." He couldn't talk about his missions. And Trev should know better than to bring any of that up.

"People are saying you were a sniper. Any high-value hits?"

"I don't think about that life anymore. We have to leave the past in the past."

They ran in silence for a minute or two before Trevor broke it again. "Big family back home?"

"Mother."

"Two mothers. Two fathers. Well, some are steps. Seven siblings. I'm the youngest." Instead of smiling, as most people did when talking about family, misery filled Trevor's face. "I guess I let them all down."

"You can't let your family down by serving your country," Cole said, because the kid looked like he might start crying.

Cole wished they could just run in silence. Movement made lip-reading more difficult. He caught what he could and guessed the rest, filled in the blanks.

"Yeah." Trevor didn't look convinced. "But going nuts." He wiped the sweat off his forehead with the back of his hand. "They have to be embarrassed. Small town, you know? Like this place. Everyone knows everyone's business."

"That just means everyone's pulling for you. In Chicago, even my neighbors don't know me. You're lucky."

"Yeah?" The kid's face cleared. "You think they're pulling?"

"I bet you're on the prayer list at church."

"That'd be nice." Trev's gaze turned heartbreakingly wistful. "I mean, I like the thought of that."

The rain that had been threatening all morning finally began with a drizzle, quickly wetting the track.

"I'm gonna peel off," Trevor said. "Neck injury. Not supposed to push it. See you around." He sprinted for the buildings.

Cole stayed on the track. He kept his eyes on the ground in front of his feet while he let his brain work on other things. He'd been here for five days—the first two days, before meeting Annie, spent with various assessments, a general orientation, a full physical, and his schedule being put together—but he still didn't have a suspect for the texts.

No obvious clues. Nobody was of Middle Eastern origin or had any connection to Yemen, as far as he could tell. He'd managed to search about half of the staff offices the other night with Annie's ID, but he hadn't found anything incriminating. He'd identified five more patients he could rule out, but what he wanted to find was the traitor.

He kept running. When he reached the beginning of the track again, he veered off toward the facilities, then ran past the buildings. He circled the front parking lot in a lazy loop.

He spent time on the front porch every day, watching cars come and go until he knew what belonged to whom. Now he scanned them again. Nothing jumped out at him, nothing too extravagant. If his target made good money selling intel, he or she hadn't spent it on a fancy car.

The vehicles ranged from rust heap to average, with an Audi and two Mercedes-Benzes representing the high end. He checked out each car he ran by up close—front seat, back seat. He wasn't looking for anything in particular, but maybe something outwardly innocent would give him a hint that the car's owner wasn't what he, or she, seemed.

He saw clothes and junk mail, an empty box, lots of crumbs. The occasional bumper sticker wasn't any more helpful either, mostly clever quips with some political snark thrown in. Libby, the reflexologist, drove a Corolla loaded with two car seats and sippy cups. The woman had twins. Their pictures were all over her office.

As Cole circled back to the modest compound of buildings, he cut through the yard. He thought about quitting, but then looked toward the woods and headed that way instead.

Restlessness and frustration pushed him. What was he missing? Was he slipping? Had his injuries affected his brain? Was he slower mentally as well as physically? Would he know it if he was, or was that something noticeable only by others?

He took the path he had walked with Annie on Monday. On the uneven ground, he immediately felt more off balance, but he didn't slow. He needed to get used to this, needed to learn to compensate for the rocks and dips, the small branches under his feet. He needed to learn his new body.

He ran, ignoring the drizzle that turned into rain, thinking about Annie's assertions that people were not to be treated like machines. Truth was, he *missed* being a well-oiled machine.

He noted the pain in his shoulder muscles. The PT guy had told him the pain came from holding his upper body too stiffly. So Cole stopped, rolled his shoulders, and stretched as best he could before going back to running.

The rain turned into a downpour. He kept going. Until he slipped. He flung out his right arm to catch himself, but, of course, his right arm didn't work, so he sprawled face-first into a puddle. The impact jarred the already injured arm, sending pain shooting up his shoulder.

Still, the pain he could handle. What he hated was the humiliation of being facedown in the mud, dammit.

He pushed himself up with his left arm, spit muddy water, wiped the dreck from his face with the palm of his left hand. Then he started running again.

He couldn't turn back now, not after falling. He had to push harder; he'd been made like that, trained like that.

He fell again, his pants and shirt completely covered in mud. His cheek stung. When he wiped the stinging spot with the back of his hand, his knuckles came away with blood. He'd cut his skin on a rock. A freaking run in the woods could draw blood from him now. *Shit.*

He pushed to his feet and ran faster. He was done with taking it slow. He was done with making allowances for his new limitations. *Done.*

He slipped in a puddle, fell, his entire weight coming down on his bad shoulder. Pain flashed hard enough to make his stomach roll with nausea. For a second there, he couldn't breathe. He rolled on his back to catch his breath. He closed his eyes against the rain and let it wash his face.

When he opened his eyes, he saw Annie peering down at him.

He hadn't heard her coming at all. If she'd been an enemy combatant, he'd be dead right now. He gave a vicious curse.

She simply held out her hand.

He held her amber gaze. He didn't want the help. Everything he was pushed him to stand on his own. But then there was this other impulse, this sudden need to take her hand, to touch her.

He reached for her before he could think about it. She smiled. And then he was standing.

He didn't want to let her go, but she pulled away, walking off the path and into the woods. He followed her.

Why? He wasn't a follower. He'd always been a leader. Yet he didn't question where she was going or why he should go with her.

She walked only fifty feet or so, to a giant tree, the trunk close to four feet wide. Pine boards were nailed to the trunk at foot-high intervals leading up. Cole looked at the tree house above them.

Annie went first, climbing easily.

He climbed after her, left hand up, then when his feet were steady on the next board, his right hand worked well enough to keep him from falling back as he reached over his head with his left again. He came out in a six-foot-by-six-foot little room that had only a floor, a roof, and half walls around it.

She sat in the far corner, cross-legged. "It's a deer blind. People used to hunt in these woods, but the area was posted after the rehab center went up. The buildings are too close. Nobody uses the blind anymore. I come here sometimes when it rains."

He sat in the opposite corner and crossed his own legs on the roughly hewn floorboards, mirroring her. Because the space was small, there was only about a foot or two of distance between their knees.

She glanced at his right cheek, then glanced away quickly.

Was he still bleeding? He wiped at the spot with his sleeve. Nothing but a few dark spots—just a shallow cut.

The rain drew a curtain around them, making their hiding spot intimate. He took another look around before returning his gaze to her. "What do you do here?"

"Meditate." She drew a slow breath that made her chest rise. "I listen to nature. It—"

She caught herself and flinched, then shot him an apologetic look. "Sorry. You're not here for a session."

"What does the rain sound like?" He remembered, but he wanted to know how she experienced it, because it was obvious that rain didn't mean the same thing to them.

While he didn't mind being wet, to him, rain had always been a nuisance. The sound of *need to wait for a better shot.* Diminished visibility. Diminished hearing, which meant someone might sneak up on them.

Annie's blissful expression said she enjoyed the rain. Her shoulders relaxed. She rested her head on the post behind her and closed her eyes. Cole's gaze skimmed her earth-mother figure, then settled on her generous lips.

"The rain on the roof is soft, steady, almost like music. Then there is a background chorus, fainter, the sound of the rain on the leaves. It's almost the same feeling as when you're listening to someone's heartbeat. Like you're listening to life itself."

Yeah. Cole was pretty sure he'd never had those thoughts about rain.

Her words made him want to lean over and press his ear against her chest, listen to her heartbeat, which of course he couldn't, even if she let him.

But even if he couldn't listen to her heart, couldn't listen to the rain, a peace descended on him from watching the quiet pleasure on her face. She wasn't a striking beauty, but her serenity enthralled him. He couldn't look away. She had reservoirs of inner peace and kindness that reflected on the outside, and both qualities drew him.

He felt the peace she brought almost like a physical presence. He'd felt it during their first session, at the clearing when he'd actually fallen asleep, then when he'd watched her snuggled up with her baby skunks, and now here in the rain. He hadn't felt peace for so long, and these moments of tranquility were a precious gift. The fresh scent of rain and forest filled him and made him light-headed for a moment.

Not ten minutes ago, in that puddle, he'd been drowning in bitterness and rage. And now . . .

The contrast was pretty stunning.

He understood that he was looking at another world, a world to which Annie was the doorway. Did he dare enter?

He wanted to tell her that he was glad they'd met . . . without sounding like a sap. He cleared his throat.

She opened her eyes and immediately smiled, as if smiling like that was nothing, as if it was as natural as breathing. "Are you feeling better?"

He was, but something inside him wouldn't let him concede that easily. "I'm not feeling worse."

Her smile widened, as if she could see right through him. "Did you hurt your shoulder?"

"Can't get much worse, can it?"

She didn't tell him not to run in the woods when the path was slippery with rain. Good. Because he didn't regret it. If he hadn't gone for the run, he wouldn't have found her.

Her glaze slid down to his muddy clothes. "Are you cold?"

She was semiwet. He was soaked through.

"Navy SEALs don't get cold."

She resisted rolling her eyes, but just.

"It's all in the training," he said.

Her clear amber eyes turned probing. "Must be difficult when someone with superhuman abilities is met with limitations."

There went his almost-good mood. "You said we weren't here for therapy."

He was willing to give nature therapy a chance, but right now he needed a break.

"It doesn't mean we can't talk. You could talk to me as a friend."

"My friends are either dead or scattered around the country at various VA hospitals and rehab centers. I'm not sure if I want new friends. Look what happened with the last batch."

"What did happen with the last batch?" Her large eyes were solemn and serious. "I'd like to know, but you don't have to tell me. Not even when we are in session. Since you already have talk therapy with someone else, we can make nature therapy a place for you to come for comfort. I'd like it to be your safe place where you relax and heal."

The sea of bitterness he'd been carrying inside nearly made him laugh. There were no safe places. *God*, the things he'd seen. The things he'd *done*. The things that had been done *to him*.

He hadn't even talked about that yet with Dr. Ambrose, his shrink. And he didn't want to talk about it at all with Annie. But the way she was looking at him, with warmth, as if she honestly cared, with understanding, and with that promise of peace in her eyes . . . If anyone could resist her, he was a stronger man than Cole.

"My spotter, Ryan, and I were sent in to take out the leader of the insurgents we were fighting," he said. "They somehow figured out we were there. Still don't know how. They had RPGs. We were both badly injured. Ryan called in for reinforcements. A chopper came. Picked us up. Ryan died five minutes into the flight."

Cole rubbed his palm over his face, dropped his hand, and looked back at her. "As we flew over the top of the hills, we came under RPG attack again. I think the first batch of insurgents radioed ahead to alert the second batch. They were ready for us."

His chest tightened and filled with something heavy, as if someone had poured liquid metal down his throat, and it cooled and solidified inside him.

"They shot you down," she guessed.

They had. "Three guys died on impact. The rest of us were pretty badly injured. We had nowhere to hide. Darkness had fallen, but the chopper was on fire, a freaking beacon. The insurgents found us within the hour. We were captured."

He couldn't talk about the six months of torture that had followed. He couldn't even think about it. Rage and grief filled him, dark images crammed into his brain. He could feel the sharp blades, the fire, the starvation, the bite of the whips. And when those things weren't being done to him, they were being done to the others, while he was forced to watch.

He squeezed his eyes shut.

The floorboards moved as Annie came over to sit next to him. She took his hand between both of hers. He wasn't aware that he'd been shaking until the shaking suddenly stopped at her touch. He opened his eyes again.

She was right there, looking at him, inches away.

He wasn't sure what was happening. He knew what he was hoping for, but he was pretty sure she wasn't going to do *that*. He kept still instead of reaching for her and pulling her onto his lap, where he suddenly wanted her.

"You are the leaves on the top of this tree," she began. "Just feel the rain and the wind. If right now, you're twisting and tearing, it's OK to feel that. Even if you feel like the storm is going to tear you right off and carry you away. Whatever you feel is valid. It's completely OK to feel it. Instead of fighting it, give it room. Say, *There you are, I see you.* For this moment, let yourself be that twisting, tearing leaf."

"You just said no therapy."

"Just two friends meditating together. If you want."

They had classes in meditation at Hope Hill. Cole sucked at it. Yet, for some reason, this time, he felt himself slip into the picture Annie painted with her words. Maybe because he did feel like he was twisting and tearing on the inside.

He'd never thought of himself as someone vulnerable. His current situation challenged his entire self-concept, his identity, everything that gave him self-confidence. He hated being reduced to a twisting and tearing thing, made to feel small and inadequate by his own body.

"Fine," he said. "I'm a leaf," he grumbled. "But if next you tell me I'm a little teapot, I'm out of here."

God, her smile lit up her whole face. And she was already the person with the most light inside her that he'd ever seen.

"We'll stick to nature images," she promised. "Now pull your essence from that leaf, pull into the branch. You are the branch. The rain and the wind are blowing, but you are solidly attached to the tree. You will bend, but you won't break."

He did as she said, picturing a sturdy branch, and felt calmer. He wouldn't break. The worst had already happened. He had lost his physical abilities, and his friends were dead. Somehow, he was still here.

"Pull in a little deeper," she told him then. "You are the trunk, and this is a mighty strong tree. You can easily stand against the wind without giving. The rain washes you. Not even the storm can move you. You are stronger than the storm."

Was he?

Yes, he was. He had strength beyond his arm, beyond the possession of all his senses. He was more. For the first time, he caught a glimpse of a different Cole Makani Hunter. One not described in medical terms, but a core, an essence not defined by his physical prowess or lack thereof.

"Let's slip deeper again," Annie said. "You are the roots. The storm is far above. You are safe, you are strong, you are connected so securely to life, nothing could tear you up. The rain feeds you. Every storm that brings the rains just makes you stronger. All that noise, all that clamor, all the drama, all the bad thoughts, that's happening somewhere far above. Down here is what matters, deep down, deep inside. This is where you live, where you grow. It's good and safe here. And it's effortless. You don't have to hold on with all your might. The earth is holding you safe. You can relax."

She let his hand go and reached up with both hands to touch his face, gently brushing the pads of her thumbs over his eyelids until he closed his eyes.

When she moved to leave him, he wrapped his left arm around her and pulled her closer until her head was on his shoulder. He held her there, without force, willing to let go if she was uncomfortable.

He hoped she'd stay. The position wasn't sexual. He simply needed the contact. Without his hearing, with his eyes closed, he needed an anchor.

Maybe, when he didn't go for more, she understood what he needed, because she leaned against him. And he relaxed. He was as relaxed as he ever remembered being.

He still wasn't 100 percent sold on meditation, but *this*—her warm body pressed against his—*this* he liked.

He didn't know how much time passed before he opened his eyes.

When he stirred, she pulled back with a soft smile. "Hey, sleepyhead."

Had he slept?

He must have. He felt rested.

The rain had stopped outside their shelter.

Before he could think of what to stay, she stood, shaking out legs that were probably half-numb from sitting. "We'd better get back."

And then she disappeared down the ladder.

But before she did . . . Cole's gaze fastened onto her muddy clothes. Mud that had transferred from him to her. An instant, visceral reaction stung him, as merciless as a whip. A voice in his head said, *That can't happen.*

The mud he was mired in, the darkness still inside, he would not allow that to touch Annie.

Chapter Ten

ANNIE LOOKED DOWN THE NARROW TRAIL, PLOTTING THE PATH OF SHALLOWEST rain puddles, unsure about what had happened in the deer blind. A small breakthrough? *That'd be nice.*

Behind her, Cole thumped to the ground surprisingly quietly, considering his size. "So that counts as a session, right? We can cross another one off the list?"

Oh. She hid her face from him so he wouldn't see that his question hurt. She'd thought they'd actually had a moment of connection up there.

Maybe she'd seen what she'd wanted to see. She knew he didn't put much faith in ecotherapy, didn't like the idea of needing help, yet the subtext of his comment was easy to read: I-hate-this-and-can't-wait-till-our-sessions-are-over . . . She felt knocked back.

Don't take it personally. He was the patient, and she was the therapist. Her feelings weren't the primary consideration. So she turned toward him to say, "Nice try," with as light an expression as she could manage. Then she walked out of the woods, waving at him when they parted at the trailhead without another word.

Thursday

As Annie slipped behind the wheel of her car the next day to go home for the noon feeding, she was still thinking about Cole. She only stopped when her phone rang.

"Want to come over for lunch?" Kelly asked.

"I can't. But thank you. I have to run home, then I have to get back to the office to catch up on paperwork."

"Are you mad at me?"

"No. It's just a stupid wall."

"You do hold grudges."

"I don't!"

Kelly remained silent for a moment, and then she asked, "Then why are things always so strained between us? I hate it. I was so excited when you decided to move back."

Annie wanted to deny the strain. She didn't want to talk about the past.

Kelly said, "It's not my fault that Gramps doted on my father while he kicked your mom out of the house. I hated it too. I lost my best friend."

"He didn't kick us out. We left because he made staying impossible. He couldn't handle his daughter having a child without a father."

"I'm sorry."

"It's not your fault." Annie closed her eyes. "I was just so damn jealous of you. And I was so mad at you. I was stupid. It's not like you took something that was mine."

"So you're not mad anymore?"

"Of course not."

"But you never want to do anything with me. Since you got back, you haven't once said let's get together. I always do, and you tell me why you can't."

Had she? Annie thought back. Yes, she had. "I'm sorry. You're right. I'm going to call you next week, and we'll grab lunch. I swear."

By the time she finished talking with Kelly, Annie had a missed call. She called back the Broslin PD and asked for Harper Finnegan.

"I think he's been trying to reach me," she told Leila.

"I was," Leila said. "We had some calls about a couple of llamas on Brandywine Road out by your place. Mike drove over to deal with traffic."

"I'm on my way."

Annie hung up and drove out of the parking lot, maybe faster than she should have, worry bubbling in her chest. Brandywine Road was two blocks from her house. She wanted to believe the llamas in trouble weren't hers, but who else's could they be?

She experienced the traffic jam first, though there was no reason for it at all now, she saw a few minutes later—nothing in the road, only people gawking. A police cruiser sat on the shoulder, and behind it, Officer Mike McMorris doing his best to keep three llamas and a one-eyed donkey in line.

How on earth?

Annie pulled up behind the cop car and jumped out. "I'm so sorry."

Mike smiled at her, bright-eyed, freckled, and without a censuring glance. He was as easygoing as they came. "No problem, Annie."

"I swear, we fixed the fence. I have no idea how they got out."

"No harm done." The guy didn't have a frown setting.

Annie grabbed Esmeralda's halter first, then Lucy's, since Lucy was the alpha llama in her little herd. "I'm going to walk them home. The others should follow."

But Mike already had them. "I'll help. They did well so far. Let's not get anyone hurt at this stage."

So they walked together, Annie in the front, Mike following a few feet behind. Everything went well, except for the occasional drivers who for some reason felt the need to beep their horns at them. The sound startled the already-scared animals and made them jump and pull away.

Annie tried not to glare at the horn blowers. She focused on her animals instead and stayed calm, knowing being calm helped more than yelling at the beeping idiots that passed.

"Hey, you know what's more amazing than a talking llama?" Mike asked from the back.

"No idea."

"A spelling bee."

Annie shook her head, but she was smiling.

Then they finally turned down her quiet street, and things went smoothly from there. When they were about two hundred feet from her house, she could see the problem. Her gate stood open.

She led her animals through, Mike behind her. The remaining two llamas were in the far corner of the yard. Dorothy the pig lay in a patch of mud nearby. Thankfully, she'd never been a runner. Annie and Mike set the escapist llamas and the donkey free, and then she walked back to the gate, Mike following once again.

The gate had a good, heavy latch that could not be opened by accident. She pointed it out to Mike. "I didn't leave it open. I'm pretty obsessive about the animals not getting out. I rarely open the gate anyway, only when I'm mowing the lawn outside the fence. I haven't mowed since last week."

"Don't touch the latch," Mike said. He could have asked, *Are you sure?* But he didn't, and Annie appreciated that.

He added, "I'll be back in a sec." And he walked back in the direction they came from, only to return in the cruiser a few minutes later.

He got out, popped the trunk, and came back carrying a little kit. "Harper mentioned your problems yesterday. Let's see if I can lift a print or two from the metal."

She watched as he carefully dusted for fingerprints.

"Two good ones." He gave a pleased grunt when he finished. "You need to come down to the station for fingerprinting when you get a chance, so we can rule your prints out."

"No problem. I can definitely do that."

He put his kit back into the cruiser, but he didn't get behind the wheel. He looked toward her garage and house. "Let me walk around before I go. I want to make sure nothing else is off. I'd feel better."

She let him through the gate, then latched it behind him.

He looked into the garage first, but found nothing out of place. Then he walked through the house, a low whistle escaping him when he reached her bathroom. "Looks as bad as it did on TV."

"You caught the morning show?"

"Saw it on YouTube."

She groaned.

"Hey. You could become a celebrity."

"Not on the top of my wish list," she said as they cleared the house.

He cocked his head, his eyes sparkling. "So you know what happens when you get stuck between two llamas?"

She raised her eyebrows.

"You get llamanated." Mike grinned.

She couldn't help smiling back at him. The joke was so bad, it was almost good.

"You want a ride back to your car?" he asked when they finished checking out the house and found nothing out of place.

"I'll get it later. I need to feed the babies."

Thank God nobody had gotten into her garage. The tiny skunk kittens still needed milk. If they got out and got lost, they would starve.

Annie gave them all extra scratches and snuggles and even extra milk. She was grateful that they were safe, and that no cars had hit one of the llamas or Esmeralda today.

She was also grateful for the time she'd gotten to spend with Cole in the deer blind the day before. He had opened up and gone along with her guided meditation. Her heart warmed at the idea of him accepting help. He needed it, but he was like a fortress. For him, admitting that he needed help was the same as admitting weakness. She understood why he'd pulled back at the end—fortresses did not advertise cracks in their walls—so she was able to set aside her hurt feelings.

She focused on the fact that he *had* relaxed with her. He had fallen asleep again.

Under other circumstances, if she was just a woman and he was just a man, the fact that he kept falling asleep on her might hurt her vanity. But considering her occupation, she knew the times that he could relax with her and trust her were a compliment.

He'd pulled her against him. She wasn't sure about *that*, about why she'd let him. She shouldn't get that close to him again, even if she didn't think he meant the embrace in any sexual way. He'd acted as if he simply needed that touch. Like he had needed his hand touching her knee at the meadow.

She even understood why. Because he couldn't hear her breathe, and with his eyes closed, he wouldn't be able to tell if she was still there. Did he need her to be there in order to be able to relax deeply enough to sleep? Was her presence like a changing of the guard? She was with him, she was on duty, so he could take a break?

He'd smelled like man, and sweat, and rain. She'd been filled with a completely inappropriate yearning to move her head to his chest and listen to the steady beat of his heart. Except . . .

Cole Makani Hunter was her *patient*.

He was a patient who needed her. And it looked like she might be able to help him. She could not mess that up under any circumstances. And she wouldn't. So Annie put him out of her mind.

After she finished with her animals, she decided to toss in a load of laundry. She put the clothes in the machine and turned it on, then straightened the laundry room. In a house full of chaos, this small act of control made her feel better.

That good feeling lasted until she glimpsed a shadow cross in front of the laundry-room window. Annie jumped, her heart beating wildly in her chest. Every word Cole had said about *escalation* rushed back.

Here comes the attack.

She should have taken Cole more seriously. She should have prepared.

She eased out into the kitchen and picked up the nearest weapon, a chunk of two-by-four from the rubble on the floor.

She gripped the chunk of wood as she listened to the footsteps on the other side of the tarp, barely audible above the sound of the blood rushing loudly in her ears.

Someone was definitely out there.

And he was looking for a way in.

Cole needed to take a step back from Annie and focus on his own problems. He went to his afternoon session with the shrink, then two hours of PT. After that, the rest of his day was open. Time to get to work.

He glanced at his cell and brought up the schedule he'd put together from observation, a list of who would be in what therapy at this time. He had patient rooms to search. He couldn't do that at night. Night was for searching the empty staff offices.

He went straight to Shane's room down the hallway from his own. The Texan's comment—*Love my country, hate the damn government*—had stuck in Cole's brain. Exactly how much did Shane hate the government? His mother had some complicated version of bone cancer. That had to cost a boatload of money, and it could be a motive for selling secrets to the enemy.

Cole popped the lock with the pick on his slightly modified Swiss Army Knife.

Room empty. Clothes tossed all over the place. While Shane probably wouldn't notice if someone turned his room upside down, not in this chaos, Cole was careful anyway.

Aware that since he could not hear anyone coming, he wouldn't have any notice, he searched for a burner phone as fast as he could. He checked under the mattress, behind the headboard, in and under the desk, the dresser, the closet, the bathroom.

He found nothing interesting other than Shane's stash of comic books about immortal warriors, the Harreda. Finished with their earthly wars, the warriors couldn't die since neither heaven nor hell would take them. They were tasked by the gods with guarding the border between heaven and hell, doomed to never find rest.

Cole could relate. He certainly felt stuck on the border of hell at times.

He hurried to the door, ready to be out of there. But as he pulled the door open, he came face-to-face with Shane. The Texan was coming back early. He had his key in his hand and a surprised look on his face.

"What are you doing here?"

"Who is it?" Annie's voice shook as she called out, reaching for her cell phone with her free hand. Her heart pounded. Sweat beaded on her upper lip.

"David," an unfamiliar voice said.

"David who?"

"The producer. From the TV station." Brief pause. "I'll come around to the front."

He did, and Annie checked him out through the window, recognized him. *Kelly's producer.*

Limp with relief, Annie leaned the two-by-four against the wall out of sight and wiped her sweaty palms on her pants before opening the door.

"Sorry if I scared you." He was only an inch or two taller than Annie, blond hair long enough to curl on his collar, green-eyed, handsome in a hot-artist kind of way.

During the TV shoot, Annie had been too nervous to truly notice him, but now she noted his sexy, shy smile. The guy was seriously good-looking. If he ever wanted to give up life behind the cameras, he could go in front of them.

Yet she felt none of the awareness that she did every time she was around Cole. She shoved that thought aside. So not going there. Ever.

David said, "I knocked earlier."

"The washing machine is going. I didn't hear you."

"I went around to see how bad the damage was. I'm sorry."

She waited for him to get to the reason for his visit.

He did, after a sincerely apologetic smile. "I came by to see if I could help with anything."

Nice of him.

Before she could say so, another pickup pulled up behind his. This one was white, with Ed's construction company's red-house logo on the side. Two twentysomething guys, all steel-toed boots and tool belts, got out, introducing themselves as Bobby and Billy. They didn't look bad either in their manly blue overalls. Apparently, Hurricane Rupert was raining hunks.

"Brought plywood," Billy said. "We're gonna replace the tarp. Plywood's more secure."

"I can help," David volunteered.

Annie thanked them all and left the men to their work. She stole one last glance at them through the window as she headed to make herself a cup of tea. *Could probably sell tickets.*

Annie decided to stay. She could catch up on paperwork another time.

While the dream team worked, she played with her animals. She hadn't spent enough time with them in the past couple of days. Before Bobby and Billy left, they promised that a small cleanup crew would come the following day to deal with her kitchen.

David lingered. "I have to go pick up Tyler from his friend's house. Single dad," he added. "And I'm sorry I can't come tomorrow. I have to work at the station."

"That's OK. I didn't expect you today. Ed's guys will take care of it."

"I was involved. I feel responsible." He looked at his feet, then looked up at Annie. "So does Kelly come over often?"

Annie did an admirable job biting back a smile. But she was screaming *Aha!* inside. Kelly had a secret admirer.

"Not that much." Her heart nearly broke at David's crestfallen expression, so she added, "Kelly works a lot. And she's an exercise nut. She's at the gym every night."

David cheered up. He was a smart guy. He was probably heading to the gym next. "Anyway"—he pulled a business card from his pocket—"here is my number. Call me if you need an extra pair of hands."

The way he'd had the card ready, Annie thought he'd meant to give it to her regardless of how the Kelly thing panned out. David was pretty nice. She could only hope Kelly had the sense to see that, if they managed to run into each other. Time for one of the Murray women to break the curse and fall for one of the good guys.

After David left, Annie ambled back into the kitchen, taking the two-by-four with her.

Oh God, the kitchen.

She itched to have her kitchen back.

What if Ed's guys couldn't make it tomorrow? He'd said they were super busy. She *did* have the dumpster. She had time. She was on a break from work. Keeping busy was better than obsessing over her problems. Especially when the mess in her kitchen was a problem she could fix, or at least start fixing.

Annie grabbed a bucket and shovel from the garage and began clearing out the rubble. And then she sent a silent request to the universe to let her have a quiet evening, preferably without Joey popping in.

The man checked Annie's office, but she wasn't there. She wasn't in her room either. He even loped around the walking trail—in vain.

He liked to keep track of her.

She liked to play hard to get.

He let her for now. He wasn't a monster. But he was in control, whether she knew it or not. Whenever he felt the need to know where she was and what she was doing, he tracked her down and watched her. *He* controlled the game.

Someday soon, he was going to teach her to check in with him regularly throughout the day. Once she understood that the continued survival of her animals depended on her obedience, she would toe the line nicely.

As he headed out to the parking lot, he caught sight of Cole walking between two buildings. Good. At least he wasn't with Annie.

Annie was home. Probably alone. Was she moving back to her house? Was she going to sleep at her house tonight?

The man smiled, thinking how much he'd missed that these last two nights. He liked watching her around town, or at work, or with her animals. But he *loved* watching her sleep.

He made a point to stop by at least two or three times a week. They'd spent many nights together. She just didn't know it.

Darkness fell by the time Annie ran out of steam, with every muscle in her body aching and shouting a protest, begging her to quit the heavy lifting. Her kitchen was in better shape, but by no means clean. She decided to listen to her body and moved on to her regular chores.

She led the grazing animals into the garage. Fed the babies again. Thought about walking out to where she'd left her car earlier and driving to Hope Hill, but she'd just have to drive back again at midnight. She didn't have it in her. Staying required a lot less effort.

She took Cole's warnings about stalkers and escalation seriously, especially after the David scare. So she lined a large basket with towels and brought the dozen skunk babies inside the house. Now she wouldn't have to go out again in the middle of the night.

She settled the little ones in her bedroom, then ate a tuna sandwich for dinner. Her stomach full, she collapsed on her bed, fully clothed. Her shower didn't work, but sleeping dirty one night wasn't going to kill her. She could pretend she was camping. She could clean up at Hope Hill in the morning.

The house was locked up tight, and the hole in the bathroom was sealed. Spending a night here should be perfectly fine.

She was so certain of that thought that she fell fast asleep. So certain that, hours later, when a noise woke her, she put it down to the house settling. The structure *had* lost two walls recently: one internal, one external. Any house would creak in protest.

She didn't think anything of the noise until she blinked her eyes open. Through the bedroom door, she saw movement in her kitchen—a large, looming man. Definitely not David this time. This guy was bigger.

Thud, thud, thud. Her heart was all clear on the danger, while her brain still tried to catch up.

Who?

How?

She'd locked up. Only her cousin, Kelly, had an extra key, and the large shape out there definitely wasn't Kelly.

The man in her kitchen had broken in. Annie was pretty sure he wasn't here with good intentions.

Even in her sleepy state, two things became immediately clear.

One: The man wasn't Joey. Joey she could have reasoned with, but the guy in her kitchen had a different shape. Thicker body. No baseball hat. Joey never went anywhere without his.

Two: The bedside clock showed five minutes to midnight. In five minutes, the alarm would go off to wake her for the midnight feeding. And the sound would draw the intruder's attention to the bedroom, to Annie.

If she turned off the alarm, the clock would beep. It beeped for any push of any button.

Four minutes.

Oh God.

Panic choked her for a couple of seconds before her brain woke up enough to find a solution. Inch by minuscule inch, she reached behind her nightstand and unplugged the clock. The clock face went dark without a sound.

The guy walked toward the guest bedroom, disappearing out of sight. For a second or two, Annie could almost breathe. But he came back into view a moment later. Did he mean to go through the whole place? If he did, in a few minutes, he would be entering the master bedroom, alarm or no alarm.

Annie eased off the far side of the bed, taking her cell phone with her. Once she moved, she could no longer see the intruder, which also meant he wouldn't be able to see her as she ever-so-slowly crept toward her half-open closet.

On second thought, she grabbed the basket of skunk kits on her way. The guy in her kitchen had to be the same guy who'd crashed her fence yesterday and opened her gate today. No way could she have more than one psycho after her.

And, if he *was* the same idiot, he'd already proven that he didn't care if her animals got hurt. The llamas and the donkey could have been easily hit in the road. Annie wasn't going to leave the kits to him.

She pulled into the back of the closet, put the basket down, and eased the door closed as far as she could without making it click into place.

She muted her phone, then dialed 911. And when she didn't speak after Leila picked up, the dispatcher said, "Are you all right, Annie?"

Because, thank God, Annie had her cell phone number registered in the local 911 database, so they had her address even when not calling from a landline. The PD began providing that service once half the town gave up their landlines in favor of their cell phones.

"If you can't speak, press one."

Annie did.

"If you can't speak because you're hurt, press one. If you can't speak because there's an intruder in your home, press two."

Annie pressed two.

"Sending a car right now. You hang in there, Annie honey, all right? Stay on the line. Harper's on duty. He's near you, and he's heading right over. He'll be there in five minutes."

Hurry. Hurry. Hurry.

Oh God.

Her bedroom door was opening. The next second, shoes scraped on the wood floor. Annie's chest was so tight, she couldn't breathe.

No matter how much Harper hurried, he wasn't going to reach her in time.

The intruder was only a handful of steps away from her. She thought about the one good self-defense move she knew, but then, through the crack in the door, she caught something black and metallic in the man's hand.

A gun?

Sooo not good.

All she had was a basket of skunk babies.

Chapter Eleven

THE CHOPPER'S TAIL EXPLODED IN MIDAIR.

"Brace for impact!" the pilot shouted.

But bracing made no difference when they hit. Cole felt as if not just the chopper, but his whole body, had exploded, as if his bones had left him, flying out through his skin.

Most of the men had been thrown free.

There was no help for the three who hadn't been.

Fire. Smoke. Pain.

Yet no one rushed to scramble away. Everyone was looking to see who needed help. When the survivors finally pulled back, they did it in pairs, the men with lesser injuries carrying those who couldn't move under their own power.

Derek's pant leg was on fire. He had Alex on his back in a fireman's hold. Alex was bleeding so hard, his blood was soaking Derek's leg and putting out the flames.

Cole's right shoulder felt dislocated. He had shrapnel stuck between his ribs and incredible pressure in his chest. He couldn't breathe. If metal had punctured his lungs, he had only minutes left. He was determined to use those minutes to drag Matt to safety.

He tripped. Went down, white-hot pain exploding behind his eyelids. Matt screamed.

Cole bolted upright in bed before he was fully awake, drenched in sweat. He was gulping for air, his chest tight.

He rubbed his hand against the pain in the middle of his chest, swore, and hauled himself out of bed. He needed a shower.

Hope Hill. Home. Safe. Annie. His subconscious mind threw words at him it thought might settle him.

He let them rumble through his brain while he stood under the spray. Afterward, he didn't go back to bed. He dressed and sat in the chair by the dark window. He stared into that darkness until his mind was empty.

At midnight, he ambled out into the parking lot, ready to go feed the skunks with Annie. He'd missed her when she'd gone to the evening feeding. He'd had group therapy. He made sure to attend those sessions and listen carefully. He'd figured with people baring their souls, he might catch a clue. He hadn't so far.

He shoved his hands into his pockets, still pissed that he hadn't found anything in Shane's room that afternoon, that he'd let Shane catch him.

"What are you doing here?" the Texan had asked when he'd found Cole coming out of the room.

"Sorry, man. Your door wasn't locked. I'm out of toilet paper. I thought you wouldn't mind if I grabbed an extra from under your sink." He held up the roll he'd picked up two minutes before, his contingency plan in case someone saw him leaving Shane's room. SEALs always had a plan for every eventuality. "I'm not gonna make it downstairs tracking down the custodian, you know what I mean?"

"Freaking bean burgers, amigo. Cooks have a fiber fetish." Shane shook his head. "Feel free to take a dump here. Just don't stink up the place."

"Nah, I can make it back to my room." Cole walked away, calling back without turning, "Navy SEAL shit don't stink."

If Shane laughed behind him, Cole didn't hear it.

He'd gotten away with the room search, but he had no new information. Daily progress: zero. As he scanned the parking lot for the umpteenth time for Annie, he kicked a pebble across the blacktop and watched it bounce into the darkness.

A dark-blue pickup pulled in. Trevor jumped out and headed straight for Cole.

"Couldn't sleep." The kid flashed a sheepish grin. "Had a craving for pizza, so I thought, why not. They have some pretty good pizza over on Main Street. Was watching TV over there. The hurricane just hit Cuba. Now it's a category three. You think it'll come up this way?"

Cole shrugged. "They usually turn out to sea."

"Yeah. Are you going out?" Trev asked in a way that said he wouldn't mind being invited along.

But Cole said, "Waiting for someone."

"Right." Trevor smiled brighter to hide his disappointment that Cole's words weren't followed by *Wanna come with us?*

"I guess I better get to bed." He walked away slowly, willing to be called back. "Have fun." He made his last attempt.

He reminded Cole of a puppy wanting reassurance and affection, wanting to be part of a pack, even a pack of two. Cole looked after him. Maybe they could hang out tomorrow for a while. Trevor had been here longer. Cole could ask him about the patients he hadn't ruled out yet. The kid was such an obvious mess, maybe people didn't think they had to be on their guard around him. Maybe he knew something that would help Cole finish his job.

Cole waited a few more minutes after Trevor disappeared inside the building. Still no sign of Annie or her car. Maybe she'd gone already. Because Cole didn't like the idea of her alone at the house at night, he hopped into his pickup and drove over.

Her car wasn't in the driveway. All the windows were dark, even the window on the garage door. She wasn't in there feeding her little stink muffins.

Maybe she'd come and gone already, spending the night with a friend instead of at Hope Hill. The possibility that that friend might be male had Cole in a dark mood as he headed back to the rehab center.

He was only a couple of blocks from Annie's when he passed a police car flying in the opposite direction. The lights flashed. The sirens blared loudly enough so even Cole caught some of the sound. Detective Harper sat behind the wheel. Cole did a U-turn and barreled after him.

When the cruiser pulled into Annie's driveway, the detective lunged out of the car and ran toward the front door. Cole didn't follow him. Annie's car wasn't there, so Annie probably wasn't there. Maybe a neighbor had seen someone skulking around the house and called it in.

That siren would have been heard from a mile away. Whoever had been in there was gone at this stage, and whatever damage he'd wreaked was done. Cole put pedal to the metal and drove for the spot on the other side of the cornfield where the path that began at Annie's fence ended.

If the intruder ran when he'd heard the siren, Cole might still be in time to catch him.

But the first thing Cole saw was Annie's car on the shoulder just half a mile from the house. *Empty.*

Now the fear hit him.

He drove past the Prius, turned down the next road, and kept going. The spot where he'd hoped to find the intruder's car stood deserted. If the guy had come this way, he was gone now. Nothing to see here.

Another U-turn and he was back at Annie's car again. This time Cole stopped and got out. The Prius was locked. He checked the ground, illuminated by his pickup's headlights. *No sign of struggle.* Worry punched him in the solar plexus anyway.

He left her car and sped all the way back to her house.

The lights were on now. He pulled up behind the cruiser, ran to the front door, found it unlocked, went in.

"Annie!"

Detective Finnegan came to greet him, hand on his holstered weapon. "What are you doing here?"

"Thought I'd help with the midnight feeding again. Saw the cruiser. What's going on?"

Annie, pale and frowning, popped out from one of the rooms. "Cole?"

"What happened?"

"Let's all sit in the kitchen. Then how about I ask some questions first?" the detective suggested, keeping himself between them. The sharp gaze he kept on Cole said somebody was in trouble.

The man took out his notepad, which already had some writing on the top page. He'd already questioned Annie. Cole wasn't surprised when the man turned to him as they sat.

"You come by often in the middle of the night?"

Shrug. "Can't sleep anyway."

The man shot a look at Annie. Because her patients probably didn't come home with her on a daily basis. Or drive by her house at midnight. Cole rubbed a hand over his chin. He sounded like a stalker.

Then he caught the wary look on Annie's face, and he felt it like a punch in the gut.

Did *she* think he was acting like a stalker? For the detective to think something like that was one thing, but Annie . . . *Dammit.*

Cole rested his hands on his knees and sat still, no sudden movements, trying to make his body smaller and less threatening. He didn't want to scare her. If he was scaring her . . .

Desperation washed through him. "I'm a Navy SEAL," he told Finnegan. "I've been trained to run toward trouble and not away from it. When something's off, I investigate. I've come out with her to feed the animals before. Tonight, she wasn't at Hope Hill. I know she's in some kind of a stalker situation. I didn't like the idea of her out here alone in the middle of the night, so I thought I'd drive over."

Finnegan looked at him as if weighing every word. He wasn't impressed by Cole's explanation. His cold expression said *he* was protecting Annie, and Cole needed to stay out of his way. When the detective turned to Annie, the question in his eyes clearly spelled, *Want a restraining order against this guy?*

But Annie said, "He's OK, Harper. He's one of the good guys."

And Cole realized only then that he'd been holding his breath for the last couple of seconds.

She should have told him to stay away, just to be on the safe side. And she'd gone way too far with calling him *one of the good guys.* She missed the mark by a mile there.

Cole didn't correct her, because he wanted the detective to think that he *was* one of the good guys. No sense getting his ass arrested tonight.

"Are you going to tell me what's going on?" he asked Annie.

And she did, beginning with someone opening her gate and her animals getting out. Then worse. *Intruder. Male. Unidentified. Possibly armed. Took off when he heard the police siren.*

By the time she finished, Cole wanted to kill. She'd been in the freaking closet the whole time, scared to death. If Finnegan had been on the other side of town and gotten here ten minutes later . . . Cole didn't want to finish the thought.

He'd been in front of her house. No lights. No car. He'd turned around and driven away while Annie trembled in the damn closet inches from danger.

She could have been killed. The thought threatened to explode Cole's head. He wanted to pull her into his arms right there in her kitchen, in front of Finnegan.

"I'll drive Annie back to Hope Hill," he said instead.

Finnegan nixed that right out of the gate. "You go ahead on your own. Miss Murray can drive her own car when we're done here. I'll escort her in the cruiser."

The dismissal rankled Cole, but he stood. He wasn't going to argue with the detective. Not yet. Not over this. Not as long as Annie was safe. But he reserved the option to stand up to the law in any number of ways if he thought they were falling down on the job. Because there was one thing everybody needed to understand here. He wasn't going to let Annie get hurt.

Cole drove back to Hope Hill and went inside. He didn't go straight to his room. He stayed in the hallway window that over-looked the parking lot until Annie drove up, the cruiser behind her. To his credit, Finnegan got out and walked her to her room.

Cole waited just around the corner. When he checked after a few minutes, Annie's door was closed, and Finnegan was walking away. Cole allowed himself to relax and went about his mission.

At two o'clock in the morning, pretty much everybody was asleep. Time to take a look at the rest of the offices he hadn't made it to the other night. But even as Cole walked away from Annie, his mind kept returning to her.

She'd taken the last couple of days pretty well, and they had been rough. But tonight was rougher. An intruder in the house would send most women into hysterics, and a lot of men too. Annie had hidden herself and calmly called the police. She hadn't fallen apart during or after.

She had courage, and courage was the quality Cole appreciated the most in people. She was no fragile butterfly flitting from flower to flower in naive abandon, living in her little, happy, peppy, tree-hugging world, as he'd first thought. Annie Murray was a strong woman.

He thought about her sitting calmly at the kitchen table and recounting the intruder episode.

He wanted her.

He wanted the generous mouth and generous body that went along with her generous soul. He wanted her soft curves. He wanted to see her amber eyes darken with desire.

The realization nearly knocked Cole on his ass. *Yeah. Worst idea ever.*

Nevertheless, he wanted to go back to her room right now and not leave. But what Annie needed overrode what he wanted. And he was pretty sure she didn't need him.

She needed someone like Harper Finnegan. The detective was young, good-looking, and carefree. He'd been clearly concerned about Annie. And the man was probably tough enough to protect her. Cole wanted her protected. Even if the thought of her with Finnegan left him filled with a dark rage.

He left the dorms and entered the main building.

The first floor held a rec room and the cafeteria in the back, reception in the front. He went upstairs where the staff offices were and pulled out the ID card he'd once again borrowed from Annie's bag earlier while she'd been rubbing her eyes and Finnegan had been consulting his notes.

Once Cole was inside, he was set. The individual offices had key locks he had no problem picking. Dr. Ambrose had one of the largest offices. Maybe because he was a PhD.

Cole entered but didn't turn on the light, not even after he closed the door behind him and closed the blinds on the window. He used the small LED light he had in his pocket and swept the gray metal desk first.

No laptop. Ambrose had taken it home.

Cole turned to the filing cabinet, picked the lock, and looked through the patient files.

He found nothing beyond a lot of psychobabble, diagnoses, treatment plans, and drugs prescribed.

Nothing useful on the bookshelf, just a million copies of *Psychology Today* and other similar publications, reference guides, two copies of the *Diagnostic and Statistical Manual of Mental Disorders*, a bunch of inspirational booklets, and self-help guides. Ambrose handed those out to patients. He'd given a handful to Cole during their first session.

Two full shelves held nothing but research books on the history of medicine, many of them on medieval practices. Looked like Ambrose had a hobby.

Cole returned to the desk and popped the lock on the single drawer. Empty notepads and a bunch of pens, a couple of thank-you cards from past patients. He closed the drawer and locked it again.

On his way out, his light fell on Ambrose's lineup of diplomas on the wall. Nothing interesting there either. Apparently, the guy had gone to graduate school in England.

Cole turned off the LED light before he inched the door open and looked out into the hallway. Nobody there. Except . . . light showed under the door of one of the offices. When Cole had come through earlier, that strip of light hadn't been there.

Whose office was that? From the outside the offices all looked the same, two rows of white doors on white walls, all evenly spaced.

Then he remembered: Milo Milton, the acupuncturist. Cole had only had one session with the guy so far. Not his favorite thing.

Cole's skin had been cut and punctured too many times during torture. He remembered the pain, even if he'd been shot up with drugs half the time. His captors had hoped the drugs would make him talk. The nightmares he'd hallucinated . . . He hated the memory. And he wasn't a fan of needles either.

What was Milo doing here at past two in the morning? The acupuncturist was thirty, into everything Eastern medicine, a giant fan of incense burning. During their one session, Cole had barely been able to breathe. He still got the pungent smell of sandalwood in his nose every time he thought of the guy.

He had a hard time picturing Milo tangled up in the transmission of military secrets. The guy was nearly as bad as Annie. He probably wished for world peace for his birthday.

As far as foreign connections went, he'd told Cole during their session that he'd been to Nepal a couple of times. But Nepal was a long way from Yemen.

Based on Cole's considerable experience, Milo was an extremely unlikely candidate.

Opportunity? Sure. *Means?* Maybe. *Motive?* That last one stumped Cole completely.

Not money. Milo believed in *voluntary simplicity*, not owning anything beyond what was absolutely necessary.

Still, Cole could have missed something.

He looked behind him. If Milo was passing on information, who was passing information to him? Maybe Milo was here waiting for the guy right now. But the hallway was dark and empty in both directions.

Cole moved forward with as much stealth as he could muster, knowing that if he made any noise, he wouldn't be able to hear it, but Milo might.

When he was at the door, he stopped. Was Milo alone? If there were people in there, if they were talking, Cole couldn't hear.

He silently cursed his CO for putting him on the job. Cole had to be the worst person for it. What gave anyone the idea that he'd make a good spy? Stupidest idea he'd ever heard. No pun intended.

He shrugged off the tension in his shoulders. The mission had been entrusted to him, so he would do the best he could.

He figured the gap at the bottom of the door to be about an inch wide. He eased his large body down onto the carpet and lined up his eye with that gap.

Having his full body on the floor was good. He hoped if someone was coming, he'd feel the vibrations from their steps. Because he sure wasn't going to be able to hear them.

The man walked the hallways, anger making his hands clench and unclench at his sides.

He'd come every night when Annie was at Hope Hill, instead of going to her house to look through her windows. He couldn't do that here. At her house, since her bedroom looked to the back, she didn't draw her curtains. Here, she always closed the blinds.

He couldn't get into her room either. That made him furious with frustration. He'd gotten into her house. Prying off a sheet of plywood had been pretty easy. Yet the memory of walking into her bedroom was less than satisfying.

He'd just wanted to watch her, to softly touch her hair.

Then he had planned to go back to the garage and butcher that damn potbelly pig. Ugly piece of shit.

He'd actually stopped by the garage before going into her house, wanting to stomp a couple of her little skunks and leave the small bodies in her bed as a warning of what would happen if she continued to defy him. But he hadn't been able to find the skunks.

And Annie hadn't been in her bed. She'd hidden from him.

And then the police came.

Then Cole Makani Hunter.

Bad, bad Annie. She had entirely too many men around her.

She was alone now, once again.

The man slowed in front of her door. Light came through the cracks. She was awake.

He hesitated. If he knocked . . . But how would he explain why he was here? He had no excuse for a visit.

Soon, but not tonight, the man promised himself as he kept walking down the hallway. Very soon, Annie Murray would understand just how seriously she needed to take him.

If he had to take out one of her animals, so be it. He'd begun his game with roadkill for the sole purpose of scaring her, but he found he liked killing. There was a primal satisfaction to ending a life and being able to watch as it happened, as the victim's eyes dimmed.

Chapter Twelve

ANNIE'S FIRST TASK FOR THE MORNING WAS TO RECONNECT WITH HER INNER peace. She needed to be in the right frame of mind for her morning session with Trevor. And she would need a strong dose of tranquility later, when she stopped by her grandfather's house to drop off some groceries.

Annie drew a deep breath. She had twenty minutes and an empty pool complex to get herself ready for the day.

She wasn't the best swimmer, but she liked the pool complex at the rehab center. The township had contributed significantly to the cost of the building, and it maintained a shared-use arrangement with Hope Hill. The high school swim team used the complex Monday through Friday from three to seven o'clock. The rest of the time, the water belonged to the recovering vets.

The Olympic-size pool, the hot tub, the sauna, and the steam room were used both by the vets and the high school athletes. The diving pool had been put in at the high school coach's request and saw most of its use from the BHS dive team.

Water had always calmed Annie. She often came to the pools when it rained too hard outside to go on her morning walk through the woods. The pool complex was a large, open space that usually stood empty during the breakfast hour.

Up on the highest diving board, Annie felt like a bird in her nest. Since the wall she faced was all windows, she overlooked the forest, still with her trees.

She wore a soft cotton T-shirt with yoga pants. She'd kicked off her sneakers before climbing up. She was positively languid, sitting cross-legged on the diving board and doing her morning meditation. One by one, her troubles fell away from her: the ruined fence, the opened gate, the intruder in the night. Yesterday's troubles could not be allowed to carry over and soil a brand-new day.

She breathed in, breathed out, and emptied her mind little by little. The wind flung rain against the windows. Trees bent in the wind. For a few minutes, Annie allowed herself to be a vulnerable little leaf, allowed herself to feel fear and anger and dismay, even helplessness. The goal of any kind of therapy wasn't to shut away unpleasant feelings. The goal was to give the patient tools to be able to deal with those feelings. So she let herself feel all the emotions that swirled inside her, and she acknowledged them. It was OK and completely normal to feel that way.

But it didn't mean she had to wallow in her feelings.

She pulled her essence from the leaf into the branch. She still felt the storm on her skin, she still bent and shook, but she could handle it. The emotions were more muted, more manageable. Bad things happened, but nothing she couldn't handle. She could stand up to this storm.

When she felt comfortable in that spot, she pulled herself fully into the massive trunk of the tree and relaxed completely. The storm was a buzz around her. It couldn't do serious damage. She'd seen storms come and go. She'd survived them.

By the time she was in the roots, she was in Zen bliss. She was one with the earth. Down there, deep inside, an incredible peace waited for her. And the best thing was that this place was always here, always waiting. She could come anytime she wanted.

A metal door slamming downstairs brought her out of her zone. She drew another deep breath, held, released, then blinked her eyes open, as reluctantly as if waking from a pleasant dream.

Far below her, Cole walked across the tile floor in nothing but a pair of navy swim shorts. She sucked in a sharp breath as her gaze focused on his powerful body.

He had scars so large she could see them from the distance, and she suspected she'd see more if he was closer. Annie looked away. He wouldn't hear if she called a greeting, and without knowing that she was here, she felt as if she was spying on him.

She should go. She would. In another minute. First she needed to catch her breath. Her gaze strayed back to him.

Water glistened on his head and wide shoulders from his shower. He stretched his muscles, and she could see for the first time the difference in range of motion between his two arms. His right shoulder was obviously stiff, and his right elbow wouldn't contract enough to bend all the way.

Was he even able to lift a fork to his mouth?

She'd never seen him eat with his right hand. She'd never seen him do a lot of things. The sudden thought of how briefly they'd known each other startled her. *Less than a week.*

Yet, even with all the other craziness going on, he spent a disproportionate amount of time in her thoughts. And in her company too. He had helped with the fence. With the midnight feedings. And when he couldn't find her, he'd come to check on her in the middle of the night.

A soft, tentative kind of longing unfurled in the middle of her chest. Suddenly she could see what life might be like with a true partner. Not a casual boyfriend, not somebody she went on dates with, but someone to share the little day-to-day things, someone who would have her back. She'd never experienced that.

She longed for a deeper connection than the ones she'd had before. *Not with Cole, though.* He was her patient. So she stashed that longing away for another day, another man.

When Cole finished stretching, he dove into the pool. He swam just under the surface of the water, both arms at his sides, his great body propelled only by his powerful legs.

Every once in a while, he came up for a quick pull of air as he swam a lap, then another and another. He propelled himself with his feet and left arm, his right arm dragging in the water.

Annie needed to leave, but she couldn't look away as he kept going, lap after lopsided lap, swimming a lot longer and harder than she could have.

He had to be growing exhausted.

When he slowed at last, she expected him to move to the edge and climb out of the pool, but instead, he abruptly sank to the bottom.

Her breath caught all over again.

Did he have a cramp?

She jumped to her feet, heart hammering as Cole lay on the bottom of the pool, an alarmingly still, dark shape.

Her chest constricted. She struggled to fill her lungs. She called without any hope that he would hear. "Cole!"

Before she knew it, her feet were at the end of the diving platform as she stared down, her heart hammering madly. God, she was up high. Cole seemed far away, the distance insurmountable: a leap over Niagara Falls.

Don't let me break my neck.

She pushed off.

She was in the air long enough for some serious regrets. Then she slammed into the water, sideways, because what did she know about diving?

For a long moment, she felt paralyzed with pain, then instinct kicked in, and she was happy to see that her limbs scrambled on their own. So far so good, except that same instinct was pushing her up. She forced herself to swim down. She didn't make it. Halfway there, a submarine hit her, propelling her to the surface.

Then Cole had her out of the water and on the wet tiles, on his knees next to her, hovering over her, his dark eyes boiling with anger. "What the hell do you think you're doing?"

Because she was still scared to death, she shouted back, a water-logged, half-choked sentence. "What do you think *you* are doing?"

"I was relaxing on the bottom until you decided to commit suicide."

Oh God. Fool much?

Her voice weakened. "I thought you were drowning."

"You could have killed yourself." His volume dropped too. He spoke in the same gruff tone that she remembered from their first encounter at the gas station. That voice still drew shivers along her skin.

He had bent to her during their earlier shouting, and their noses were now mere inches apart. His massive chest was heaving almost as hard as hers. Hers from effort, his from anger.

That hungry-bear look came into his eyes.

For a stunning, crazy moment, heat flared between them, arched like lightning, and she couldn't breathe at all. Not a single oxygen molecule. Or maybe she just imagined that the heat was something mutual. Because the next second, he pulled back, his face completely blank as he ran his large hands over her limbs.

She felt hot and cold at the same time. The best she could do was whisper. "What are you doing?"

"Did you break anything?" His hands didn't stop roving over her. "Dislocate anything?"

She tried one limb at a time. Everything ached, but everything moved. When she was sure that she hadn't broken any bones, she sat up. This brought them closer together again. Too close. Too much awareness.

He sat back on his heels, ran his palm over his bald head. His dark gaze wouldn't leave her face. "You took ten years off my life when you stepped off that diving board."

"You saw me?"

"I noticed you up there when I came in."

Right. He'd been a sniper. He probably saw things that escaped normal people. She had to remember this in the future. Cole Makani Hunter missed nothing.

"You didn't call up to me," she said.

"Looked like you were meditating."

He stood and reached out a hand to her. She accepted the help but let his hand go as soon as she was standing. When his gaze dipped to her chest, heat tingled through her.

"Don't do that." His voice was suddenly the rough rasp of a dying man.

"What?"

But because he wasn't watching her mouth, he couldn't see the question.

Her gaze followed his to her chest. *Oh God.* Her giant, hard-from-the-cold-water nipples were nearly poking through the thin white cotton of her sports bra and shirt.

She crossed her arms, but from the deep groan that escaped his chest, she was pretty sure he could still see the offending peaks.

"Just," he said as if speaking from the bottom of a well, "suck them in or something."

Part of her wanted to laugh, but the expression on his face was so intensely focused and tortured, she couldn't. Cole was looking at her nipples. As if he was affected by them. As if he was struggling with desire and—

Finishing the thought might make her faint, so she didn't. "I need to go. I have a session in fifteen minutes. I need to change out of these wet clothes."

He raised his gaze at last. He shifted his weight, an uncertain look on his face—which was startling, because little about the man was uncertain. He looked as if he was about to say something and was still tasting the words to make sure they were the right ones. But in the end, he only said, "Have a fun day."

She had her doubts about fun. She'd settle for a day that didn't leave her bleeding. Beyond the visit with her grandfather, she was also going to get Ed's estimate for the house today.

Cole stepped away from her. The tension eased between them. She could finally draw a full breath.

OK, go, go, go. She nearly ran to get her sneakers. She pulled her sopping socks off before she shoved her feet into the shoes.

Cole was back in front of her before she tied the laces, holding two white towels out for her. "Dry yourself with one, cover yourself with the other."

She was grateful that he didn't offer his hand to help her up this time. She was in no shape to be touching him.

She stood on her own and grabbed one of the towels from him. "Thanks." She dried herself with brisk movement, her brain cells playing ping-pong with the one question she didn't want to be thinking.

What had just happened here?

OK, so Cole was into nipples. Like *really* into them. *God, the look in his eyes.* A nipple fetish? It happened. It had nothing to do with her. Could have been worse. He could have focused on all her flabby spots revealed by her plastered-on clothes.

Maybe any nipple would have riveted his attention. According to his file, he'd been depressed for a while. By his own admission, he'd spent a month locked into his apartment with nothing but his weapons for company. Before that, he'd been in a hospital and rehab. The last time he'd seen nipples might have been a long while back. With hers right in his face, he was just remembering what they were.

She tossed the wet towel on a plastic chair.

He snapped the dry one open. "Arms out."

When she obeyed, still bamboozled by the sight of so much naked male chest so close to her, he wrapped the towel around her gently, lopsided, the right side hanging lower than the left. His hands didn't drop away from her body when he was finished.

His gaze slipped to her lips. The air between them thickened, charged with undisguised desire.

His fingers clenched on the terrycloth. His jaw tightened. His warm breath fanned her face. "I wasn't going to do this, dammit."

And then he kissed her.

She was no tough cookie. She capitulated the second his lips touched hers. Her body simply said *yes* and went for it.

His firm, warm lips pressed against hers, and he nuzzled her, nibbled her, prompting her to submit. She did.

She let him draw her against his wide chest as he angled his head to deepen the kiss.

Her brain had to be somewhere on the bottom of the pool. Because no way was she kissing a patient, in the pool complex, where anyone could walk in.

And with that thought, she regained sanity at last, enough to tug away.

Leave. Now. But she couldn't. All she could do was stare at him, at the heat in his eyes that threatened to blister her.

"I'm sorry," she blurted, clutching her towel. Swallowed. Panicked. Took a quick step back. "That didn't happen."

He growled and advanced. "The hell it didn't."

Right. What was she thinking? What had Cole said about denial and hand grenades? Denial was not the way to go, and certainly not in a professional capacity.

"If you want to file a complaint, I completely understand."

His head dipped forward like an angry bear's. "What are you talking about? I kissed you."

"I shouldn't have let it happen."

"You think you could have stopped me?"

"A *no* would have stopped you. I didn't say no."

His lips flattened.

"I don't think I can have sessions with you," she said, and hated that she'd caused this. That her lack of judgment would take something away from Cole that he needed.

"No."

"Cole—"

"You're right. Nothing happened."

"And it's not going to happen again. Not even if we're not having sessions. Anything between us is completely unethical." She begged him silently to understand. "We can't be more than friends. And if we can't manage that, we can't be anything."

He reached for her. "Annie—"

She'd made mistakes with men before, but never this big. "I need to go." She ran.

By the time she changed in her room, then walked to the conference room for her morning session with Trevor, she should have had her emotions under control. She didn't. She pushed Cole out of her mind, regardless. Not all the way—that seemed impossible—but enough to be able to function in a professional capacity. *Focus, dammit.*

Trevor deserved her full attention.

Technically, Annie was still on vacation, but Trevor was a fragile case. And she was on-site anyway. So she'd uncanceled their session.

When his face lit up as she walked into the room, she knew she'd done the right thing.

The conference room was light and airy. A dozen chairs surrounded a large poplar-wood table in the middle, one wall all windows, another decorated with three dozen orchids, an installation she had put in. The flowers cheered up the place. With this many, a handful was always blooming.

"How are you, Trev?"

He stood from his chair, like a gentleman from some old movie. She wasn't sure whether he stood because he had that kind of manners, or excitement simply pushed him to his feet. "Good. Well. I think I kinda made a new friend." As she sat, he plopped back down again. "Too bad we can't go for a walk in the woods, huh?"

"We'll go tomorrow. If the rain stops. Who's your new friend?"

"Cole. He's a Navy SEAL." The way he said the words, admiration and respect in his tone, Cole might as well have been a celebrity or some major sports figure. Trevor grinned. "He said you were great."

"Did he?" And why did her heart leap at the news? She wanted to ask for details, but suppressed the urge. She wasn't here for self-gratification. "He's all right, isn't he?"

"Yeah."

She approved of Trev making friends. He was high-strung, too wired most of the time, jumpy. He was a good kid, but a lot of the other patients had their own jumpiness, and sometimes they stayed away from him. He took a lot of mental energy.

"So what are we going to do today?" he asked.

She nodded toward the large cardboard box she'd put in the corner early that morning. "I was hoping you could help me repot the orchids."

He was on his feet in a blink. Then right next to her in two seconds, so close that their elbows bumped together. "Sure. I mean if you ever need help with anything . . . I'd love to help."

She definitely got that. She had to bite back a smile. He was so eager. He clearly liked the idea of *giving* a hand instead of being the broken one who *needed* a hand. Annie relaxed. Today's improvised therapy was going to work.

"So we have the bark," she began. "It's wet. I soaked it for an hour this morning. Then we have some orchid food. That's pretty much all we need."

"The old bark can go back in the box?" He was already opening the flaps.

She nodded. "You know anything about houseplants?"

He gave a sheepish smile. "My mom has a few. But, I mean, us boys don't pay no mind to them."

"Maybe when you go home, you can surprise your mom with a nice orchid."

He looked at her as if she'd invented beer in a can or something equally earth-shattering. "She'd love that."

"Then your brothers will be jealous that they didn't think of it first. You'll definitely be the favorite."

He laughed, still a pretty rare occurrence. "I'm already the favorite."

Because they were bumping elbows again, she stepped back and put some space between them. She picked up the next orchid.

By the time she glanced at Trev again a few seconds later, he had shut down. Eyes lifeless. Mouth grim. She could almost see the dark cloud that enveloped him.

He was like that most of the time, actually. He was usually at his lightest at their sessions. She knew he liked her. She liked him too, a lot, as a younger brother.

Trev's nearness didn't make her feel any of the crazy impulses Cole's did.

Cole . . . Annie could and would resist the physical attraction she felt for him, but so much more than that drew her to the former SEAL. She enjoyed his wry sense of humor. She admired his instinct to help and protect. She respected his inner strength.

He hadn't made peace with his new life yet, but he never used injury as an excuse. He was gruff on the outside, but he felt deeply. He was still grieving his friend Ryan.

And then there was the way Cole sometimes looked at Annie, that hungry grizzly look, as if he wanted to devour her. The memory of that look sent heat tingling through her.

Don't think about it.

"The roots need light." She dove into work. "So don't bury them too deep or too fully. Orchids grow in just a little dirt in the crook of the branches of host trees. I mean, look at those roots. You think they wouldn't be able to hang on to anything, but they do."

"They just hang on with these little things?" Trev ran a finger over a pale-green air root.

"Through storms and everything. You ever seen a tropical storm?"

He nodded, still touching the root. "I was assigned to JTF-Bravo in Honduras for a while before our unit was shipped over to Afghanistan."

She picked another orchid off the wall and gently tugged it out of its pot. Inside the clay pot, another plastic see-through pot held in the bark. "You have to let some light reach the roots. That's important."

Trev's shoulders relaxed as he began copying what she was doing.

She was suddenly glad for the rain. She had already done the same leaf-branch-trunk-root meditation with Trev that she had done with Cole, but Trev hadn't responded fully. She suspected he viewed himself as . . . if not broken, at least definitely breakable, fragile. He couldn't relate to the mighty-oak symbolism. But he could relate to the weak roots of the orchid. If those little roots could hold on, then so could he.

Trev and Cole becoming friends was a good thing. Maybe Cole could be the strong, sturdy tree that sheltered a more fragile plant that didn't have massive roots, just little air roots. Weaker roots that needed something to hang on to, in order to live.

Recovery had stages. Right now, Trevor needed that support, that shelter. And maybe he needed it from a friend, from someone who was kind of like him. Words weren't always the same when they came from a therapist.

When he looked at Annie next, some of his darkness was fading around the edges. "You think I could take one of these orchids back to my room with me?"

She smiled at him. "Sure, Trev."

More of his darkness melted away.

Trevor was definitely making progress. And Annie couldn't have been happier about that. With everything she was, she sensed a breakthrough just around the corner for him. She couldn't wait.

Soon they were both grinning.

She'd messed up with Cole, but she was definitely doing something right with Trevor. She needed to keep her mind focused on that.

Don't think about the kiss. Don't think about the kiss. Don't think about the kiss.

Chapter Thirteen

NOON FOUND COLE ONCE AGAIN LEANING AGAINST HIS TRUCK IN THE PARKING lot outside Hope Hill. He watched the facilities and the people hurrying between buildings, coming and going from lunch. None of them looked like a traitor. He needed progress. One damn clue. Anything. Those burner phones the traitor used had to be somewhere.

He had only three more offices to search, and seven patient rooms.

He'd gotten an eyeful when spying on the acupuncturist, but what he'd seen hadn't exactly moved him forward.

Milo had had a young woman with him—maybe the girl was twenty, if that. They'd both been naked. Milo had been on the treatment table, acting out some fantasy, the woman's lips moving up and down an impressive erection. But the sex act wasn't what left Cole mentally scarred. What had him jerking his head back was the fact that Milo had about two dozen stainless-steel needles sticking out of his ball sack.

Like a freaking porcupine down there.

Who did that?

First thing this morning, Cole had canceled all his scheduled acupuncture treatments.

Since that left a hole in his schedule today, he'd gone swimming earlier than usual, and . . . *Annie.*

Her mad dive into the pool, the way his heart stopped, her see-through shirt, the way his heart stopped again—he didn't know what to do with any of that. He knew what he *wanted* to do. He wanted to kiss her again.

He didn't go to her morning feeding with her. He'd tracked her down and offered, but she'd said Detective Finnegan would be stopping by. The man had more questions and wanted to look at the house and yard again in the light of day.

Maybe he'd find footprints.

Instead of going with Annie, Cole had texted his mother, checking in—she was fine, other than some big drama at the knitting club. After she finally let him go—once he agreed that Letty was definitely copying her colors—he went for a run and bumped into Trevor on his way back. Trevor had been sitting in the courtyard with a sketch pad.

"Didn't know you were an artist," Cole said.

"Planning a new barn for my mother. She loves her horses." He showed Cole his drawings. "I work on it every day. Takes my mind off other things. Kind of relaxing."

Cole was glad to see the guy relaxed. He left Trev with a few encouraging words and went back to his room to text his CO with an update. They'd agreed on regular check-ins.

His CO texted back.

Msgs are still going to Yemen

2 in the past 3 days

And Cole thought, *Shit.*

Then noon rolled around, and Cole found himself in the parking lot once again.

"Need some company?" he asked when Annie showed up.

Her gaze hovered in the vicinity of his neck, and she wouldn't look any higher. "Thanks, but I'm good. I have some errands to run. I won't be back for a while."

He shouldn't have said anything about her nipples back at the pool. The sight of her clothes stuck to her body had poleaxed him. His body stirred at the memory.

"I'm going crazy in this place," he said. "I need to get out for a while. You said we could be friends."

After a moment, she gave a reluctant nod.

Relief loosened the tension in his shoulders. "Truck?"

"Car. I have to get groceries."

He went around to the Prius's passenger side.

"Finnegan have anything new?" he asked as he got in.

"Not yet."

"I don't like the idea of you going to the house alone."

She didn't tell him to mind his own business, but she looked as if the words were on the tip of her tongue.

Don't think about her tongue.

They took care of the animals and bought groceries. They also stopped by the small PD so she could be fingerprinted, which took less than ten minutes.

When she drove by her house, he said, "You missed the driveway."

"The food is for my grandfather." The skin tightened around her eyes. "Sylvia, his housekeeper, has a bad back. She can't carry heavy grocery bags anymore."

Annie's stiff posture said there was a story there somewhere about the grandfather. For one, Cole wondered for the first time, why wasn't she staying with the grandfather instead of at Hope Hill?

Annie drove to the end of the block, turned right, drove past the cornfield, turned right again at the next stop sign. She pulled over in front of a hundred-year-old brick farmhouse. "You don't have to come in."

Cole was already reaching for the handle. "I don't mind. I'll help you carry the groceries."

She was so clearly dreading the visit, he almost told her to stay in the car and he'd carry the bags in, but he had no right to interfere in her family business.

They found the eighty-something man alone, sitting in his striped blue pajamas in the kitchen, reading the paper. He didn't smile at Annie, didn't hug her, didn't thank her for the food.

"Who's that?" were the first words out of his mouth, his eyes slanting toward Cole.

Annie turned toward Cole as she responded. She hadn't once forgotten, from their first session, that he needed to see her lips. "A friend from Hope Hill. His name is Cole."

"One of the looneys?"

"He has trouble with hearing, so if you talk to him, you have to turn toward him. He needs to read your lips."

Instead, the old man turned away, but not enough so Cole couldn't read his next question. "You sleeping with him?"

He read the words almost as clearly as he read the disgust and censure on the old man's face.

Annie's expression tightened. She began putting food in the refrigerator while Cole hesitated, unsure how to defend her.

The guy was old and frail, his disapproval the strongest thing about him. A two-hundred-pound Navy SEAL mowing his ass down wouldn't be right. And he was Annie's grandfather. She clearly cared about him enough to help him.

She shot Cole a let-me-handle-it look.

So Cole stood there, fuming silently. He prayed the old geezer didn't lay into Annie again, because Cole wasn't sure he'd be able to keep from saying something he might regret later.

"Sorry about that," Annie said when they were back in the car, her slim hand hesitating on the key in the ignition.

"You have nothing to apologize for."

"We don't get along."

"Why?"

"When my mom was twenty, going to college at WCU, she got pregnant by an older guy in town. Turned out, he also got another woman pregnant at the same time. He chose the other woman and the other kid."

Annie's face was so studiously impassive, Cole knew the rejection still hurt her.

"So then my mom quit college to raise me. She went to work as a cashier at the grocery store. We spent the first eleven years of my life living with my grandfather. He called my mother a slut and a whore at least fifty times a day, until she couldn't take it anymore. She got a new job in Delaware, and we moved there."

Her expression had been closed and her muscles tight since they'd pulled into the driveway, but now the look in her eyes turned dark and bleak.

"What happened in Delaware, Annie?" Cole asked as softly as possible, and held his breath for the answer.

She stared past him, out the passenger side window as her lips formed a single word. "Randy."

"Who is Randy?" Other than a man Cole needed to kill.

Her gaze snapped to him, as if she'd only now realized she'd spoken out loud.

"He was my mother's boyfriend." She drove away from the farmhouse. "Need to go anywhere before we go back to Hope Hill?"

She straightened her spine, filled her lungs, and turned her tight expression into a neutral one. From the way she was desperately avoiding looking at him, he was pretty sure no further questions on the subject would be answered.

He glanced at the clock on the dashboard. "I have PT in half an hour. I'd better get back."

Even if what he really wanted to do was go wherever this Randy lived and ask the asshole what he'd done to put that look into Annie's eyes.

She drove in silence.

"I'm going to your feedings with you from now on," he said. "Until they catch the intruder, you shouldn't go alone."

He was aware that he wasn't giving her a choice. He couldn't. Her safety wasn't up for negotiation.

He expected her to push back.

"Harper said the same thing. That I shouldn't go alone," she said instead. "OK. Thanks. I appreciate it." And then she added, "Sorry about my grandfather."

"You don't have to be sorry on my account. But he should treat you better."

He wondered if the old man put her down regularly like he'd done with that are-you-sleeping-with-him comment.

Yet Annie still took care of the man. She was not only courageous, but she was loyal too, another attribute Cole valued highly.

He wanted to protect her. He was going to go with her again at six and at midnight.

After that, he was going to search the three remaining offices. Hopefully without running into someone else with needles in his ball sack.

Chapter Fourteen

ANNIE RESCHEDULED SOME OF THE SESSIONS SHE'D ORIGINALLY CANCELED FOR the week, including an informal activity at three o'clock. She sent out a round of text messages. Five guys showed, which wasn't bad on last-minute notice.

"Grab some shovels and buckets," she told them.

Would have been nice if Cole had come.

As soon as the thought surfaced, she shook it off. She needed to be glad that he wasn't here. She'd been serious when she'd told him she couldn't help him anymore as his therapist. She had to be circumspect at work.

And outside of work?

He wouldn't let her go to the feedings alone. Probably only because his default setting was *protector*.

Don't read anything into it.

Maybe she should have sent him away when she found him waiting for her in the parking lot, but she couldn't.

Because he needed the normalcy of the chores?

Because she liked his company?

Both? Neither?

Her thoughts and feelings were a swirling mess when it came to Cole.

She was smart enough to know when she was in trouble.

Yet when he lumbered up as the group headed to the back of the buildings, her heart leapt. She acknowledged it, but remained firm in her decision not to encourage the attraction.

She nodded a greeting, then turned to lead the group, not stopping until they reached the designated spot.

"So we'll mark out the spots for the trees, then start digging the holes. We need holes about two inches deeper and two inches larger all around than the root balls. Everybody who didn't get a shovel needs to start carrying water."

None of them ever complained about having to do something physical. Getting them to talk or consider taking some of the alternative-treatment methods seriously was like pulling teeth. But if hard work and muscle were needed, they were there.

Cole carried water. Digging one-handed would have been awkward for him. Annie made sure not to pay any more attention to him than to the others. He was preoccupied, doing the work, but his attention was clearly not on his task. He almost planted one of the trees without taking the burlap off the root ball.

"Why are we planting two of everything?" Dale, a recovering burn victim and former marine, shouted over. "OCD?"

At the moment, the brand-new orchard consisted of two cherry trees, two apples, two pears, two plums, two sour cherries, and two peaches.

"I'm experimenting with what'll grow well in this soil," Annie said. "We'll plant more of whatever produces well."

The property had plenty of space, and if they grew more fruit than the cafeteria needed, they could always donate the rest to the Broslin food pantry.

"Why not plant one of each, then?" Dale wiped his hands on his jeans. "If you're not sure they'll all make it."

"Most fruit trees need two of a kind for cross-pollination," Kyle, a farm boy from Iowa, told him.

"They don't look too good." Dale had doubt written all over his city-boy face.

"They're going dormant for the winter." Kyle rolled his eyes.

And Annie added, "Best time to plant them."

The trees wouldn't bear fruit for years. None of the men who planted today would be here for the harvest. They wouldn't benefit. They were planting for others.

They talked about that as they worked on the orchard. Annie considered the concept of continuity important. She wanted them to viscerally understand that there was a future—a future that could be bettered by simply working on things today.

She hoped the message reached Dale, specifically.

Most of her patients lived in the past—had trouble letting go of the past, of things that had happened to them, things they had done. She had to coax most of them to live more in the present. Not Dale. Dale lived too much in the present. If something didn't work right now, it was never going to work. If he had trouble sleeping right now, he was never going to sleep again. She'd done several visualization exercises with him in the past couple of weeks about what his ideal future would look like. He had a lot of trouble with that.

In his mind, the way things were—especially bad things—was the way they were always going to be.

Annie wished Trevor had been able to attend the tree planting, but Trev had PT. The planting would have probably been too strenuous for him anyway. Titanium screws held his neck together.

The guys did a great job with the task, the trees popping into the ground one after the other. Annie was pleased.

She was also far too aware of Cole in a way she wasn't aware of the others. She wanted to think the reason was because he was bigger than everyone else. And, also, she had to be aware of him to make sure she turned toward him when she spoke, so he could read her lips. Except, if she was honest with herself, her awareness of him went beyond that.

She had to admit that she was aware of him as a man. When he passed by with a bucket of water and brushed her arm, she nearly jumped out of her skin.

She was aware of his shifting muscles as she watched him lift a hundred-pound root ball with one hand. Every time he came within ten feet, her entire body focused on him.

She had to get over her stupid and extremely inappropriate attraction before he noticed. And before others noticed. None of the men were fools. If anyone figured out how stupid she was being, her credibility with her patients would be ruined. Not to mention her continued job prospects at Hope Hill.

"I'll take that." Cole popped up at her elbow as she reached for the cooler the cafeteria had packed for them.

She'd wanted to eat at least a snack outside with the group under the sky, in the orchard they were planting—another connection.

Cole reached around her and took the cooler, his arm brushing her shoulder. Once again, lightning sliced through her. Before she could step back, he was gone, taking the cooler to the picnic table in the center of the future orchard and dropping it in the middle.

Dale opened the top. "Egg-salad sandwiches." He picked one along with a bottle of water, then looked back in. "Got some tuna too."

The guys gathered around and sat. Annie rubbed her arm where her skin tingled, then went to join them.

She had no plans to sneak in any therapy. A shared meal, community, nature, and good work all contributed healing power.

The picnic table could easily sit eight average people, but some of the guys were pretty big, especially Cole and Dale. Their warrior bodies took up a lot of space. Only when she stood next to them did Annie notice that there wasn't enough room for her at the table.

Cole sat on one end. As Annie prepared to sit on an overturned bucket, Cole leaned into the row of massive soldiers next to him and pushed them over. He barely exerted himself, but the row moved, until Dale fell off on the other end.

"Make room for the lady," Cole mumbled under his breath as the others laughed, Dale taking his dethronement in stride and claiming the bucket.

Nothing for Annie to do then but sit next to Cole. She made sure to keep an inch or two between them as she dropped her hands onto her lap. She didn't want to reach over Cole for a sandwich and accidentally press a breast against his arm. She wasn't that hungry anyway.

"Can I grab you something?"

They were so close to each other, she could see the golden flecks that ringed his dark irises. His gaze dropped to her mouth as he waited for her answer.

He looked at her mouth a lot. She knew he had a perfectly good reason. Awareness zinged through her anyway.

Knock it off.

"An egg-salad sandwich and a bottle of green tea would be great."

He turned to grab what she'd asked for and handed it over, keeping his gaze on her mouth in case she asked for something more.

The guys talked about the game they'd watched on TV the night before. Cole didn't join in.

She was as acutely aware of his silence as she was of his body. It occurred to her that his need to read lips might be even more isolating than she'd realized before. Maybe he felt uncomfortable watching other men's lips. Or maybe other men didn't talk as much to him because having another guy stare at your mouth for an extended amount of time was weird. Not to mention, trying to follow a conversation among six people had to be challenging. Just finding the speaker would take time, making Cole miss part of the conversation. And if two people spoke at the same time?

Annie didn't have a large family, but she was friendly with a lot of people. She talked to a dozen different people a day. Cole's isolation made her heart hurt. She wanted to lean into his massive side and put her arms around him.

Bad idea.

She snapped herself right out of it and was so studiously professional for the rest of the day, it made her teeth ache.

After the break, they finished planting the trees. All went well, until the very last one, when Dale stabbed the shovel into his foot, right through his sneakers. He swore. Blood ran everywhere.

Kyle just laughed. "City boy."

The others too were more amused than worried. Apparently, their idea of grave injury was on a different level than Annie's.

Annie's head turned woozy at the sight of flowing crimson. She stepped forward anyway, her heart pounding. "Let me see."

Cole came through between them like a bear galloping through the woods. He tackled Dale at the waist and kept going, slinging the big fellow over his shoulder. "I'll take him in for first aid."

"Put me down, dammit." Dale's voice was strangled with embarrassment.

Cole couldn't have heard, but he responded anyway, probably because Dale was trying to break away. "Wouldn't want you to die from your little paper cut."

The rest of the guys laughed, then went back to work. They watered everything they'd just planted. The forecast promised plenty of rain, but they still gave two full buckets—carried from the showers at the pool complex—to each tree.

After they finished and cleaned up the site, they headed in for a real meal—dinner. Annie usually ate with the patients, but today she sat at the staff table and chatted with Dan Ambrose about a new study on behavioral therapy. By the time she finished eating, she needed to head back home again.

Cole waited for her in the parking lot as usual, leaning against his silver pickup, looking as if he didn't have a care in the world.

"I'll drive you."

She was ridiculously aware of his gaze on her lips, his wide shoulders, his strength that had propelled her out of the pool that morning . . . and how much she liked his company.

"You don't have to do this. It's not your job to protect me."

He gave a one-shouldered shrug. "I've decided I like driving a pickup and doing the country-boy thing. It's definitely not Chicago's South Side. And I'm finding the gentleness of the llamas healing. As a therapist, you shouldn't discourage me from a healing experience."

"Don't mock my llamas," she said, but got into his pickup.

"Who says I'm mocking?"

She tried not to like his wry humor so much. She failed. Gave up. "Thank you for helping Dale." He'd been back by dinner, with stitches.

"The guy needs to cut down on the bean burgers."

"You didn't have to carry him."

For a long moment, Cole didn't respond. Then he said, "You don't like blood."

Oh. Had that been why he'd barreled into the situation? To get Dale's bleeding foot away from her as fast as possible? Had he done it to spare her?

"Why?" he asked.

And because her defenses were suddenly down, she responded. "Childhood trauma."

"Want to talk about it?"

"Hey, who's the therapist here?" She tried to regain their earlier, light tone, resisting the dark memories that threatened to pull her back into the past.

"Hey, look who's stalling."

When she still wouldn't say anything, he asked, "Would this be related to Randy?"

Her chest clenched. "Do you always remember every word everybody says?"

He shook his head. "I remember the people I want to kill."

"Don't make me put *homicidal impulses* in your file."

"Those threats are getting old. You're not my therapist."

"You should keep up with the green therapy on your own." She jumped on the subject change. She didn't want to talk about Randy.

Cole huffed. "Let me guess. Barefoot. Will the earth absorb my murderous impulses through the soles of my feet?"

"Laugh all you want. It works. Ecotherapy solves problems."

"So does a nine-millimeter bullet," he said under his breath.

His massive biceps stretched his navy cotton shirt. He was 100 percent male, 100 percent soldier. Nothing she said was going to soften him. And she didn't really want him to change. She liked him way too much the way he was.

Once they arrived at her house, Cole helped her muck the soiled straw out of the garage and lay down new bedding.

"You need a barn," he called after her as she picked up the wheelbarrow handles.

"It's on my wish list."

"So what's this Randy guy's last name again?" he asked in a way-too-casual tone as she passed him.

She turned so he could read her lips. "Give it a rest."

She came back in, warm from all the physical work. She'd be more comfortable finishing up in fewer layers. She stopped inside the open garage door and started to pull off her sweatshirt.

"Stop." His voice was strong enough to freeze her with the shirt over her head. "Don't move."

"Is it a spider?"

She loved all God's creatures, but . . . she had nightmares that the tarantula she'd rescued last month had hidden her eggs somewhere in the garage before her untimely death. In those dreams, the eggs hatched, and the baby spiders came to get her for not protecting their mother from the goat's chomping teeth.

"Get it off! Please get it off."

Dammit, he couldn't see what she was saying. She tried to wiggle her face free, but he was next to her by then, and he caught her wrist.

Thunder rumbled through his voice, the tone sharper than she'd ever heard from him. "Who did this?"

She had no idea what he was talking about until his finger glanced over the naked skin of her rib cage. Obviously, her T-shirt had ridden up. Then she forgot about the T-shirt as she realized what he was talking about. She'd been put off too, when she'd changed earlier and seen all that black and blue on her side.

She tugged to pull her arms down, but he held them fast. She wiggled her head and finally freed her face. "I hit the water the wrong way when I dove into the pool."

The message his dark eyes were transmitting switched like a traffic light from *murder* to a more subdued *All right, nobody has to die.* He quietly swore as he let her go, tugged her T-shirt down, tugged the sweatshirt off, and hung it on the peg by the door.

He pointed at the stacked bags of pig feed by the wall. "Take a break."

She did, but only because her skin was still tingling where he'd touched her, and she needed to regroup.

"What else do you need done?" he asked.

"The animals need to be watered."

"I'll do that. You sit right there and tell me all about ecotherapy. I'm ready to listen."

Sure he was. "Don't think I don't know you're faking interest just to keep me sitting." But, of course, she couldn't resist. "What would you like to know?"

"Did you learn it in college?"

"I studied psychology. Kept feeling that I needed more. Like if someone had panic attacks, we just tried to make it easier to deal with them. Mantras and visualizations to make it less scary, to make it go away faster. I wanted a solution that would prevent the panic attacks from happening in the first place. Thyroid disease or even celiac can cause anxiety. No amount of talking about your feelings is going to fix that."

He watched her lips as he worked.

"I did a lot of extra reading," she told him. "I believe that physical and mental health are part of a larger system and can't be treated separately. Our physical health and mental health are not separate from the health of our environment."

"Makes sense."

"I interned at a counseling center that had all these middle-class women as their clients. Great houses in the suburbs, great jobs, or some didn't even have to work. And they were all falling apart. I swear some of them were in worse shape than the military vets I'm treating now. These women were popping pills like you wouldn't believe. Not to mention self-medicating with wine."

Cole quirked an eyebrow.

"These women told me," she continued, "that they felt as if the world was rushing by them at a hundred miles an hour. And they felt impelled to keep up, even at the cost of their health and relationships. A million meetings at work, then a million after-school activities for the kids, then making costumes for the plays and baking cupcakes for the fund-raisers. And the hairdresser and facials and the trips to the gym for maintenance, and shopping for the right clothes for just the right image."

Cole leaned the broom in the corner, outside the llama pen so neither Esmeralda nor Dorothy the pig could eat it. "How did you fix them?"

"I didn't fix them. I can't fix anyone. All I can do is share some ideas people can use to fix themselves."

"And what did you share?" His gaze hung on her face, as he was genuinely interested.

"Not me. My mentor. I was basically there to learn and handle the paperwork. But Susan shared that it's OK to get off the train. She got me thinking that maybe what's outside the train is actually your true life. All the little moments when you stop to smell the roses. A lot of the other stuff is just noise."

"Pretty deep for an intern."

"I was a total nerd. I just followed Susan around, when she would put up with me, and read the rest of the time." She'd spent pretty much every minute of her college years with her nose in a book.

Cole leaned against the door frame. "What did you do after college?"

"Worked with inner-city kids in Philly. There's a concept called *nature deficit disorder*. The idea is that not spending enough time in nature negatively affects people's psyches in ways they don't realize. A foundation put up the money, and we did nature activities with at-risk kids who live in the concrete jungle. Spent a lot of time at Fairmount Park after school."

"Did it work?"

"Spectacularly. Missed days at school went down by forty percent. Incidents of in-school violence went down by fifty-four percent. Graduation rate went up by thirty percent."

He watched her, and he must have picked up on her mixed emotions, because he asked, "But?"

Melancholy filled her. "We had a four-year grant. The foundation's idea is to give worthy causes three to four years to prove their concept. They figure other investors or some state or federal funds will take over at that point."

"And that didn't happen?"

"The city didn't have the budget. The state is into rural development right now. They think Philly already gets more than its share of state funds. As for federal aid, there are areas of the country in much worse trouble than the Northeast. We couldn't get funding. The program shut down."

"You hated leaving the kids."

Someone else might have said, *Tough losing a job like that.* But Cole knew what hurt her most. The thought swirled around in her chest, unsure where to nest.

"Some of the kids still keep in touch. We text."

"I'm glad you found your way here."

"I was lucky that a position opened up at Hope Hill. It's not like there are a million openings for ecotherapists."

He pushed away from the door frame to pick up an empty bucket. "Tree hugging is vastly underrated. It'll catch on. I mean, what's not to like? Right?"

"Definitely the next big thing." It hit her how much she loved spending time with him like this. How could the two of them together feel so right even as she knew, with her rational mind, that a relationship between them would be all wrong?

When she heard a car pull up, she was grateful for the distraction. She went to see who it was. Then her stomach clenched when she spotted Joey's camo-painted pickup in the driveway behind Cole's.

Joey cracked the driver's side door to get out.

Dammit, Joey. "I can't talk to you right now."

He paused with the door half-open and pushed his red baseball hat up his forehead an inch with a finger. "I can't take a no for an answer again. You have to give me time to explain."

Then Cole strode past her, heading Joey off before Joey could even get out. When Cole pushed the pickup's door closed, Joey rolled down his window, a wary look on his face. "Who are you?"

Cole said, "You need to leave. You won't be stopping by again."

Outrage reddened Joey's cheeks. "I'm Annie's boyfriend. Who the hell are you?"

"I'm the guy you'll be seeing through your tears when I rip your balls off."

Good grief.

Annie flinched as she stood in the doorway. She didn't need Cole to defend her. But she knew she couldn't stop Cole, and Joey needed a wake-up call. As unpleasant as their conversation was, maybe it was something Joey would finally take seriously.

"You don't come by," Cole said. "You don't call. You don't run into her in town." He took a step closer to the pickup. "If you see her on the street, you turn and start walking in the other direction before she even notices you. Am I clear?"

Joey cast a hurt look at Annie. "Don't do this to me. You can't choose this guy over me, Annie. Not him."

Cole fisted his left hand and punched the pickup's door so hard he dented it.

"What the hell, man? You can't do that!" Joey scrambled to roll up his window. When the dented door wouldn't let him, he switched his efforts to backing out of the driveway. Then he was off, his mouth moving, probably swearing. Annie could no longer hear him.

By the time Cole came into the garage, Annie had the first-aid kit ready.

"Anger management. It can do wonders." She twisted the top off the peroxide bottle. "Let me see that hand."

"You don't have to."

"I want to. Having to look at a few drops of blood isn't going to kill me. Neither of us believes in indulging our weaknesses."

Cole held out his busted knuckles for her. The damage wasn't as bad as it'd been back at the gas station.

He scowled. "Somebody had to talk to the kid."

"That was you talking?" Annie shook her head as she cleaned Cole up. "Band-Aid?"

"Don't bother," he said, and went back to work.

When Cole finished filling the outside troughs with water, they fed the skunk kittens together, then drove back to Hope Hill.

"Thanks," she said into the silence.

"For what?"

"Everything."

He nodded.

Come midnight, he once again insisted on going with her. She didn't even bother resisting. She'd been dreading having to go back to the house alone in the middle of the night.

Cole said little. He was preoccupied. Annie was too. The whole time he was helping her, she lectured herself over and over. *Don't get used to this. Don't get used to this.*

The man in the window watched Annie return to Hope Hill in the middle of the night, once again with Cole. Anger built a fire in his gut.

Were they sleeping together? They had to be.

He'd seen that kiss at the pool, had been walking by and happened to look through the glass.

Rage fisted his hands now as it had then.

He did *not* share.

As Annie had not been smart enough to heed his previous warnings, he was going to have to be clearer.

He thought of her stupid pig. Then the one-eyed donkey. She could be changed into a blind donkey fairly easily.

Yet maiming or killing one of Annie's animals no longer felt like enough punishment.

Whoring herself to Cole was a personal affront. The punishment too would have to be personal.

Annie would bear his retribution on her flesh. He had so many wonderful tools. His pride and joy. He'd made them all himself.

She wasn't going to like his tools. His mother certainly didn't. But how else was one to teach stubborn women?

Chapter Fifteen

Saturday

ANNIE PUT OUT MORE HAY FOR THE LLAMAS AND THE DONKEY THE FOLLOWING morning, but her mind wasn't on what her hands were doing. She'd stopped by the post office on her way over from Hope Hill and run into one of Joey's uncles, a burly guy who reminded her of Big Jim. They all had that big-boned look in the family. Which made her think . . . what if it'd been Big Jim in her house the other night?

Joey wouldn't have sent his cousin to scare her, but this was just the kind of thing Big Jim would come up with on his own, if Joey had complained to him about Annie. Big Jim might have figured if he scared Annie good, she wouldn't want to be in the house all by herself and she'd ask Joey to stay with her.

She dropped the last of the hay and reached into her pocket for her phone, but then she left it there. For one, she hadn't spent enough time with Big Jim to recognize him by shape alone, and she'd caught only a few glimpses of the man in her dark kitchen. She just wasn't sure.

And if she told Harper about her suspicions, he'd go and talk to Big Jim. And Big Jim wasn't as nice as Joey. He'd come over to Annie's and throw a fit.

If it'd been Big Jim trying to scare her the other night, then most likely, if she left things alone, he wouldn't come by again. He didn't have that kind of attention span.

Had he really had a gun? She *had* seen a glint of black metal. But she couldn't imagine Big Jim trying to shoot her. What would be the point? What she'd seen was probably a flashlight. She'd been so scared, her brain must have jumped to the darkest conclusion.

Annie filled the bucket with water and filled the troughs, then stilled when the prickly sensation of being watched crept up her spine. She glanced toward the house. Right. She wasn't alone.

Ed had sent the cleanup crew: two of his nephews. They were dragging a four-by-four out the back. They weren't part of Ed's regular crew. His regular crew was putting siding on half a dozen houses in the new development down the road, on Victoria Circle. They couldn't take time off, not with all the rain from Rupert in the forecast. Hence the nephews. The boys didn't have a ton of construction experience, but they had all the muscles of eighteen-year-old high school athletes, which was all the cleanup required.

And then David Durenne showed up again. The producer didn't have to go into work at the TV station until noon, and his son, Tyler, was at a birthday party.

Annie was grateful for the help. Grateful enough to invite Kelly over for coffee, but Kelly was closing on a home for a client and couldn't leave. So much for playing Cupid.

Annie finished her chores, then left the men to their work and drove back to Hope Hill, listening to the weather report on the way.

Hurricane Rupert was sweeping through the Bahamas. It had spent most of its strength in Cuba, so it'd been downgraded to a category 1 hurricane.

She didn't see Cole again for the rest of the day, although she kept catching herself looking for him. She hadn't seen him since that morning when she'd run into him crossing the courtyard, and he'd offered to blow off a couple of his sessions so he could go with her to her feedings. She had thanked him, but declined, reassuring him that she wouldn't be alone since Ed was sending over people. He had promised to go with her at midnight.

Annie completed her afternoon sessions, then she grabbed a quick dinner in the cafeteria with a handful of her patients. After dinner, she drove back to the house for the evening feeding.

David was gone, but Ed's nephews were still there, as promised. They had an away game the next day, so tonight they were going to keep going with the cleanup until they finished.

They were sweeping up the last of the rubble when Annie left to drive back to Hope Hill at seven. She had to give it to them, they were hardworking kids.

She took Reservoir Road as usual, the fastest way to work. At this time of the evening, with the sun setting, the drive offered a spectacular view. The soft light of the setting autumn sun gilded the water with a golden glow. The breathtaking serenity was so awe-inspiring she decided to bring a Hope Hill group here for a meditation walk next week, if not sooner.

Screech. Crash.

A dark SUV hit her from behind.

Adrenaline slammed into her. She gripped the wheel. *Ohmygod. People, pay attention!*

She couldn't see the driver, not with the last rays of the sun turning his windshield into a mirror.

Her instinct was to brake, and she had her foot on the brake pedal before she changed her mind. At any other time, she would have put that bump down to an accident, but she'd just had an intruder at home. Instead of pulling over to exchange insurance information, she kept going. They could both pull over a few miles down the road at the gas station.

Bam. The SUV hit her again.

OK. *That* couldn't be by accident. Her heart raced. *Don't panic.*

Annie sped up to get away from whoever was behind her, but that meant she had to keep both hands on the steering wheel. She couldn't call for help. Her phone was in her purse on the passenger seat.

The SUV caught up. This time, it hit her little Prius harder, with intent, pushing her toward the shoulder.

Her breath caught. Less than five feet of grass stood between the road and the water. She was not a good swimmer. Not even in a pool—forget the giant reservoir. In the dark.

She pulled to the left so far that she was in the opposite lane. But the SUV kept bumping her, kept herding her to the right. No other cars in sight. Where was everybody? She was on a back road, but still.

Cold fear rode her.

She drove as fast as she dared, but not nearly as fast as she wanted. If she went too fast and the idiot hit her again, she might lose control, spin out, and end up in the water. She held the steering wheel in a death grip.

She didn't dare take her eyes off the road to look in the rearview mirror.

Joey?

Or was it someone else? This didn't feel like Joey. Joey drove an old camo-painted pickup.

Except . . . he *did* have access to a bunch of cars. The gas station had a repair shop in the back.

Focus on the road. She would think about the who and the why after she survived. *Go, go, go.*

She had maybe five hundred feet left before she'd pass the end of the reservoir and be surrounded by dry land. The SUV's driver knew it, too, and rammed her again, harder. Her teeth snapped together so fast, she nearly bit off her tongue. That her airbag hadn't gone off yet was a miracle.

Four hundred feet to go.

Bam.

Three hundred feet to go.

Bam.

She skidded onto the shoulder, fought hard, and veered back onto the road as her heart threatened to burst with panic. She had to stay on the pavement.

Two hundred feet.

The sun dipped below the horizon.

Bam.

One hundred feet.

BAM!

Annie's Prius flew off the road.

The car rolled. Her purse slammed into her temple a split second before the airbag slammed into her face. Then the side airbag slammed into her shoulder.

She was still screaming when suddenly everything stopped.

For a moment, she was too stunned and shocked to move. Then a whole new wave of panic hit. *Oh God, the water.* Was she in water? She scrambled to see.

Dark sky. A stand of trees up ahead. The car was right side up, having done a full roll. But she was still on solid ground. An overwhelming sense of gratitude filled her even as her heart still madly pounded.

She beat the airbags back and scanned the twilight as she sobbed for breath, desperate to see who was out there.

What did he want?

Would he come now to finish her?

Chapter Sixteen

ANNIE PEERED THROUGH THE WINDSHIELD AND CAUGHT MOVEMENT BY THE road. Fear screamed, *Get out! Run!*

She turned off the engine with a shaky hand. The locks popped. Then common sense returned. *Nonono.* She grabbed to lock the doors again. She needed to just sit tight until the police came.

Phone.

She released the seat belt and swept around for her purse with her right hand, searching the passenger-side foot well.

The sharp knock on the driver's-side window had her jerking forward so hard she smacked her head into the console. She turned, caught sight of a shadowy face, but then recognition hit before she could scream.

"Are you OK?" Pete the mailman shouted from the other side of the glass.

Breathe.

Annie straightened in her seat and pushed the door open. "I think so." *Breathe.* "Did you see a dark SUV?"

"I saw taillights. Nothing else."

As she moved to get out, Pete put a hand to her shoulder. "You might have injuries you don't realize. Let me call an ambulance."

"And the cops." She lay back against her seat, every inch of her sore. "Ask for Harper Finnegan."

Pete sat on the grass. "My knees are shaking. Sorry." He dialed. "Are you sure you're OK?"

Before Annie could answer, the other end picked up, and Pete reported the crash.

Annie closed her eyes, willing her heart into a normal, steady rhythm instead of weak, panicked flutters. *It's over. I'm safe.*

She could move everything—she tested herself limb by limb. A few spots seriously hurt, but nothing was broken.

She raised her fingers to the place on her neck that burned, but she felt no wetness, no blood, thank God. She turned her head to look in the askew rearview mirror. With the door open, the dome light was on.

Just an abrasion. She flinched at her reflection, reached up, then dropped her hand. She was too far gone to fix. Her hair was a mess, wide-eyed shock on her face. She looked as if she'd been tumbled in a dryer.

She *had* been tumbled.

Breathe. She chose to focus on the positive. At least the airbag hadn't broken her nose.

"I'm fine," she said, not so much to Pete, but because she needed to hear those words herself.

Long breath in. Hold. Slow breath out.

OK, she could do that. She could calm down. She knew how. She had this.

But as shock ebbed, anger took its place. If she found out that Joey had been in that SUV, or his popcorn-for-brains cousin . . . She was going to revise her principles of nonviolence and strangle the idiot. This went *way* beyond stupid.

She stilled.

Yes, it did, didn't it? Whoever had been in the other car had gone way beyond scaring her.

She couldn't see Joey, or even Big Jim, running her off the road like that, then driving away. But if not one of them, who?

She could not have another stalker, could she? What were the chances?

Long breath in. Hold. Slow breath out. That worked, so she kept the breathing technique going. She didn't want to start hyperventilating and scare Pete even worse.

Then Harper Finnegan arrived, sirens blaring, the ambulance right behind him.

Harper made sure she was OK before he moved on to police business. "I'll take pictures and measurements, write up what's here, then I'll meet you at the ER," he told Annie while the EMTs fussed over her.

"I'll go with her," Pete offered, still pale as a postal envelope.

Annie shifted as one of the EMTs checked something on her back, pulling up her shirt. She wanted family with her. *Would Kelly come?* Did she want to call Kelly?

She looked back at Pete. "I appreciate the offer. But let me call my cousin. She can meet me at the hospital. Could you please find my bag for me? It's somewhere in the car."

The ride to West Chester Hospital took only twenty minutes. The EMTs kept her entertained on the way, working to determine whether she had a concussion, taking her blood pressure, then starting an IV. They put her in a neck brace, even though she told them she didn't need it.

They asked her about her older bruises. She told them about her mad dive into the pool. They made her work at convincing them that she wasn't a victim of domestic abuse, which she liked, because it gave her hope that if someone else *was* abused, the EMTs would help her, or him.

All Annie wanted was some kind of cream for the stinging abrasion on her neck, some kind of ointment with lidocaine. Of course, that was the one thing they didn't have in the ambulance.

They did let her call Kelly.

"Are you OK? I'll meet you at the hospital. I'm leaving right now."

For some reason, Annie's eyes filled with tears as she thanked her cousin.

Pain pounded in her head. She closed her eyes and focused on her breathing.

She had about five minutes of rest before they were at the ER. She told the EMTs she could walk. They insisted on pushing her on a gurney anyway. She was taken right through into a small evaluation room that had green curtains for walls. The nurse who popped by a second later, a Hispanic woman called Maria, took Annie's vitals again and checked the IV.

"Dr. Chen will be with you in a minute." Maria gestured with her head toward a short, older gentleman who had just walked into a room on the other side of the nurses' station. Before she left, she drew the green curtain that turned the bed into a sterile cocoon.

And then Annie was alone, closed in.

Kelly will be here in a minute.

When heavy footsteps headed her way, she looked toward the sound. Then a large shadow fell on the green divider. *Definitely not Kelly.* And not Dr. Chen either.

The hefty outline of the man in her kitchen flashed into Annie's mind. Her heart clenched as she stared at the curtain. Then anger flared. She was *not* going to be a sitting duck again.

She grabbed for the IV stand.

Chapter Seventeen

COLE PULLED BACK THE CURTAIN AND STOPPED IN HIS TRACKS. ANNIE WAS sitting in bed, lifting her metal IV pole, ready to swing.

"What are you doing?"

She put down her weapon and lay back on her pillows, the fight going out of her. "I thought you were someone else."

She'd been scared. A bruise darkened her pale cheek.

Cole's hands clenched into fists at his sides. His heart beat the old war-drum rhythm he'd thought would never sound inside him again. The war drum demanded death.

A red abrasion on her neck looked as if someone had tried to choke her.

"Seat belt," she said when she caught him staring.

"Who was it?" He kept his voice even, because flying into a rage wouldn't help Annie, and he'd come to help if he could.

Her chestnut hair spread on the hospital pillow in twisted tangles, almost as if floating in water. He thought of the dark waters of the reservoir where he'd been told the accident had happened.

She could have gone in and not come up again.

He fought the urge to reach out and fold her into his arms.

"I couldn't see," she said.

Fear clouded her eyes, which did nothing to dampen his murderous impulses. Her fear slammed into him like a torpedo into a submarine and ripped his guts apart.

"How bad is it? What did the doctor say?"

"I haven't seen him yet," she said just as the man showed up at Cole's elbow in a white coat with a black stethoscope hanging around his neck.

The doctor began to speak, but he had his head turned toward Annie, and Cole could only see that the corner of the guy's mouth was moving. He stepped out to give the doctor space and give Annie privacy. Cole wasn't the husband, or the boyfriend, so he had no right to be there.

The thought bothered him more than it should have.

He shoved his hands into his pockets and turned his back to the curtain.

A woman was running down the hallway toward him. She resembled Annie—except blonde and with a lot more makeup, clothes tight instead of Annie's easy, natural style.

Cole recognized her from TV. Annie's cousin.

"In here." Cole nodded toward the curtain behind him. "She's OK. The doctor's with her."

"Thanks. Hi. I'm Kelly."

Cole took the offered hand. "I'm Cole. From Hope Hill."

"You work together?"

"Not exactly."

"Oh." Kelly pulled her hand back, probably evaluating just how crazy he might be.

"I'm going to get a cup of coffee. Would you like some?" he asked, because she suddenly looked uncomfortable with him, and because he didn't want to chat, didn't want to explain that he was deaf.

He didn't want to go through the whole ritual of the surprise, then the apologetic murmurings, then the pitying looks, then the awkwardness of the person not knowing how to talk to him. The whole one-act play when the other person pretended hard that everything was A-OK, while acting completely weirded out.

He couldn't read Kelly's lips because she suddenly dropped her head, looking down at her boots, but he got enough from the shake of her head. *So no coffee.*

Cole walked down the hallway and kept on walking until he found a waiting room with vending machines, where he pushed the button for espresso. He took his time drinking as he worked on sorting himself out, the blonde already forgotten.

His mind was full of Annie.

Everyone at Hope Hill kept telling him that denial was a bad thing, as if Cole didn't already know that. Combat didn't allow for denial. Threats had to be immediately assessed so they could be immediately eliminated. When you saw a suspicious package on the side of the road, it did no good to pretend it probably wasn't an IED.

And it did no good to pretend that his interest in Annie was strictly friendship.

He didn't think about his friends a hundred times a day. He didn't run his day so he could spend as much time with them as possible—wouldn't have, even if they weren't scattered across the country. He didn't want to touch his friends so badly that not doing so required all his military discipline.

So Annie was more than a new friend to him.

Annie Murray was the first woman he'd been attracted to since he'd gotten home from overseas. Maybe more than attracted. And that hadn't happened since . . . ever.

He'd never had trouble finding a willing woman, but he rarely thought the requirements of a relationship were worth the benefits. Some women specifically targeted Navy SEALs. Weird groupie women who wanted a SEAL boyfriend for bragging rights, for the whole my-boyfriend-can-beat-up-your-boyfriend thing.

Like his last relationship, Evie.

"Mark called me a bitch," she'd whine. "He's totally stalking me. Are you going to let some punk talk to your girlfriend like that?"

To which Cole would say, "What did he say, exactly?"

"Get out of my house, you crazy bitch." Evie included hand gestures for full dramatic effect. "He scared me. What if he hit me?"

"How is he stalking you if you were at his house? Stop freaking going over to him, Evie."

At which she usually exploded, accusing Cole of not caring.

He learned over the years that *not caring* was code for *not doing what I want.* The few relationships he'd had were all based on what a woman wanted from him. Bragging rights, his combat pay, protection. He didn't much mind.

He'd wanted things too: peace and companionship, a warm body to come home to when a mission ended.

As he drank his bitter coffee in the hospital waiting room, he thought about what he wanted after Hope Hill, about going back home to Chicago. When he'd first arrived here, he couldn't wait to be back in the solitude of his apartment. And now . . .

He thought about having someone with a soft smile who brought him enough peace so that he fell asleep next to her. Someone who, at the same time, challenged him, called him on his bullshit.

Cole tossed the empty cup into the garbage and swore under his breath, because, of course, the whole time he had an image of Annie in his head.

Annie Murray was the woman he wanted.

He'd barely stopped himself from hauling her out of the hospital bed and into his arms. He wanted to pick her up and carry her off to someplace safe.

This is a hospital. She's safe here.

Trouble was he didn't want to trust her to others. *He* wanted to keep her safe. *He* wanted to take care of her.

Seeing Annie hurt brought out two visceral responses in him: the overwhelming need to hunt down and kill whoever had hurt her, and the need to celebrate the fact that she was alive. In his head, the images of that celebration looked a lot like passionate lovemaking.

Except, he couldn't kill the guy who'd hurt her, even if the cops caught the bastard. Beating someone to death would be a one-way ticket to prison, and Cole would die before he'd be locked in a cell again. Also, Annie wouldn't want violence.

Making love to her . . . He suddenly wanted that more than he wanted his next breath.

Cole headed out of the waiting room, back to her, reaching Kelly outside the green curtain just as the doctor was leaving. The little man didn't look grim, nor did he shout orders for CAT scans and emergency surgeries, but still Cole couldn't relax.

He should have let Kelly go in first, give the cousins a few minutes alone, but he stepped through the curtains right behind the woman. Annie could send him away if she wanted.

"I have a bruised rib and a mild concussion," she said instead, with a smile as if sharing good news. "I'm being released."

Fine, that last part worked.

Kelly stepped up to the bed to squeeze Annie's hand. "You can come home with me. I brought you clean clothes, in case you needed some. Comfortable, in case you're sore. Sweatshirt, sweatpants."

Cole stepped forward. "I'll take you back to Hope Hill."

Kelly shot him an annoyed look that asked why he was even there.

"You have to work tomorrow," Annie told her. "Hope Hill will be fine. Half the staff there has one kind of medical training or another. If anything comes up, help will be at hand."

Some of Cole's tension relaxed.

Kelly wasn't as happy. "Are you sure? Having you over would be no trouble. I swear. I can take time off from work."

"I have a bunch of my stuff at Hope Hill already. Maybe the hot tub will help me get rid of some of the aching."

Kelly hesitated, but after a moment, she nodded. "I'm going to call you and check on you in between each showing. I only have half a dozen appointments scheduled."

"You'll have to let me know if you have any weird clients." Annie made a valiant attempt to grin, but as she shifted on the bed, the grin turned into a grimace that said she was hurting. She pushed the covers back anyway as she looked at Kelly. "Could you please help me get dressed? I'm ready to get out of here."

Cole took that as his cue to step outside again.

Fifteen minutes later, they were in the car. Since Annie sat in the passenger seat, the seat belt touched her neck on the right side. The strap didn't rub the abrasion on her left that had turned yellow once a nurse swabbed the wound with iodine.

Cole put the key in the ignition but didn't turn it. Instead, he looked over at her, the bright parking-lot lights illuminating her face through the windshield. "Are you hurt more than you let on?"

"Sore." She sighed. "How did you know I had an accident?"

"I was with Finnegan when his radio went off. He hasn't discovered anything new in your case, so he's circling back. He had more questions about how the two of us became such close friends so fast. He wanted to know why am I going to midnight feedings with you. He tried to pin down whether I'm obsessed with you in a stalkerish, want-to-put-you-in-the-trunk-of-my-car kind of way."

"You don't have a trunk. You drive a pickup."

"Exactly what I told him."

"I should text him to let him know I'm heading to Hope Hill." She dug through her purse, then pecked out a message. "He was going to come to the hospital after he finished recording the scene of the accident."

"Care to tell me what happened?" Cole's fingers tightened on the steering wheel.

She gave a tired nod, then began with leaving her house. By the time she was finished with the story, the plastic was creaking from the pressure of Cole's grip.

She finished with, "It wasn't an accident."

The war drum started up inside him again, but all he said was, "You know you can call me at any time, right? Day or night."

She watched him, her gaze growing even more troubled. "I appreciate that, Cole. But—" She glanced away, then back. "I probably shouldn't even have accepted this ride. I should have had Kelly drive me."

If she had, Cole would have followed right behind them. He couldn't leave her unprotected. Yet he was aware that Annie hadn't asked him for protection.

"I'm worried that you're about to tell me to get lost." He made a point to relax his hands on the steering wheel, ease his shoulders and his tight expression, so he wouldn't look like a maniac. "I need to make sure that you're all right. OK? Until Finnegan catches the guy."

He stared straight through the windshield as he asked, but then stole a glance at her to catch her answer.

"Why?"

"I can't stand the thought of you getting hurt. You're like one of those mythical woodland creatures that protect the forest. I feel like if anything happened to you, something important would be lost from the world."

"A mythical woodland creature? Like an elf?" She huffed out what he knew had to be a laugh because the corners of her mouth turned up before her lips slightly parted, and her eyes crinkled. "I think elves are lanky and willowy. Definitely taller and skinnier than me. Also, pointy-eared."

"A shorter nature-related mythical creature, then, with round ears."

"A gnome? Are you seriously calling me a garden gnome right now?" Her eyes crinkled again.

A rare sense of contentment filled him. Air rushed into his lungs, as if he'd just come up from a deep dive.

He started the car and pulled out of the parking lot. She closed her eyes, and he let her rest. The night landscape flew by them, endless fields. Little more than farms lay between West Chester and Broslin.

When they reached Hope Hill, he parked as close to the entrance as possible. "Stay put. I'll come around."

He opened her door and lifted her out of the pickup. "Put your arms around my neck, and hold on. I'm going to carry you to your room, and since I only have one good arm, I'd appreciate it if you didn't fight me on this. I don't want to drop you."

Before she could object, he added, "This is me helping you, because right now you need help. Like I acknowledged that I needed help and let you help me with the tree meditation back in the deer blind."

"I don't remember you ever acknowledging that you needed help."

"It was there. You had to read between the lines."

"Those lines must have been in small print."

"Be that as it may, this is me helping."

"This is me not protesting," she said as he began walking toward the building.

She was too tall to weigh nothing, but he had no trouble carrying her. He'd carried gear twice her weight, hour after hour, over rough terrain. Sometimes under enemy fire.

At her door, he set her down, but he kept an arm around her waist, holding her close to him. And then he let all good sense leave him and went with impulse. "This is me kissing you."

He paused a beat to give her time to say no.

She blinked at him, her eyes going wide. But she didn't move.

He dipped his head. Just a kiss. He was the wrong guy for her, he got that. But he needed to feel her lips under his right now, needed to feel her alive and well after the scare she'd given him.

One kiss and then he would give her up. He was disciplined enough to do it.

Heat gathered where their lips met, slow and heavy heat that settled into his entire body. The need to pull her to him full-length and grind his hardness against her soft places was nearly irresistible. He dropped his hands from her hips to stop himself.

Not going to happen.

Just one kiss.

Harper Finnegan's arrival helped Cole keep to that limit. Cole didn't hear the guy walk up behind him, but Annie's eyes suddenly flew open, and she jumped back, flushing crimson. Finnegan must have made some noise, scuffed a foot or cleared his throat.

By the time Cole turned around, the detective had his eyebrows halfway up his forehead, an amused expression on his face. "Good to see you doing well, Annie."

She blushed deeper.

"Let's have a chat," the detective told her.

She opened her door. Was that a slight tremble in her hand? Cole's whole heart trembled.

"Come in, Harper," she said.

"Mild concussion," Cole spoke up, not missing that the invitation hadn't been extended to him. "She probably shouldn't sleep."

Then he nodded at the detective and strode away.

Even if the sight of another man walking into Annie's room just about killed him.

Chapter Eighteen

HARPER SAT ON THE ONLY CHAIR IN THE ROOM, WHILE ANNIE SAT ON THE BED, doing her best to lock Cole's kiss in the farthest corner of her mind. Later, she would take it out, look at it, think about it, yell at herself for allowing it, but she couldn't do that right now.

"I want you to know that I'm not taking the attack lightly," Harper was saying. "If we had a better budget, I would ask for around-the-clock protection. But even if I did, it's almost never approved after a single attempt."

Annie kept upright with effort. She was exhausted and hurt—not just physically, but emotionally. She hadn't been aware that any-one hated her, let alone hated her enough to want to kill her. When Harper asked her if she had any suspicion who might be doing this, she told him just that.

"With my fence hit and the gate left open, I thought it might be Joey," she said. "Maybe he's thinking if he scares me, I'll be too frightened to stay alone at night, and I'll ask him over, give him a chance to win me back. But I don't think he would hurt me."

"He's not an angel, but he's more of the drunken-brawl type when he's hunting for trouble." Harper tapped his pen on the notepad he held. "I'll track him down and see where he's been for the last couple of hours. He drives a pickup. Are you sure the car you saw wasn't a truck?

"Yes." A sudden thought squeezed her heart. "His mother has a dark-blue SUV."

"I think you're right. She usually parks it in the driveway, so that'll be easy enough to check without a warrant." Harper paused a beat. "Anybody else?"

She shook her head, then regretted even the slight motion. Her head was beginning to hurt again.

"How about here at Hope Hill?" Harper asked. "An angry patient? Some people with PTSD can become violent."

She had two dozen patients. She considered them, one by one. Yes, some were depressed, some had anger-management issues, some had anxiety. But she could not classify any of them as a danger to others. If she did, she would have reported it to Dan already. Hope Hill was a rehab center, but not for severe psychological cases that required a locked psych ward and a lot more supervision than they had here.

"I don't think it's a patient."

Harper paged back in his notebook. "Every page of this investigation has Cole Makani Hunter's name on it. I'm not a big believer in coincidence." He asked his next question in a careful tone. "I saw that kiss. How involved are you two?"

"Not at all." She jumped up. Her head pounded. She sank back onto the mattress again. "What you saw was a mistake. I'd appreciate it if you didn't tell anyone. I was shaken up, and Cole was . . . feeling protective, and . . . I should have stopped him. There's not going to be a next time. I swear."

Harper's skeptical gaze said he didn't entirely believe her. "Just because you don't think you're in a relationship doesn't mean he's on the same page. Maybe he's the one who wants to scare you so you go to him to feel safe." He tapped his notebook again. "Usually, when the same guy's name comes up over and over in an investigation, it means something."

"It's not him."

"He didn't run you off the road. I'll agree on that. I was with him when the call came in. But he could be behind the incidents at your house."

They went around on that point for another few minutes. Then Harper had her tell him everything about the accident all over again, starting with when she'd first noticed the SUV behind her.

She finished with, "I wish I could remember something helpful."

Harper stood to leave. "Call me if you remember anything new at all."

He tore a sheet from his notepad and scribbled a phone number on it. "That's my private number. If you feel that you're in danger, you call 911 first, then you call me immediately after."

On his way out, Harper stopped by the door. "You gonna be OK? I could stick around for a while. My shift is almost over. I doubt I'll get another call tonight."

"I'm good. I'm just going to watch TV. Thanks anyway." She walked over, and when he left, she locked the door behind him.

She was barely halfway to her bed when someone knocked. Did Harper forget something? She opened the door.

Cole stood outside. He looked tired and rumpled, and like the man she wanted to kiss again. She swallowed a groan. That'd better be the painkiller talking.

His gaze sharpened, his forehead furrowed into a deep scowl. "What are you doing opening the door without asking who it is first?"

"Don't yell at me." She let him in. "I have a headache."

"I wasn't yelling."

"You were talking sternly."

The corner of his mouth did that almost-twitch.

Don't think about the kiss. He's only looking at your mouth to read your lips.

"What are you doing here?" she asked.

"People who have a concussion aren't supposed to stay alone."

"Mild concussion."

His expression said he wasn't impressed by her nitpicking.

She didn't have it in her to argue with him. "You can stay half an hour, if it makes you feel better. You don't need to stay all night."

"I won't. At midnight, I'll go feed your small herd of skunks. I figure you can handle an hour alone. As long as you promise not to lie down and fall asleep."

She couldn't say no to his offer to take the midnight feeding. She hadn't asked Kelly because her cousin had made it clear in the past that she was not going anywhere near the skunks. The skunklets wouldn't starve in a single night; they'd be just extra hungry by morning. But if they didn't have to go hungry, Annie would definitely prefer that.

The fact that Cole thought of her skunks had to go into the same vault where his two kisses were locked away—things she'd think about later. "Thank you."

He gave a one-shouldered shrug. "No big deal. Unless I get sprayed. If the little stinkers spray me, you're going to owe me for the rest of your life. Just so we're clear."

"You ever need a kidney, I'll hand one right over."

He smiled.

She wanted to step into his arms and lay her head on his chest. *Stupid. Stupid. Stupid.*

She glanced at the bedside clock that showed past eleven o'clock. She gestured him to the chair and went to sit on the bed as she had with Harper. Except Cole took up a lot more room, both physically and emotionally. She was aware of him as she hadn't been aware of the detective.

She cleared her throat. "Now what?"

He pulled a deck of cards from his pocket. "We'll play strip poker."

She had to work on not laughing. "I don't think so."

"Fine. Regular poker." He murmured something under his breath about people who had no sense of adventure, then shuffled the deck and dealt. "Did you like Broslin when you were a kid?"

She looked at her cards and practiced her best poker face. "I always liked the woods. Always liked nature and animals. I grew up on my grandparents' farm. When my grandmother was still alive, they grew soybeans and raised goats. My grandmother made goat cheese and soap from goat milk."

"I don't think they have goats in Chicago," Cole said. "Not the part where I lived. And in my neighborhood, people mostly went to the park to buy drugs."

She thought about that as she played her cards. "That could be a problem. You didn't grow up with the idea of nature as a good place."

"I saw plenty of nature in the service."

She considered that for a few seconds. "Yes, but when you were in some desert or on an Afghan hillside, you were there expecting to kill or to be killed."

The very thing that had been a source of peace and nourishment for her, had been a place of deadly danger for him. Her heart cracked.

"I don't mind walking through the woods with you," he said. Then he added, "You should take another couple of days off from work."

"It's not like my work is difficult. The woods are my healing place. I'll just walk through slower than usual. Helping others will stop me from thinking about my own problems all day."

"But no more sessions with me?"

"No. Sorry." Definitely not after that second kiss. She cleared her throat. "We can go for walks as friends."

His eyes said he had some very definite opinions on *friends*. He didn't voice them. Maybe he didn't think she could handle it.

He was right about that.

He glanced at the clock, put his cards on the small desk face-down, then stood and fixed her with a stern look. "Don't look at my cards while I'm gone. If you do, I'll know it."

"Sure you will."

"It's a Navy SEAL thing."

"Omnipotent?"

"Damn near."

If her head didn't hurt, she would have shaken it.

He pulled a paperback from a side pocket of his BDU and handed the book to her. Derek Daley: *Revenge Games*.

"Pretty good thriller. Friend of mine wrote it." Pride crept into his voice. "Derek was one of the other POWs with me. He kept himself alive by making up stories in his head. And then he kept us alive by telling us the stories. After we got back, he wrote one down in the rehab hospital, and it got published. He's doing pretty well. Big-time author now."

She set the book on the table. "Thanks."

"If you start getting sleepy, start reading." He held out his hand. "Keys?"

"I don't lock the side door on the garage. There's nothing of value in there."

His gaze sharpened with disapproval. "Someone could be in there waiting for you when you go in."

Before today, she would have laughed that off. Now a shiver ran down her spine. "I'm not sure if I ever had a key to that door. I don't think I got one when I bought the house."

He looked back from the door. "I'll put on a new lock for you in the morning."

"Cole!" she called before he could turn away. But suddenly she didn't know what she wanted to say exactly or how to say it. "I don't expect your help. None of this is your responsibility."

Then she wanted to groan because that didn't come out right either.

He held her gaze for a long moment. She thought she caught a flash of longing, but that wasn't possible, was it?

"Lock the door behind me. And don't fall asleep," he ordered before he walked away.

All day, Cole had had a weird itchy feeling, not anything as pronounced as a premonition, but a sense that something bad was about to happen. The same sixth sense that had saved his life at least half a dozen times overseas. *Better not go into that cave. Better drive in the middle of the road instead of on the right side of the bridge.*

Back then, he'd paid attention. Now, he shook the faint prickling off. He wasn't in hostile territory any longer. Random bad moods and anxiety were part of the whole PTSD mind trip.

He drove to Annie's place, parked at the end of her street, walked to the house, and walked around the property.

Nobody in the backyard, or at the edge of the cornfield. Nobody in the house. Nobody in the garage.

He managed to feed the skunks without getting sprayed.

He lay down like Annie usually did and let the little stinkers crawl all over him. Their soft warmth felt nice. Just lying there in the straw with the folded-up comforter under his head, he could see there was peace to be found here, maybe even for someone like him.

He wouldn't have minded staying a few extra minutes. But because he didn't want to leave Annie alone too long, he got going.

Hope Hill slept as he walked in. Her door was locked. He knocked. She opened.

"Didn't I tell you not to open this door unless you ask who it is first?"

She looked like she was fighting not to roll her eyes. "I was expecting you."

He walked in, locked up. The clock on the nightstand showed one in the morning.

She yawned. "I'm tired. When can I sleep?"

"Is the headache getting worse or better?"

"Better."

"Let's stay up a few more hours."

She watched him as she sat on the bed and scooted back far enough to rest her back against the headboard, taking her cards with her. "Do you miss the navy?"

After a couple of seconds of thinking, he said, "I miss my team."

"Do you have any brothers or sisters?"

He picked up his cards. "Only child."

"Sounds like your mom really cares about you and worries about you. I'm glad she talked you into coming here. Do you feel like the therapies are working? It's not that bad here, right? It's good to learn new things."

"Let's say, I'm less resistant to ecotherapy than I was in the beginning. It's not completely uninteresting." Nobody was more surprised than he was.

A smile softened her face. He felt like a bastard for giving her such a hard time before. He could have been more open-minded. It wouldn't have cost him anything.

"Human beings evolved as part of nature," she said, "and lived in nature for ninety-nine percent of our history. Locking ourselves away in cities is a recent development."

"Like taking a tree, putting it into a small pot, and bringing it inside."

She smiled wider. "You were paying attention."

"You were so earnest. I didn't have the heart to tune you out completely."

"I'll take what I can get." Then she said, "I love the holistic approach of nature therapy. That neither the body nor the mind is isolated, but part of a system. And that system is part of an even larger system. Working on depression with meds is like working on the motor of a car. But without changing the oil. Without changing the broken motor mount. Without putting gas in the tank and water in the radiator."

She paused, her gaze searching his face. "What? You think me talking about cars is stupid, don't you? OK, I don't know that much about cars. I just try to come up with stuff guys can relate to."

"I think you talking about cars is unbearably sweet." And it made him want to kiss her again. He tried not to think about the fact that they were in her bedroom, behind locked doors, with her in bed, not three feet from him.

"We use the systems concept in the SEAL teams," he told her. "Going after insurgents, we didn't just go after insurgents. We went after why they were in a place to start with. Did the locals support them? Why? How do we turn that support to our side? Stuff like that."

"Exactly." She played the last of her cards.

He almost felt bad about showing her his.

She groaned.

He gathered up the cards and shuffled. "Want to play another round?"

"Sure."

So they played cards and talked until six in the morning, Annie losing while enthusing about the role of nature in healing, Cole listening and beginning to see her point.

God, he wanted to get into that bed with her. The need for her thrummed through his blood. She reached for a pillow to put behind her back, and, for a second, her shirt stretched over her breasts. He wanted to . . .

He had to hold his cards over his lap to cover his body's response to that thought.

At six o'clock she said, "I want to take a shower before I grab some sleep. I think I've stayed awake long enough."

"Don't lock the bathroom door. The second you feel dizzy or faint, you crash something to the floor. I'll feel the vibration."

Was she blushing? She turned away so fast, he couldn't tell.

She grabbed clean clothes and retreated into the bathroom. He put away his cards and paced the room, thinking about the hit-and-run, needing to figure out what he could do to keep her safe.

She was out in fifteen minutes, wrapped only in a large towel, and Cole had this instant fantasy of her dropping it and stepping toward him. But even as his body responded to the images in his head, her hand clutched the towel tighter. Her gaze skipped him completely, darting to the door of her room.

"What's going on in the hallway?"

Something's going on in the hallway? He hadn't heard a thing.

A whole insurgent brigade could be out there with machine guns, coming for Annie, and he would never have known it. *Shit.* What had he been thinking setting himself up as her protector? Who was he kidding?

He scowled as he went to yank the door open, with more force than necessary, but not all the way. He didn't want people in the hallway to see Annie in a towel.

About half a dozen patients were milling around, shock on their faces. Everybody was talking at once, but at the wrong angle for Cole to read lips.

"What happened?" he asked, loudly enough to be heard.

Isak, a twentysomething beanpole from Arkansas, responded, and Cole's hand clenched on the doorknob, the words hitting his chest like bullets.

"He's . . . They just found him," Isak said, pale and shaky. Then he realized he'd left out a crucial piece of information, and added, "Trevor committed suicide. He's dead."

Chapter Nineteen

ANNIE SAT IN THE EMERGENCY STAFF MEETING, NUMB. LAST NIGHT'S CAR crash was nothing compared to this morning's terrible news. She'd be willing to roll off the road all over again to have Trevor back.

Her phone pinged with a weather update. Hurricane Rupert was moving up the East Coast, but staying out at sea. She flipped the phone facedown. She didn't care.

Dan Ambrose reached for her hand on the conference table and gave it a gentle squeeze before pulling back. "You shouldn't be here. You're not well. Go lie down."

"I want to be here." She couldn't sleep if someone offered her $1 million for ten minutes' rest.

Trevor was dead.

She looked around the table. They all had failed him. *She* had failed him. She felt the crushing weight of personal responsibility.

"We are going to offer emergency counseling, free of charge, to everyone who needs it, for as long as they need it," Murphy Dolan, the program director, said. "Staff and patients alike. The police are coming to interview everyone before they officially rule it a suicide. I'm going to request that if a patient asks, the officers let a therapist sit with that patient through the interview session for support. I hope they'll let us do that much, at least. Detective Chase Meritt is lead on the case."

Dan began to rise, then sat back down. "This is going to be devastating for our patients. Hope Hill is supposed to be their safe space. I hate to say this, but Trevor's suicide may trigger other suicide attempts. Statistically speaking."

Annie nodded. Dan was only saying what they were all thinking.

"Let's head that off at the pass," Murph told them. "That's our number one priority. Number two priority is to figure out how Trevor got his hands on enough meds for a fatal dose."

"Do we know what he took?" Libby, the reflexologist, asked. The young black woman had the most amazing intuition of anyone Annie had ever met. Somehow, Libby always knew exactly what to say to a patient. People at Hope Hill loved her, and she loved them back. The news of Trevor's death had hit her hard. Her eyes were red from crying. She looked heartbroken.

Murph's response was tight with tension. "Not until the autopsy comes back."

Annie squeezed her eyes shut at the thought of sweet Trevor on a cold stainless-steel table at the morgue, but she couldn't shut out the image.

Murph cleared his throat. "There's something else. I found out something last night that I was going to share with staff and patients today, but now I'm not sure if we shouldn't wait telling the patients."

The people around the table fell silent.

"I do a one-week follow-up with patients postdischarge," he said.

They nodded. They all knew that. Part of the Hope Hill aftercare.

"I haven't been able to reach Mitch Moritz. I finally caught up with his wife. Mitch was in a fatal car accident on his way home from here. Apparently, he fell asleep and drove into oncoming traffic."

Annie gasped.

Libby clutched a hand to her chest. "Where?"

"Maryland. Maybe half an hour after he left here."

For a moment, everyone was too shocked to speak.

"Under the circumstances," Dan said, "I think we should hold this information back for now unless someone specifically asks after Mitch."

The rest of them nodded.

Annie felt too numb to say anything.

Murph kept the meeting short, and then everyone left to focus on the patients, to help where they could.

"I'm officially back at work," Annie told Murph as she headed out. Her vacation was over. "I can put in as many extra hours as you need. And I'm going to carry my cell phone all day, so anyone who wants to talk to me can reach me."

She definitely expected Detective Meritt to call her for an interview at some point, since she'd treated Trevor. But when, at midmorning, her cell phone buzzed with a call from the police, the caller was Harper.

"I have an update for you, although it's not exactly progress," the detective said on the other end. "Joey Franco has no alibi for last night. But neither can I find any proof that he was involved in your hit-and-run. No damage to his truck, no damage to his mother's SUV, none of the neighbors heard him come or go in the middle of the night. He says he was home alone, sleeping. I don't even have enough to bring him in."

"Thank you for checking." She didn't know what else to say.

She was relieved, because she didn't want to think that Joey hated her enough to want to kill her. But she was also disappointed, because she wanted the guy who ran her off the road caught so she could feel safe again.

Annie headed back to her room to grab a couple of painkillers from her purse. Her headache was gone, but her body was even more sore than it'd been last night. She walked through the rec room and for a minute studied the half dozen guys there. The TV was on, but nobody was paying attention to the game, and a grim mood filled the room.

They asked how she was. They'd all heard about the car accident. She told them not to worry.

Then, on impulse, she asked, "Anybody want to go for a walk?"

Brett, an army colonel who'd lost a kidney and half a lung to an IED, asked, "Like group therapy?"

"Just a walk." Whether they called the walk official therapy or not, it'd still help.

She wished Cole would go with them. As soon as they'd found out about Trev this morning, Annie had to run off to the emergency meeting. But she was worried about Cole. What happened to Trev had to bring back memories of Cole's father's suicide. She wanted to seek Cole out to make sure he was all right. But she had other patients.

Brett stood. "Sure. I'll go."

Three of the other guys stood with him.

As the group crossed the courtyard, Cole jogged up, joining them, nodding a greeting, which all the guys returned with obvious respect. Despite his disabilities, every time she saw Cole in a group setting, the other men were always deferential to the Navy SEAL.

He had incredible presence. The first time she'd seen him, she'd been scared of him. But then she'd gotten to know him. And now, she never felt as safe as when she was with him.

She was glad he'd come. A hard knot inside her relaxed at his presence.

He looked shaken but OK. He was dealing with Trev's suicide, but she wanted to talk to him about it anyway. She needed to catch him one-on-one later.

The man who watched the small group from across the courtyard wasn't pleased. His gaze settled on Annie. She refused to learn her lesson. And catching her on her own was increasingly more difficult. She was never alone these days.

The Navy SEAL, especially, had appointed himself her constant companion. He was a big guy. It'd take a lot of drugs to eliminate him. And he wouldn't go as easily as Trevor had. The SEAL was always alert, never let his guard down for a second, not even here.

The man in the window watched as Cole maneuvered himself so he'd be walking next to Annie.

Another suicide would be suspicious right now.

Car accident? The SEAL did drive.

No, that'd raise questions too. Mitch Moritz's car accident had just been discovered by the staff.

The man thought carefully and considered sedatives, something that would knock Cole out just long enough to drown him during his morning swim.

So much to do. Both at work and at home.

His mother wasn't doing well. Was she dying at last? Dark fury sliced through the man at the thought. His mother could not die. She still had a lot to atone for.

He wanted Annie to meet her. He needed to set that meeting up sooner rather than later.

Annie didn't take her sneakers off as they reached the path. Neither did anyone else. The ground was still soggy from the rain the other day.

They walked in silence. The wind in the trees, the birds, even the sound of squirrels darting around in the underbrush were all an instant balm to her soul. That Cole didn't benefit from any of nature's song saddened her.

They walked in a loose formation. After about two miles, she steered them off the path to a spot she'd discovered only a few weeks before, a spot that would be new for everyone.

The clearing was tiny, maybe twenty feet across, nearly a perfect circle framed by seven oak trees. When she'd found it, her first thought was that it was a sacred place.

"You think someone planted the trees like that?" Kevin asked.

She sat at the foot of the nearest oak. "It looks pretty natural."

Thick roots protruded from the earth, keeping her off the damp ground. "I'm guessing there's rock under the topsoil. Maybe even one giant rock. The trees couldn't grow on top it, so they grew around it." She leaned back against the trunk.

The others followed her example, some folding their legs, others stretching and opening them, Cole crossing his ankles.

Annie hadn't planned it, but there were six of them and seven oaks. One solitary tree was left without a human, almost as if waiting for Trevor. Maybe his spirit was here and they just couldn't see his body.

"Why did he do it?" Brett asked, and everyone turned to Annie for the answer.

Probably none of them would think about much else. Her heart ached for the pain on the faces around her. The wound of Trevor's loss was too fresh, too jagged, still bleeding.

Annie told them the truth. "I don't know. I wish he had asked for help."

"Maybe for a second he didn't see the way out," Kevin said. "But you don't make a decision based on your worst moment. You ride out the worst. Then you work on making the next day better."

Annie offered Kevin a watery smile for having listened during their previous sessions. He'd clearly internalized what they'd talked about. Trevor's death filled her with despair, but Kevin's remark made her feel as if, in some small way, she *was* making a difference.

Brett bumped his fist against his solar plexus as he looked at Annie. "It hurts in there. You got an exercise for that?"

Liam groaned. "Don't get her into therapist mode, man."

"We can certainly do a meditation," she said, ignoring the subtle rolling of eyes around the circle. "Since you guys are begging for it."

That drew some half-hearted protests. Truth was, they liked to resist ecotherapy, but almost as if for form's sake. They all identified as tough, unbreakable warriors. Needing medical help—surgery or PT—was one thing. But the men felt they shouldn't need alternative therapies, especially therapies that worked on thoughts and feelings. Some believed needing that kind of support meant they were weak.

"It takes a strong man to ask for help," Cole offered. "The weak can't. All they have is ego. They have to play it tough. The real tough guys, they don't have to play anything."

That pretty much ended any resistance. If the SEAL was on board, everybody was on board.

"So just lean against the tree behind you," Annie began, shooting Cole a look of appreciation when he looked at her at last. "You can close your eyes or not, as you wish," she said for the others. "Draw a deep, cleansing breath through your nose. Hold it. Let it out through your mouth."

She made a point to relax her own shoulders. The kind of energy she projected would make a difference. She waited until everyone got in a couple of nice, calming breaths. "Good. Now let's do that again."

They breathed silently for a minute.

Cole was watching her mouth. Since he'd kissed her, she'd been more aware of that gaze than ever before.

"Obviously," she said, "we all have feelings and thoughts about what happened this morning. I am sure we all have things we wish we could tell Trev."

Several of the men murmured their agreement; others nodded.

"Let's do that."

A couple of the guys stiffened. In general, they didn't like talking about their feelings in a one-on-one setting, let alone in a group situation. Most of her group therapy consisted of simply working or walking out in nature together. Her main goal was to make her patients feel better. She tried to do whatever it took to achieve that.

"Let's all silently talk to Trev for a couple of minutes. Visualize the words you'd like to say as swirling lines of letters, flowing around inside your chest. The words flow, not out of your mouth, but out your back and into the tree behind you. They travel up the tree trunk, into the branches, into the leaves. From the tips of the leaves they will rise invisibly, like the breath of the tree, up and up, all the way to Trev."

She fell silent, closed her eyes, and sent her own words.

Oh, Trev. I wish you'd come to me. I am sorry I didn't pay more attention. I am sorry I was caught up in my own nonsense. I wish you'd felt all the love everyone had for you. I know that in that dark moment, you couldn't see the light, but I wish you had waited just another minute to see the clouds part. I wish you peace, my friend.

She did a few more cleansing breaths as she wiped away her tears.

Then she said a prayer for Mitch Moritz too. He'd been so excited about going home to his wife and kids. Annie couldn't even image how devastated they must be at his loss.

For a moment, she thought about whether Murph was right not to tell the men that Mitch had died. In the end, she decided she was glad it was Murph's call to make and not hers.

When she opened her eyes, she saw that about half the men were still doing the exercise. The other half, including Cole, were finished, eyes open but not looking at anything in particular, the men lost in thought.

She let another few minutes pass before she said, "You all know that there is help available, right? I am available. Around the clock. I'll be actually staying at Hope Hill for the foreseeable future."

Kevin said, "Yeah."

Then Liam said, "Thanks."

"Things are good," Brett told her.

Even Rob—the most taciturn of them all—chimed in. "Not gonna do anything stupid. You can have my word on that. Don't spend all your day worrying about us."

Annie smiled at him. Three complete sentences were more than she heard out of Rob sometimes in a whole therapy session.

Cole just nodded.

Annie wasn't sure whether he'd come along because he truly wanted the walk and talk, or because he'd appointed himself to be her protector. Either way, she was glad he'd joined them.

She pushed to her feet and brushed off her pants. "How about we go back to the path and finish the loop?"

Brainlessly putting one foot in front of the other while soaking up the silence of the woods was a meditation in itself.

All five guys decided to go with her.

Once again, they were walking in a loose formation, in a single line, since the trail was narrow in most places. For the most part, they walked in silence.

Annie moved up next to Cole. "How are you doing?"

"OK."

"This must bring back memories of your father."

"I was chained to the wall in a cave when he died. I didn't find out about it until we escaped and I got back home."

"That had to be difficult."

"More difficult for my mother. She had to deal with the funeral, and everything else, alone."

"If you want to talk about it . . ."

"Not right now."

He hadn't ruled out later. She hoped he *would* come to her.

She hadn't figured out yet how to handle what was happening between them. Ignore? Discuss? Avoid all contact?

She didn't want to avoid him.

She wanted to . . .

God help her, she wanted to walk into his arms and ask for another kiss. She wanted to comfort him, and she wanted to be comforted by him. She was smart enough to know that she was in trouble.

Cole walked the path, staring at the ground in front of his feet. He wanted to be alone in the woods with Annie. He wanted her in his arms. He wanted to kiss her until the hurt and pain disappeared from her eyes.

Trevor's death had shaken her.

It'd shaken Cole too. He should have paid more attention to the kid.

He swore under his breath.

He'd almost talked himself into believing that the treatment was working. But it wasn't, was it? Nothing they did at Hope Hill had helped Trevor, and he'd been there for some time. Trevor had *not* been helped.

Maybe Cole could have helped the kid, if Cole hadn't been so focused on his mission and Annie. Those hadn't worked out either anyway.

He hadn't been able to protect Annie. And he was letting his mission down too. Failing to achieve his mission objective burned him.

Except . . .

He might not have a clue about the traitor, but he was beginning to have a terrible suspicion about the op in general. What if his mission was fake?

Maybe there was no traitor. Maybe his CO had invented the texts to make sure Cole entered rehab. Maybe Cole had been tricked into therapy.

Maybe *that* was what he needed to investigate.

Chapter Twenty

Monday

COLE SPENT SUNDAY NIGHT LOST IN PAIN—THE CHOPPER CRASHING, PEOPLE screaming, burning. He woke swimming in sweat and pushed out of bed for a glass of water. Falling back asleep again took forever, and when he finally nodded off, his nightmares thrust him back into endless, bloody torture sessions.

He woke in a dark mood. He insisted on going with Annie to all her Monday feedings and wouldn't take no for an answer. She was smart enough to know that her safety should come first, so she agreed. But she kept a distance between them that Cole hated.

She'd listened to the radio and updated him on Hurricane Rupert—still out at sea, but causing heavy rains and major flooding in the Carolinas. She refused to talk to him about anything but the weather. Or his father. But Cole refused to talk about that.

He couldn't wait until the police nailed her stupid ex's ass. Cole was tempted to nail it for them. Once she was safe, he could leave Hope Hill. He was no longer even sure why he was here.

Both his CO and Cole's mother had suggested therapy before, but Cole had refused. Of course, when the request for the undercover work came up, he'd agreed in a heartbeat—despite the therapeutic setting. An op was an op. He'd never thought he would get to go on another mission again.

Would his CO trick him like that? Lie?

Or was Cole being paranoid?

For the last couple of days, he'd felt . . .

Unbalanced was the word Annie had used. Cole had been that when he'd first arrived at Hope Hill. But he'd regained some of his balance since, one piece at a time.

Now he felt not so much *unbalanced* as *unsettled*. He kept having the unsettling sensation that he wasn't remembering something, that something was off. He wasn't seeing something he needed to see.

When he'd felt like this in the service, he'd known to look at the roadside for IEDs, or at high ground for an enemy sniper. But where to look here?

He sensed a threat.

Real or PTSD?

His nightmares were getting worse and more frequent.

Once Annie's attacker was caught, once Cole found the traitor— or confirmed that he'd been sent on a fictional mission—he would leave Hope Hill, he decided.

Nothing could keep him here then.

Except Annie . . .

He wanted Annie—any way he could get her. As a friend. As a lover. He voted for a combination of both, if possible.

But the truth was, Annie was better off without him. Cole might not be broken, but he wasn't whole either. And his status as a patient at Hope Hill, where she was a therapist, was freaking her out. For a tree hugger, she was certainly conventional.

He wished he could tell her the truth, start over. *Hi, I'm Cole. Undercover investigator.* Not *your patient.*

He liked kissing her. And he wasn't going to lie to himself; he was thinking about kissing her again. He was thinking, and definitely dreaming, about going past kissing.

He wanted to know what her long legs looked like out of her khaki cargo pants. He wanted to see her chestnut hair tumbling over her naked shoulders. He wanted to know what she'd look like tangled in the sheets on his bed.

She deserves better.

He needed to leave this place before he got any stupider.

Annie was in her bed, snug and safe—the only thing he needed to know about her, Cole decided as he walked down the hallway that night after the midnight feeding. He was proud that he'd kept his distance all day, even if, at times, he'd wanted to fall on her like a ravening beast.

He stopped in front of Trevor's door.

The police tape was gone. Trev's death had been officially ruled a suicide.

Cole opened the door to a bare room. Somebody had already cleaned up and mailed Trevor's belongings to his parents.

What would happen to the body? His parents would want him home in Montana. If the coroner had released the body, Trev could be on his way home already.

He's never going to build that barn. Cole looked around for the kid's sketchbook, but that too had been taken. Good. His parents should have it.

Except . . .

Yesterday morning, in the strange round clearing, the group had talked about how Trevor had been carried away by one hopeless impulse, one moment of darkness. He had not understood that the clouds would part again.

Cole accepted that sometimes suicide happened like that. It had with his father. But Trevor had taken a fatal dose of meds—a dose that would have taken weeks to collect, saving his pills. So the suicide couldn't have been a decision born in a bad moment.

And even while Trevor had been collecting pills to kill himself, he was also preparing for the future, drawing a barn. He'd been excited about going home and building that barn for his mother. The two facts didn't mesh.

Yet depressed people's moods could fluctuate several times a day. Maybe in his light moments, Trevor had prepared for the future, and in his dark moments, he had prepared for death.

What the hell did Cole know? He wasn't a therapist.

He turned to leave, then stopped when he stepped on something. He crouched to examine the small piece of black plastic he'd missed on the dark-gray carpet. He picked it up, put it on his palm, then looked at the floor again, more closely this time.

Two more pieces lay near the empty garbage can. *Could have come from anything. A burner phone someone smashed up before getting rid of the evidence?* The thought gave Cole pause.

He collected the pieces using only his fingernails and dropped them into his pocket before he left. He would put the chunks of plastic in an envelope and send them to his CO. If the man thought they were something, he could send them on to a lab.

Had Trev been the traitor?

Cole hated the thought. Yet he couldn't discount the possibility. His mind churned as he tried to build a case around what few clues he had.

Trevor upset. Trevor asking questions. Trevor taking his own life. Black plastic.

Tuesday

As Cole lay in bed, he chewed over every detail, every minute he'd spent with Trevor. He didn't get more than half an hour of rest toward dawn.

When he woke up, a text message waited on his phone, a note from Annie that she'd gone to the morning feeding early. Finnegan had called her. Joey was in jail. She was safe.

Cole grabbed his phone and texted her: What happened?

She texted back: Joey's cousin picked up a car in West Chester. Joey helped. They're both in jail for grand theft auto. Harper's working on changing it to attempted murder.

Cole typed: Any proof they pushed you into the reservoir?

And Annie sent: Cousin has a black Chevy Blazer. Front end smashed. That's why they went out looking for another car last night.

Think he was the intruder at your place? Cole hit "Send."

A couple of seconds passed before her response came: Maybe Joey complained I wouldn't take him back. Wanted to scare me a little?

Running you off the road is more than just scaring you a little, Cole responded.

And she sent: Got carried away? Kind of a boozer.

Cole wanted to talk to Finnegan. Would the detective disclose anything about the case? Probably not. Still, Joey and his cousin were behind bars—progress. And when the paint on Annie's back bumper matched, they'd stay behind bars. Cole liked that even better.

Another message popped up from Annie: Any sessions this morning?

Cole typed a quick response: Ambrose at eight.

As long as Annie didn't need him, he might as well go for a run in the woods before the session with the shrink. Even if he'd much rather be with Annie, helping her with her animals. Not that she really needed his help. She was as self-sufficient as they came. And now she didn't need his protection either. Annie was safe.

Cole went for his run, showered, then headed off to see his shrink.

"Cole." Ambrose greeted him and pointed him to the armchair across from his desk. He knew better than to point him to the couch.

Nobody was going to put Cole on his back, a fact he'd explained to the guy right at the beginning, in no uncertain terms.

"How are you feeling?" As usual, the man poured them both a glass of ice water from the carafe on his desk.

"How does anybody feel after what happened with Trevor?"

The man watched him. "Any thoughts that maybe Trevor was right, maybe that's the solution? Any dark or suicidal thoughts at all?"

Cole drank. You confessed suicidal thoughts to a shrink, and next thing you knew, you were transported to a locked facility. He'd seen it done at the vet hospital where they'd initially treated his shoulder.

"Nope," he said, and made sure to look sincere.

"Were you and Trevor friends?"

"Barely." If he said yes, Ambrose would want to spend more time on the subject. Yet denying Trev also felt wrong.

"How does this affect you in light of your father's suicide?"

"My father's suicide was a long time ago. I've dealt with it. This brings back some of the pain. Some of the guilt. But when a person makes a decision, there isn't much anyone can do to stop them. You can't monitor someone twenty-four–seven."

"All right," Ambrose said after watching him for a couple of seconds. "How about your other issues? Are you making progress there? Flashbacks?"

"No."

"Nightmares?"

"Sure."

"How bad? Would you call them night terrors? Do you wake up heart pounding, screaming? Do you wake up to find you've maybe moved off the bed, walked across the room without realizing?"

"Once or twice."

"What were the dreams about?"

Cole leaned back in the chair. They'd been through this before. "Same old memories."

"The crash?"

"That and other things. Sometimes I dream about the RPGs hitting the hillside. Sometimes I dream about the chopper going down. Sometimes I dream about what happened after."

And sometimes, lately, all three, in one night, coming out of one nightmare only to enter another, and then another.

"Ready to talk about what happened after you were captured? I think it could be important for your recovery."

Cole drew a deep breath, huffed it out. "No offense, doc, but I don't think you could handle it."

"You could decide to trust me and give me some credit."

He didn't want to. The only staff members Cole had any real respect for around here were the guy who ran the place, Murphy Dolan, and Annie. Not that the rest were bad or incompetent, but their perpetual pretend cheerfulness grated after a while. The whole *Oh, you're doing great* mantra. *Oh, you're doing so much better.*

He didn't feel better. Except when he was with Annie.

Ambrose asked a few more questions, his voice an annoying drone. He had a knack for wanting Cole to talk about the exact memories Cole wanted to forget.

He rubbed his arm. Man, that burned. He looked down and saw the blood where a jagged piece of metal had sliced through muscle. His ears were ringing. The chopper was down.

Eighteen people. They'd been heading to Kandahar Air Base. The helicopter with the special-ops team had already been en route when they picked up his call for help. They had immediately detoured to save Cole's and Ryan's asses.

The onboard medic was hooking Ryan up with blood, O negative, but Ryan was bleeding out faster than the blood was flowing in. The medic was bandaging him up, putting pressure on the worst spots.

Ryan screamed.

The next scream was weaker. They couldn't hear it over the whoop, whoop of the chopper blades.

Then Ryan's eyes rolled back in his head. His body convulsed. They held him down. The medic opened Ryan's mouth to make sure Ryan wouldn't bite off his own tongue.

There were at least a hundred special ops at Kandahar Air Base: army spec ops, rangers, SEALs. The guys in the chopper had just rooted out a warlord in the foothills.

The chopper was cresting the last hill. Night was falling. None of them looked out. They were all looking at Ryan, who was now unnaturally still.

The medic started CPR.

Then the medic stopped CPR. He shook his head, his blood-smudged face etched in misery.

Cole roared, ordering him to start again if he didn't want to be tossed out of the chopper.

A couple of guys grabbed Cole to hold him back.

Then nothing.

Then pain.

Then the realization that they were on the ground, crashed. Pain in his arm. Blood. The chopper burned. Men around him were dead or dying.

"That's quite a bit of progress," Dr. Ambrose said with a pleased smile.

Cole returned to the present with a start. He was back in a too-white room at Hope Hill, where everything was too organized, from the books on the shelves to the miniature orchids on the windowsill. Nobody sitting in an office like this could ever imagine the chaos of the hillside.

He blinked at Ambrose.

How much had he told the man? And how on earth had Ambrose gotten to him? That droning voice must have done it. Hell, Cole felt half-hypnotized. *Shit.*

He pushed to his feet. He needed to get out of here. The too-perfect office and the too-pleased doctor were suffocating. Nauseating. His stomach rolled.

"I'll see you on Thursday," Ambrose called after him.

Inanely, Cole thought, *Not if I see you first.*

He stumbled down the hallway. *WTF?* He hadn't taken sleeping pills for the past couple of days. Annie had been in danger, and he'd wanted to stay sharp.

He glanced at his cell phone. Ten past nine. He made it across the exercise yard and headed to the woods. He didn't go too far down the path, just to the first large tree. He sat at its base and leaned his back against the trunk.

He could actually smell burning flesh.

He'd gotten burned on his leg when the chopper had gone down, although not as badly as some of the others. Then he'd gotten burned again during torture. Later, he'd gotten tattoos to cover up the worst of the branding.

He could hear the whoop, whoop of the chopper, so realistic that he looked up, hands in tight fists.

Nothing but blue skies above.

Then he heard the RPGs. They'd exploded on the hillside before the chopper ever showed up. His flashbacks were coming out of sequence.

He kicked at the dirt, rage boiling through him. He hadn't had flashbacks before he'd come to Hope Hill. Nothing like this. Instead of helping him, the therapies were just messing with his head, making him worse.

He tried to do the breathing Annie had taught him. He tried to meditate, focus on the tree behind him. When he couldn't, he brought up Annie's amber-colored eyes in his mind and focused on her.

He focused on her faint smell of lavender, and after a few deep breaths, he couldn't smell burning flesh anymore. He focused on her smile, and the invisible chopper stopped whoop-whooping overhead. He focused on the way her soft lips had felt when he'd kissed her.

The chaos inside him settled.

The woods were all right. She had been right about that. The woods brought peace. She had given him this. So he wasn't going to repay the favor by messing with her life. He was going to leave her alone.

He hadn't realized he was so screwed up, but *damn*. Ten minutes ago, he'd felt like a live grenade with the pin pulled.

He wasn't getting better. He was getting worse. Decisions were going to have to be made.

Chapter Twenty-One

ANNIE WATCHED AS COLE EMERGED FROM THE FOOTPATH. HE LOOKED AT HER, his face closed, his body language spelling out IMPENETRABLE FORTRESS. As if he were back at the beginning, as if the past week or so of progress and therapy, the tentative connections they'd made, were gone.

"You OK?" she asked when she reached him, her heart twisting. Had Trev's death hit him even harder than she realized?

"You going for a walk?"

She nodded.

"I'll go with you."

"Aren't you just coming back from one?"

"I was sitting with a tree."

She couldn't help but smile. "Come along, then. Do you want to take your boots off?" The ground was dry today, the weather back to warm.

He shoved his hands into his pockets as he shook his head.

The silent no didn't surprise her. His military boots were part of his armor. Trevor's death had been a setback. The shock and grief would be a setback, one way or the other, for most of the people at Hope Hill.

Annie kicked off her Keds to show that nothing was wrong with being vulnerable either.

They simply walked together for an hour, enjoying the comfort of walking through nature with another person. Being alone with nature was one kind of therapy. Being not alone was another kind. The mere presence of another person at a time of trouble could make a huge difference to the psyche.

They offered nothing more and nothing less to each other than their presence, their silent support, the safety net of *I'm here if you need to talk.* Some incredibly small things could, at times, make the greatest gift.

The tension of Annie's rushed morning leaked away; the earth drew it out through the soles of her feet. She also gave credit for this welcome measure of peace to Cole and his large, protective, reassuring presence.

When he'd helped her with the animals, she'd wondered what it would be like to have a partner in her rescue efforts. Now she wondered what it'd be like to have a partner to be with in general. She caught herself and put those thoughts away.

The man watching from the window allowed himself a smile. While Cole headed back to the facilities after their walk, Annie headed to the parking lot.

The SEAL was no longer shadowing her every moment.

She must have rebuffed him. *Good.* She was smart. She must have realized that the SEAL wasn't for her.

That little car accident had snapped her to her senses after all. The wake-up call had been just what she'd needed.

He'd been so mad about her letting the SEAL kiss her, he almost hadn't cared if she lived or died. But now he was glad she hadn't gone into the dark water.

Watching her, playing with her, was too much fun.

She could give him so much more pleasure. *Soon.*

He was damned tired of waiting. Yet, once he'd done with her all he wanted to do with her, he would have to kill her.

Would a third death within a week, all connected to Hope Hill, be suspicious? He straddled a fine line. Mitch's death was being investigated by the Maryland State Police. Slowly. Trevor's death wasn't being investigated at all. Broslin PD had put the case to bed the same day.

Yet, overconfidence had brought down many a smart person. The man was determined not to be one of them.

The SEAL was still alive—instead of floating in the pool—because of that.

And Annie was allowed to go on and break more rules. Up to her. If she did, her punishment would be that much more severe.

The man smiled, picturing a good, hard punishment and all that it entailed: apologies, begging, and tears—all too late. He wanted complete submission. He was ready for the end game.

Libby the reflexologist worked only half days on Tuesdays. Since Annie lived on the way, Libby drove her home so Annie could feed her animals lunch.

Libby's car smelled like baby powder. They talked about her twins, who were begging for a pet. Annie mentioned that she had a cat who'd be soon done with his cast.

After Libby dropped her off, Annie took care of her small herd. Then she made a shepherd's pie from the ground meat she had in her freezer and the wilting vegetables she had in the crisper. Since she'd been living at Hope Hill, she hadn't been cooking at home. She needed to use up the food in her fridge before it spoiled.

When the meal was done, she split it into six individual portions. She put three of the plastic containers into a grocery bag and walked it over—hiking through the cornfield—to her grandfather's.

"Where's your sailor?" was the first thing her grandfather asked when Annie stepped into his kitchen.

"He's not my sailor."

He harrumphed at her response. "Kelly told me you were in an accident. She was here this morning." He wouldn't look at her. "You all right?"

Concern? It'd be a first. She put the food in the fridge. "I'm fine. Thanks." Then she added, "It's shepherd's pie."

"Kelly said your fancy piece of a foreign car was toast." Was that satisfaction in his voice? But then he added, "You can take the truck if you want."

She stared at him.

Gramps hadn't driven in about a year. His blood-pressure issues made him too dizzy to be behind the wheel. But he'd never offered the truck to anyone, never even thought about selling, as far as Annie was aware.

"Thanks." The word came out uncertain.

He looked at her when he snapped, "I don't want that emotional-woman crap."

OK, then.

"Key's by the front door." He turned to the TV and flicked it on. She was dismissed.

She was used to it. "See you in a couple of days."

She stopped in three or four times a week. Kelly did the same. Sylvia, the housekeeper, had been upgraded to twice weekly, from Fridays only, to make sure someone saw the old man every day.

Annie walked to the garage and got into the truck—clean, save the dust that had accumulated on the outside. The pickup was older and more beat-up than she remembered. When was the last time she'd been inside it? Before her mother had moved them from Broslin.

Don't go there.

She turned the key.

Nothing happened.

Dead battery? She was almost relieved. The thing was a massive gas guzzler. The Toyota dealership had promised that a loaner would be ready for her at one point today. She'd much prefer that.

She locked up the garage and then walked through the backyard and into the corn, her mind on her grandfather's sudden softening. Resentment rose inside her. *Now* he wanted to give her a vehicle? He should have helped back when her mother needed the help.

Instead, he'd kicked them out of the house. If he hadn't, her mother would never have met Randy. Annie rubbed the heel of her hands over her thighs as she walked.

Don't think about it.

The wind picked up, ruffling the cornstalks around her. They towered over her, boxed her in.

A noise came from her right, gone before she could identify it. The wind? A deer?

The sun slipped behind the clouds, and immediately the temperature dropped, reminding her that summer was over. She rubbed the goose bumps on her arms.

The wind strengthened. Something touched the back of her neck. She jumped and swirled around, gasping.

Oh. A foot-long corn leaf whipped around on the stalk right at her neck. *Just a leaf.*

Then that noise came again. She was amazed that deer would still come to feed considering how much poison the guy who leased the land sprayed on his crop.

Annie hurried forward, shivering. Odd bits of noise, different from the wind, kept following her. Almost as if the deer was pacing her, maybe ten feet back and to the left. She couldn't see the animal through the forest of green stalks, had no idea why a deer would follow her.

Then she thought, *What if it's a stray? A scared dog that needs help?*

She stopped.

The wind had blown in some clouds. She couldn't leave an animal out there, especially with all that bad weather coming.

"Hey, puppy," she said in a soothing tone. "Where are you?"

No barking, no whining. Yet something definitely moved in the corn.

She felt anxious suddenly. For no reason, since both Joey and Big Jim were in jail.

She resisted the urge to hurry home. Instead, she turned toward the noise to see if there was an animal that needed her help.

Cole stared at the text that came from his CO: No transmission today. No transmission yesterday either.

Trevor Taylor. Cole hated typing the name. Looks like he was our guy.

The CO sent back: Sudden attack of conscience?

Maybe, Cole typed. Then he added, Nothing in the room other than the plastic I sent. His belongings have been mailed home already.

A couple of seconds passed before the response popped up. I'll send someone to his parents.

I'm finished? Cole texted.

You should complete your treatment.
Yeah. No. Cole typed: Checking out.

If you're sure. Anything you need?
Cole sent a single question: Any news about the guys?

Matt is being released from Walter Reed.

Matthew Halpern had been the pilot of the chopper that crashed, the youngest person on the team. Cole had been worried about the kid. His injuries had been hard on him. So Cole's next question was: Did they fix his legs?

He waited several seconds, but the CO didn't text back.

Matt's legs had been crushed when the chopper had been shot down. Nobody had thought Matt would make it through the night, let alone the six months of brutal captivity that had followed.

Cole was pretty sure he knew what had kept the kid alive. Matt had had this photo, hidden in the sole of his shoe, the engagement photo of his older brother and his fiancée. Matt would take it out when their captors weren't looking and stare at it, run his thumb over the image.

They'd all assumed he was close to his brother, that thinking about his family kept him going. But Cole had seen the photo up close once. The glaze had been worn off the woman's face.

When they'd finally escaped, they'd carried Matt out of the country, over three hundred miles of rough terrain. He'd cursed at them the whole time to leave him behind. They wouldn't.

Cole thought of him, in a wheelchair for the rest of his life, hopelessly in love with his brother's wife. *Hell of a way to live.*

Cole swore under his breath. Then he refocused on the mission at hand.

He sent one last text to his CO: Let me know when you find out about Trevor.

The response popped up within seconds. Will do. Take care.

Cole was still thinking about Trev when he went to find the program coordinator. Had Trev's lost-lamb act been a trap? He'd befriended Cole with it. Maybe he'd befriended others the same way. He'd acted so messed up, people lowered their guard around him. Maybe he'd been able to get sensitive information out of the others— previous missions, troop movements.

Cole tried to remember every word they'd exchanged. Had he told Trev anything he shouldn't have? He didn't think so. But that he might have, given more time, bothered him.

He'd meant to, planned to, hang out with Trevor.

He walked to Murphy Dolan's office. The door stood open, Dolan behind the desk.

He spotted Cole. "How is it going?"

"I'm checking out." Cole didn't take a seat.

The last time he'd been in this office had been his first day at Hope Hill. Dolan's space was pretty bare-bones: desk, chair, and file cabinets. About half the size of Dr. Ambrose's, which said something about Dolan. He wasn't an egomaniac. Searching Dolan's office had been dead easy. The most interesting thing he'd found was a chocolate stash.

He was an OK guy, had been a local cop at one point, according to Annie. Cole could see it, something in the way the man watched him. According to Annie, Dolan had been in the Army Reserve. Cole could see that too. A man could leave the military, but the military never left a man.

"Can we do something for you that we haven't been doing?" Dolan asked. "I know Trev's passing has been hard on everyone."

Cole shook his head. "Time for me to move on."

Dolan hesitated, as if he was thinking about trying to talk Cole out of leaving, but after a few seconds, he said, "All right. I'll schedule exit sessions with your treatment team."

"Yeah. Thanks."

Cole left the man and walked through the facility. He pulled his phone from his pocket and texted Annie. Where are you?

He wanted to tell her about his decision in person.

She didn't text back. Maybe she was in a session with one of her patients.

Chapter Twenty-Two

ANNIE WANTED TO BEAT HER HEAD INTO THE STEERING WHEEL. SHE'D LOST HER cell phone in the cornfield. At least the Toyota dealership had finally delivered her loaner so she could drive herself back to work. Otherwise, she would have had to ask her cousin for a ride.

She never did find a stray, or any other animal that needed her help. She'd gotten home chilled through, wet from the drizzle that had caught her. She'd be lucky if she didn't catch a cold.

She stopped by the AT&T store, picked out a new phone, filled out the paperwork, then drove to Hope Hill.

The staff break room was buzzing when she walked in. The conversation still centered on Trevor, but when Kate saw her, she said, "Hey, Murph's been trying to reach you."

"Lost my phone."

Dan strolled over. "He's setting up appointments for exit sessions for the Navy SEAL. He's checking out."

Annie stopped where she stood, a mix of feelings crashing through her: surprise, regret, betrayal. She couldn't believe Cole didn't tell her during their walk that morning that he planned on leaving.

She hated the thought of not seeing him again, not going on walks with him. That he'd no longer help with the midnight feedings left a hollow feeling in her chest.

She tried to shake off the hurt. Considering how her heart leapt every time she thought of the gruff SEAL, some distance between them was a good thing. The relationship wasn't appropriate. Her life would be easier if he wasn't here.

She kept telling herself that.

But then, when she was back in her room, and he came to see her, all she could think of was how much she was going to miss him.

He took one look at her face and said, "You heard."

She nodded, drinking in the solid shape of him that filled her doorway, that solitary way he had about him, the intensity of his dark eyes.

He stepped inside and closed the door behind him.

Before she could say *You shouldn't be in here,* he said, "You weren't answering your phone."

"Lost it in the cornfield."

Anger flashed through his gaze. "You shouldn't go into the cornfield." Then he asked, "Joey still in jail?"

She wanted to turn from him so he wouldn't see the mixed emotions on her face. But if she turned, he wouldn't be able to read her lips, so she faced him. "Harper is going to keep them the full seventy-two hours. He's playing them against each other. He thinks one will finger the other for driving the SUV the night I was run off the road."

She couldn't think about Joey. "Why are you leaving?"

Cole stepped closer. "I want you to know that you've made a difference for me, Annie. Thank you for making me think about things I wouldn't have thought about if I hadn't come here."

238

"Did any of it help?" She didn't want him to leave, but she had no right to ask him to stay.

"I think so. Yes."

"But you're leaving."

"I've started having flashbacks." His voice tightened. "They're pretty bad."

Her heart leapt, aching for him. "Have you told Dr. Ambrose?"

"Not yet."

"Tell him in your exit interview."

"I will."

"Are you sure you have to leave?"

A sour smile turned up the corner of his lips. "I feel crazier than when I got here. Maybe if I stay, I'll go off the deep end."

"Or you'll start seeing that therapy works, and you'll stick with it." She wrapped her arms around herself. He had been tenser this last day or two. She'd chalked it up to her accident and Trevor's death. "I'm worried about you."

He held her gaze for an endless, charged moment. His voice was soft. "Why are you worried about me, Annie?"

She gave him half the truth. "I worry about all my patients."

Disappointment flickered across his face.

She wanted to tell him that she would miss him, but that would be inappropriate. So she said, "Would you please reconsider?"

"No."

She couldn't badger him, even if the thought of his leaving was a deep ache in her chest. The decision had to be his.

"Annie . . ."

Her heart rate sped from his gravelly tone. And then he closed the distance between them and kissed her.

Somehow this kiss was more devastating than the ones before, maybe because he was leaving, and this was the last time.

He wasn't tentative. He kissed her the same way as he did every-thing else: a full frontal assault. In her mind, she was resisting, or was about to resist. She *wanted* to resist. Unfortunately, her body went for full capitulation once again.

She barely processed the thought that he had his lips on her before he swept inside and claimed all the hidden places of her mouth, leav-ing her with the shattering feeling that he was claiming all the hidden places of her heart at the same time.

This right here was the danger of opening herself to patients and encouraging them to open themselves to her. She had opened, and Cole had marched right in. And not just into the foyer, as she'd meant, but into every room she had.

Her head buzzed, her eyes drifted closed, her hands went to his massive shoulders. He was pressing against her as if he meant to climb inside her. He pressed and pressed until the back of her knees met the bed.

He laid her down, never moving his mouth from hers, never slowing his plundering.

Then he settled over her, keeping most of his weight on his elbows, but letting his body press against hers so she felt him firmly above her, nestling her into the mattress.

His knee parted her legs, and then he was suddenly between them, pressed against her apex where a low, dull pulsing began. She groaned at the overwhelming sensation of him on top of her.

He dragged his mouth to her chin, down her neck, and nibbled on her collarbone while one hand moved to her breast. Her body arched against her will, pushing a hard nipple into his palm.

Something fluttered low in her belly, probably her ovaries waving twin white flags.

He yanked her T-shirt and bra down until he bared what he needed. When his hot lips closed around her nipple, a sound of alarm escaped her because she understood suddenly that she was powerless to stop him. She didn't *want* to stop him.

"I've wanted to do this since the gas station," he said in a ragged whisper before descending on her swollen flesh again.

"Please don't make me fall in love with you," she whispered over his head, her eyes squeezed tight, her hands on the soft bristles of his head.

Unaware of her words, he suckled her with heated passion. Then he laved her with leisure. The next groan that left her mouth was a sound of pleasure mixed with embarrassment because she just realized that she'd been grinding herself against him.

She was wet and ready for him. He reached for the button of her pants. He would, within seconds, find out just how much she wanted him.

Now. Stop him now.

But her pants were sliding down already, a few inches past her hips, and then his hand was in her underwear.

He had two fingers at her opening, his thumb on her clit. He pressed the thumb down. His fingers slipped inside her at the same time, stretching her.

She bucked against him. "Cole." *Stop. Stop. Stop. This isn't right.* But out loud she just repeated his name again. "Cole . . ."

His thumb pressed down again, and she flew into pieces, her body madly contracting around his fingers.

She was dimly aware that he was pushing down his own pants, that his hard, hot erection was bobbing free against her thigh. Then his fingers were on Annie's pants again to remove them, so she could open her legs wider.

As the fabric brushed against her scars, she jackknifed, "Wait." She had to push his hands because he wasn't looking at her lips.

His gaze, startled and murderous at the same time, met hers. "What happened to you?"

She tried to shove him away. She might as well try shoving a boulder. She reached to pull up her pants, her face flushed with heat, but he wouldn't let her.

"Annie? What is this?"

She yanked harder, and he let her go at last. She scrambled up the bed to the headboard, pulling her pants up and dragging the coverlet over herself as she went.

He pulled up his own pants, then remained kneeling on the mattress, sitting back onto his heels. "When?"

She wasn't ashamed of her past. The past wasn't her fault. But she didn't like sharing the story. Still, after what had just happened, Cole was hardly a stranger.

"It happened after my mother and I left Broslin. After my grandfather kicked us out."

"So you were what, eleven?" His voice was tighter than she'd ever heard it before.

She swallowed. "About that."

"What happened?"

"I don't want to talk about it."

He waited. Silently. Unmoving.

"Randy had a thing for blood."

"Is he still alive?"

"I don't know. Haven't seen him since we left him."

The glint in Cole's eyes said he might be looking into the matter sooner rather than later.

"What did he do?"

Her heart pounded. The only person she'd told was Dan, since he was her therapist. Dan had helped her deal with the past and put it behind her.

"All right." Cole opened his arms. "You don't have to tell me. Just come here, please."

Instead, she pulled the cover up to her chin. "Both mom and Randy used to get paid on Fridays. So Saturday morning, my mother would go to the grocery store, and I'd be home alone with Randy all morning."

Cole held her gaze, the skin tightening over his cheekbones, his mouth pressed in a near-flat line, his eyes growing cold, then colder.

"As soon as she was out of the driveway," Annie said, "Randy would clean off the kitchen table." Immaculately disinfected it with vinegar. The smell of vinegar made her nauseated to this day. "Then he made me climb onto the table, and he tied me to the legs."

A muscle ticked in the left side of Cole's face.

"He would lift my skirt." She rushed now, wanting to get to the end. "Then he took his straight razor, made a cut, and just watched the blood well."

Cole's chest rose and fell as if he were struggling for breath.

"He said he was opening me up to let the naughtiness out. The blood washed it away. He was mesmerized by the cutting. He'd be staring for ten, sometimes fifteen, minutes before wiping off the drying blood then putting on a sliver of bandage."

"For two years?" Cole's voice was hoarse. "Every week?"

She nodded. She had more than a hundred white lines crisscrossing her inner thighs, making the skin look like the skin of a cantaloupe.

Cole was there then, so fast she barely saw him move, and the next second she was enfolded in his strong arms, his lips pressed to the top of her head.

She lifted her chin so she could finish the story. She looked into his tumultuous dark eyes. "The second year, as he was getting nearer and nearer to my private parts, I figured out that when he reached that far, he was going to open me up and make me bleed another way."

Cole's arms tightened around her.

"Then one day," she said, "while Randy was at work, my mom packed us up and moved us away without any explanation."

"Do you think she knew?"

"I don't think she did. She'd never caught us. After we moved, she never said a word about suspecting anything. I think they had a falling-out about something else."

Cole kissed her forehead, then when she closed her eyes, he kissed her eyelids. She felt doubly wrung out, first from their physical intimacy, and now by the stress of reliving the past.

Then Cole pressed a kiss to her mouth, but even that chaste kiss was too much suddenly. He felt so right in her bed, with his arms around her, yet she couldn't refuse to acknowledge how wrong it all was. He was a *patient*.

She pushed against his chest until he released her and pulled back.

"Annie?"

"This is not right. Even if you're checking out, it's still not right. You need to leave my room. This is completely inappropriate. I apologize for what happened before."

Thank God, he didn't ask for what, because she wasn't sure if she could say, *I apologize for having an orgasm on your fingers.*

She felt raw and stripped bare. Too much had happened in the last hour between them. She was unsure about most of it, except for one thing: she shouldn't have let him into her room to start with.

"It's all right." He moved to hug her again. "Annie, listen—"

"No." She scrambled off the bed, putting distance between them.

A determined light came into Cole's eyes. "I need to tell you something."

"There's nothing to say."

If he wouldn't go, then she would.

Annie buttoned her pants and ran.

Chapter Twenty-Three

KELLY MADE ANNIE CHICKEN SOUP FROM THEIR GRANDMOTHER'S RECIPE. THEY
bundled up on Kelly's couch with their bowls, surrounded by pillows
and blankets as if in a nest, and watched *Bridget Jones's Baby*.

The one-bedroom condo was a showplace. Kelly's house had had
to be sold to pay for the divorce, the leftovers split with Ricky, her
cheating-ass ex. Kelly had rallied by buying this condo, doing a full
renovation almost all by herself, and making it so resplendent, home
magazines should be standing in line to feature the place.

Serene, pale-taupe shades dominated the color scheme, accented
by lots of French linen, bouquets of live lavender, and on the walls,
black-and-white art photos of Paris, London, and Budapest.

Annie sank into the calm, sophisticated energy of the place as the
TV flashed image after image of the delectable Darcy.

They'd both seen the movie before, so they talked about Cole over
Hollywood dialogue.

"You're falling in love with him?" Kelly wanted confirmation.

"We can't have a relationship."

"Is he married?"

"No. He is a patient."

"And there is no way around that? You said he was quitting."

Annie sagged against the back of the couch. "I don't know. We only had an intro session. But I'm at Hope Hill as a therapist, and he was there as a patient. I crossed the line already. It's a huge breach of ethics."

She wanted to turn back time. "I should have stopped him right when he first kissed me."

"Exactly." Kelly jumped to her defense. "It's all his fault. He started it. Want me to make a house collapse on top of him?"

"I can't believe you're talking to me about collapsing houses."

"Too soon?"

Annie groaned.

Kelly finished her soup and put the empty bowl on the side table. "If you want to hate him, then I'll hate him too. Want to talk trash about him? Who needs giant muscles anyway, right? Or a chest that wide. You'd probably spend the rest of your life trying to find him shirts that fit. Nobody needs that kind of grief."

She pulled her knees up and wrapped her arms around them, her face tilted toward Annie. "And, seriously, if his *thing* is as big as the rest of him . . . wouldn't that hurt? Would you really want to limp around day after day?"

Annie squeezed her eyes shut, but she couldn't help the laugh that bubbled up in her throat. "Stop. Too much. Could we please not talk about his penis?"

"Have you seen it?"

"Kelly!"

"What? I've been divorced for ten months. Ten. Months. Throw the poor divorced woman a bone. Pun intended."

Annie had to set her soup down so she wouldn't spill it as her body shook. "Get your own boyfriend."

"It could happen." Kelly's tone turned sly.

"Who?"

"David Durenne. The producer from the TV station. I think he likes me."

Annie snorted. "You think? He carried you out of my collapsing house in his arms."

"I thought we weren't talking about collapsing houses."

"My bad. What's happening with David?"

"He keeps sending me clients."

Annie said, "He came over to the house to help a couple of times after *the incident that shall not be named*."

"Maybe he thinks of us as charity cases? Helpless spinsters?"

"Or maybe he's a nice guy. The whole time he was at my place, he kept asking about you."

Kelly's eyes lit up. "Really?"

"He has a son. Tyler."

"I know. He told me over lunch the other day."

"You had a date?"

"Ran into him at the diner. He came over and asked if I minded if he sat with me."

"He's not a doctor or a lawyer."

Kelly let her head drop to her knees. "When I said that, did it sound as incredibly shallow as I think I did?"

"You were pretty focused on marrying one or the other."

Kelly lifted her head, frowning. "What I really meant was, I'd like a man who knows how to work hard and has initiative. A man who sticks with things. I can't afford another deadbeat husband like Ricky. I need someone self-supportive. An adult."

"How long do you have to pay alimony?"

"Three more years." The words floated on a pool of misery. "But I'm off the hook if he gets married again."

"Are we rooting for the hairdresser?"

"I guess. But we're still wishing that she pokes her own eyes out with her giant fake fingernails."

"Are we mean girls now?"

"We're wishing for immediate injury. Any wounds she suffers will heal by the wedding. No ruined wedding pictures."

Annie stirred her soup and deadpanned, "We are two classy ladies."

Kelly looked away.

Annie lowered her bowl to her lap. "Aren't we?"

Long silence. Then Kelly said quietly, "I had a breakdown at the grocery store the other night." She pressed her lips together.

Annie waited her out.

In a couple of seconds, Kelly gave a big sigh and made a face. "I was getting chicken breast and looked at the steaks. You know how Ricky always liked a good steak. No matter how I was scrambling to pay off the mortgage early, he liked his food, and he liked his cars. I used to beg him to cut back on spending, at least while he was out of work."

Annie didn't know much about all that. Kelly was divorced by the time Annie had returned to Broslin. But Ricky sounded like a jerk, so she nodded.

"Anyway, I had a hard day. I was tired. It was the day the alimony gets deducted from my account, and I was thinking how I was still paying for his steak dinners. So there I was, standing at the meat counter, and I broke down in tears." She covered her face.

Annie put an arm around her.

Kelly looked up. "So then Loretta Bailer stops next to me, and, of course, she thought I was crying because I was missing Ricky. So she says, 'He ain't worth cryin' over, honey. Hell, he messed around with me long before the hairdresser floozy. With other women too. He was always a dog, Kelly. You were just too busy with work to notice."

Annie's jaw dropped. "Are you kidding me?"

"I wish." Kelly groaned. "She thought she was consoling me! Like she was doing me a favor by telling me Ricky had slept with her, so I could stop crying over Ricky."

Annie couldn't find the words, so she made what she hoped was a suitably horrified expression.

"That's not the worst," Kelly said.

"It has to be the worst."

"I threw a lamb chop at her."

Kelly's flinch said she was embarrassed beyond words. She always tried to remain professional and upbeat. She had clients she needed to think of. Everybody knew her in town. She'd helped half the people with their houses. She had to protect her reputation.

She was not the type of woman to lose it in public.

Annie understood all that, but the image of a lamb chop in Loretta's face was too much. She broke out laughing.

Kelly threw a pillow at her. "Not funny."

Except, a second later, she was laughing too. They were laughing so hard, they collapsed against each other.

"Who do we know on the grocery-store security team?" Annie asked when she could breathe and speak. "I want to see the security video. I'm willing to pay for it."

Kelly shot her a dark look. "Keep it up and you get no dessert."

Then they were both distracted by Darcy getting frisky with Bridget.

Once that tragically short bit of cinematic brilliance ended, Kelly said, "I've known for a long time that Ricky wasn't right for me. I married him back when I thought the cutest guy was the right guy. But I've realized that the right guy is the one who goes and feeds your skunks at midnight."

"I have no idea what you're hinting."

Kelly nudged her. "I think Cole is the right guy for you. From the moment he met you, he's been there for you at every turn. And you light up when you talk about him. Even when you're mad at him."

Annie pulled back into the corner of the couch. "That's the problem. I'm a therapist. He's a patient. I'm the one who's supposed to be there for *him*."

"You should have seen him at the hospital after the accident. He's mad about you, Annie. He looks at you like Darcy looks at Bridget."

Annie's heart clenched.

"Do you think you're falling in love?" Kelly asked.

"Yes." The single word nearly made Annie hyperventilate.

I'm falling in love with Cole Makani Hunter.

Scary, scary thought. She didn't know what to do with the realization. She couldn't possibly follow up on her feelings, could she?

"There are plenty of people in this world who never find true love." A shadow crossed Kelly's face. "Those who do have the responsibility to make it work."

"You'll find your true love."

"If I do, you can be sure I'm not going to waste it. And don't tell me to mind my own business. We're cousins. It's my job to stick my nose into your business. It's in the cousin handbook of rules."

Annie bit back a grin. "I'm glad we're cousins. I'm glad I came back to Broslin. It's nice to have family."

And it was nice to have love too—both the love of family, and the love Annie felt for Cole.

Cole Makani Hunter was worth fighting for, she decided.

Chapter Twenty-Four

Wednesday

COLE CAUGHT UP WITH ANNIE EARLY THE FOLLOWING MORNING AS SHE WAS brushing the donkey in the garage.

Since Esmeralda had a bad habit of trying to bite his butt, Cole stopped in the doorway. "I'm sorry if I pushed too hard last night."

Annie set down the brush. The light came in through the window behind her, painting her chestnut hair golden. With her animals around her, she looked like some ancient earth goddess.

He couldn't read the expression on her face as she walked toward him. At least this time she wasn't running. But would she send him away?

"Nothing that happens between us is wrong," he told her.

She stopped in front of him. And then she kissed him.

For a second, Cole couldn't move. He'd come here to plead his case. He wanted to confess how he felt about her.

He'd prepared for a difficult encounter. Instead, she fried his brain with a kiss.

Before he could show her how much he loved this change to his plans, she was pulling back, stepping away, obviously misinterpreting his lack of response. "I'm sorry. I shouldn't have done that." She flushed. "I thought you wanted . . ."

He reached for her, but she took another quick step back and held out a hand to ward him off, a torn expression on her face.

"I do want to." He'd never been surer of anything. "There is no reason why we can't."

He reached for her again, and this time he caught her. "I never officially agreed to become your patient. We've never had a single official session. All we had was an introduction. So, in case I wasn't clear before, no thank you, I will not be entering therapy with you, Miss Murray."

He kissed her. This time, she didn't pull away. He could have lived the rest of his life with her soft body pressed against his, his heart bursting with her silent admission that she wanted him as much as he wanted her.

"What changed your mind?" he asked, long minutes later.

A rueful smile turned up the corners of her lips. "Every day, I tell people not to be afraid of their emotions. I was at risk of turning into a hypocrite."

"I thought it was my irresistible charm," he teased her, brushing his lips over hers. "Are you sure it wasn't just the muscles?"

"That too."

"What else?" He sneaked a hand under her sweater and up her side, stopping when he finally cupped her breast, the feel of her sending heat through his body.

Her eyes glazed over. "I don't know. I can't think."

"Good answer." He sealed his lips over hers again.

Her hands explored his back as she melted against him.

He broke the kiss to close the door behind him, and then he pulled her sweater over her head.

The herd was outside. It'd been raining all morning, but they were getting a brief break in the weather. The donkey had already run off to join the pig. The cat was sleeping. So were the skunk kits, snuggled together in their basket. Annie had probably just fed them. The raven was looking the other way.

Cole and Annie had as much privacy as they were going to get here, and he didn't have it in him to wait out the long minutes it'd take to carry her inside the house.

He unbuttoned only the top button of her shirt, then pulled that over her head too. Then he kissed her breasts, as much as her bra allowed—modest and probably organic cotton. Sexiest thing he'd ever seen.

When she tugged on his shirt, he shucked it off, and then he spread the comforter over the clean bedding of straw and lowered himself, pulling her down on top of him. She slid into his arms without hesitation, laying down a path of kisses from his forehead to his lips. No games. She didn't shy away when he unclasped her bra and removed the soft fabric.

The sight of her generous breasts rendered him stupid for a second. He was so hard it verged on the uncomfortable. He shifted her under him, careful to keep most of his weight on his elbows. His right shoulder wasn't flexible, but it would hold his weight.

She pulled up her knees, and his hips settled between her thighs. He'd never wanted anything half as much as he wanted to be cradled in her body. He still couldn't believe this was happening, still half expected her to change her mind and run off like a startled deer.

They kissed and groped like freaking teenagers, and laughed, and fumbled with shoes, pants, and underwear, breathless by the time they were both naked. Her scars still startled him. He wanted to love her and protect her for the rest of his life.

He found the condoms he'd bought on blind faith, then dropped his wallet on the top of their clothes.

When he entered her, she trembled, and so did he. He finally truly did feel like a leaf twisting in the wind. Except for the part that felt like a good, thick, sturdy branch.

Cole felt completely whole for the first time in forever—as if his soul had come home, as if he'd found his roots, his safe place.

He loved Annie with everything he had in him.

Now I'm balanced, he thought. *In this moment. With Annie.*

He couldn't tell her that yet. He didn't want to rush her again, didn't want to scare her. He would give her all the time she needed to grow to love him back.

Afterward, when she lay on top of him, her heart hammering over his like a summer storm's pounding rain, he felt something soft brush against his foot. He tilted his head to see. The skunklets were coming over to join the snuggle.

He groaned.

She looked up. "What is it?"

He kissed the tip of her nose. "I admit, I might have fantasized once or twice about us making love. I hoped to eventually seduce you in a field of flowers. I never thought we'd be making love in a field of skunks."

She grinned and kissed the tip of his chin. "You don't seem terrified."

"I have no regrets. You?"

Stupid, stupid, stupid. Shouldn't have asked that. Why bring it up when everything was going so well? Did he need to hear it so badly?

Annie was pulling back already. Guilt replaced the bliss on her face. "The ethics guidelines advise a two-year wait period after therapy is terminated, before patient and therapist can have a sexual relationship." She swallowed hard. "I didn't . . ."

He understood without her having to finish the sentence. She hadn't meant to go this far. At least, not yet.

She slipped off him and began pulling on her clothes. Her flight instinct was kicking in.

Exasperation washed through him as he came up on one elbow. "I'm not now, nor ever was, your patient."

He appreciated her ethics; he really did. But if she thought he was going to give her up for the next two years over some random, stupid rule, she was crazy. He wanted her again, already.

"I wasn't anyone's patient," he told her. "I was at Hope Hill undercover, to investigate a case."

Time stopped.

Her eyes snapped wide with shock. "You weren't a patient. You didn't come for therapy?"

"That was my cover. I was investigating someone."

"Who?"

He wished he could tell her, because, clearly, this was the moment for truth between them, but he couldn't. So he just shook his head. "The point is, you don't have to worry about impropriety."

She looked at him as if the words coming out of his mouth didn't make any sense. Her breath caught, as if he'd stabbed her in the chest. He could almost see the metaphorical blood he'd drawn.

"What case?"

Man, he was messing this up. She was supposed to be relieved.

"I can't talk about that. But we're OK. You and I are fine to do whatever we want to do. Annie, I—"

"Stop." She held up her hand, palm out. Her mouth tightened with pain. He beautiful eyes swam in gut-wrenching disappointment. "You came to Hope Hill under false pretenses? So every word you've ever said to me has been a lie?"

"Of course not every word. Annie, listen—"

"I can't." She cut him off, the broken look in her eyes killing him.

She blinked. And Cole could almost see the wheels turning in her head as she said, "My ID card. I keep misplacing it lately." Her gaze sharpened with suspicion. "Did you have anything to do with that?"

"I borrowed it now and then." *For good reason, dammit.* Cole reached for her. He had to make her understand. "Annie . . ."

She shrank back—as if she no longer knew him, wanted him. As if she loathed him. "You used me."

She turned another shade paler, as if she were bleeding out right in front of him.

"What we have—"

"We have nothing." Her eyelashes trembled. "Nothing we had was ever real."

Cole's heart drummed madly. Cold panic surged through his veins when he finally began to understand how much he'd hurt her.

"Oh God. The Murray curse strikes again." She said the bitter words. "I'm just too stupid to learn." Her lips wobbled. "Please leave."

Her eyes glinted with tears, devastation in her expression, in the way she held herself, as if on the verge of collapsing.

Jesus. He'd made her cry. Cole's gut twisted.

"Annie, please." He came to his knees, then to his feet. He couldn't lose her.

"No."

She gathered herself, right in front of his eyes, in that indomitable way she had. As if she were a mighty oak and he just a passing storm, and she wasn't going to allow him to shake her.

Desperation sliced Cole's heart into ribbons. He was losing her.

"Annie . . ."

But she pointed at the door. "I mean it, Cole. Get out and don't ever come back."

Chapter Twenty-Five

ANNIE'S STOMACH FLOODED WITH ACID, WHILE HER HEART THUDDED HARD IN a race to see whether she'd have a heart attack or an ulcer first.

She had given Cole more of her heart than she'd given to any man. She had ripped her chest open for him and let him see the bleeding memories of her past. She'd shown him *everything*.

But for him, their entire relationship—every day when she'd been agonizing over falling for him—had been playacting. He'd used her for *access*.

Betrayal wasn't a large enough word to describe what she felt.

She wanted to go to the deer blind, but the mocking ghost of Cole's presence would be there. Same at the sacred tree circle.

She wanted to run into the woods and lose herself. She wanted to run so deep that pain couldn't find her.

There was a different woods past the far edge of the cornfield where she'd never taken Cole or any of her patients. She rarely went there herself. The place had been the site of a Revolutionary War battle. She always felt as if ghosts walked among the trees there.

At the moment, Annie felt like a ghost herself.

Tears rolling down her face, she dove into the corn and headed for the far edge.

Thursday

Dr. Ambrose had prescribed Cole's meds, so he had to meet with him to discuss what Cole would like to continue and what he'd like to discontinue. Their appointment was at ten o'clock. Other than that, Cole canceled the rest of the exit sessions that had been scheduled for him.

He was grateful for the effort people at Hope Hill had put into making him feel better, but he wasn't in the right frame of mind to make nice all morning. He didn't want to see anyone but Annie, and Annie didn't want to see him.

Cole was ready to get out of there. Not that he would be able stay away.

His plan was to go home, move out of his apartment, and ship his stuff up here. Before coming to Hope Hill, he'd done mostly Internet work, reviewing security protocols for various companies. He could pick up more work like that, and he had money saved from his active-duty days.

He would do whatever it took for Annie to forgive him.

If she made him wait two years, then so be it.

He wanted a chance with her. If he couldn't convince her, if she still said no, he'd accept her decision. But he wasn't going to throw away the possibility of a future with her because of their first fight.

Cole walked into Ambrose's office.

The shrink looked up. "I'm sorry to hear that you're leaving. Please, have a seat."

Cole didn't expect to stay long enough to make sitting down worthwhile. He sat anyway, to be polite. "Just the way it played out."

The man studied him carefully and poured them both some water, the ice clinking in the carafe. "So, what's on your mind this morning?"

Annie. Annie had been on Cole's mind most of the time since he'd met her. Not that he'd tell Ambrose.

"Getting back home," he said instead.

"Back to the same old same old?"

"I don't think so. I'd like to think I've learned while I've been here."

Ambrose offered an easy grin. "We certainly hope so."

Cole hesitated a moment before he asked the question that had been bouncing around in his head for the past day or two. "Does PTSD have a memory-loss component?"

"It can. Why do you ask?"

"I keep feeling lately that I should be remembering something that I don't. It's right there under the surface. I can almost see it, but then I can't."

Interest glinted in Ambrose's eyes. "Stay. Then we can work on that together."

"I'll probably remember on my own. Lying in bed last night, I almost had it. It might come to me if I do some meditation."

They talked about that, then his meds. He didn't want to renew his prescriptions, but understood that some of the meds couldn't be stopped abruptly if he didn't want withdrawal to knock him on his ass for the next couple of days, even weeks. So they set up a schedule to wean him off the drugs. Ambrose made a pitch that needing pills didn't mean Cole was weak.

Something Annie would say. Cole tried not to think about the fact that Annie hated his guts now. He'd return. He'd grovel. He'd do whatever he had to, to earn her forgiveness.

Ambrose's advice on Cole's future treatment plan took longer than Cole thought it would. Next thing he knew, a full hour had passed.

He thanked the psychiatrist one more time, shook the guy's hand, and went to pack.

He swung by Annie's room on the ground floor. Knocked. She didn't open up. Maybe she had a session.

He pulled out his phone to text her. Can I see you before I leave?

Frustration shot through him when he remembered that she'd lost her phone. She hadn't given him her new number. He had no way of reaching her before he left.

Maybe it was for the better.

He deleted the message as he headed upstairs to his own room.

She needed time to process everything he'd told her yesterday. He would contact her later. Her e-mail address was up on her animal sanctuary's website. That'd work.

Cole had lunch at the cafeteria, then drove to the airport through sheets of rain. He dropped his rental and checked in. By the time he made it to gate twenty-seven, the sign was up that his flight had been delayed due to the weather.

He went to grab coffee. He had his friend Derek's thriller in his suitcase. Maybe he'd finally get to finish the book.

He didn't. As rain slammed into the terminal windows and the sky darkened, another announcement flashed onto the display screen next to the boarding gate, updating to a longer delay. Cole was fine one second, then knocked sideways the next by the sudden flashback of him running up an Afghan hillside with Matt across his shoulders.

We walked three hundred miles, because the nearest US Army base was in Bagram.

Cole blinked hard, reaching out to steady himself on the armrest of his chair. *Who said that?*

Then the voice continued. *Officially, there are no special ops stationed there, but it's an unofficial staging base for black-ops missions.*

He blinked. Shook his head. *Who would know that?*

He did. *He* had said those words. *When?* He had no memory of the conversation.

He pushed up from the gray plastic chair, strode to the window, and stared into the roiling clouds of the approaching hurricane. A military plane might take off in weather like that, but no way a civilian aircraft was going to. Nobody was flying out of Philly tonight.

Looked like Hurricane Rupert has just made landfall at Chesapeake Bay, coming fast this way.

He paced along the window. The flashbacks wouldn't leave his head. When had he talked about Bagram? He didn't discuss Bagram with anyone, ever.

He ran his hand over his shaved head. Why would he say something like that? To whom? He couldn't untangle the jumble in his mind.

Had he said those words at all, or was it some kind of false memory? Was he now, in addition to flashbacks, hallucinating too?

He almost regretted ever coming to Hope Hill, ever letting the shrinks stir up the past in his head. *Almost*, because he couldn't regret meeting Annie.

How many SEALs were at Bagram the last time you were there?

OK, he had not said that. He closed his eyes and could see someone's lips move, forming the question.

Cole could clearly envision a man's mouth. But he couldn't see the face that went with it.

The walls of the terminal closed in on him. He grabbed his phone to call Annie, then swore. He needed her new number, dammit. She was the only person he 100 percent trusted at Hope Hill.

Cole leaned his forehead against the cool window, not hearing the rain outside, but feeling the vibrations as the heavy drops hit the glass. When and where had he been questioned? He wanted to pin down the sudden flashbacks. He needed to recover the memory of the face that went with the lips that asked him questions nobody should have asked him.

The last time he'd been questioned like that . . .

A flashback from one of the endless torture sessions of his captivity slammed into him. Cole broke into pacing again. He needed to work off the excess energy that sought a violent outlet, exhaust some of his murderous rage. He needed a clear head.

When was the last time you were at Bagram? How many troops were there at the time?

Had he answered that? He couldn't remember. Frustration pumped through him.

Who was the senior brass at the base?

Cole knew the answer. But had he told?

You were shot down in a chopper. Black Hawk? How many of them did the base have?

He stopped as lightning crackled through the darkening sky, the floor shaking the next second. He could actually hear the thunder, but only as if from a great distance, or as if he were deep underwater.

The thought that speared through his mind hit him as hard as if he'd been struck by that lightning bolt. He didn't remember where or when those questions had been asked, but he clearly remembered *lip-reading* them.

His hearing hadn't been injured until they were escaping. The damage had happened in a drag-out, to-the-death fight with one of the guards. So the questioning Cole was remembering so suddenly couldn't have happened during the six months he'd been a POW.

The memory had to be more recent. When and where?

Hope Hill. His subconscious mind kicked up the answer. Hope Hill had a traitor who dealt in information.

Cole's mind buzzed like a whole flock of incoming choppers as he thought about all the pills he'd taken while he'd been at Hope Hill. Any number of people around him could have switched out a sleeping pill for something else. What had he been given?

Scopolamine came to mind, used in the twenties by police departments to interrogate suspects. Not only did it loosen people's tongues, but they couldn't remember the interrogation afterward. It was banned for police use now. Any evidence gained with the help of scopolamine was inadmissible in court, but the drug was still around, used in small doses to prevent severe motion sickness.

A traitor slash spy could certainly gain access to a couple of pills easily enough. Except that the traitor at Hope Hill was Trevor.

Or was he?

Trevor had had a scar on his lower lip, part of the injury that had put titanium pins in the kid's neck. But the mouth in Cole's newly recovered memories, the mouth that had asked him those revealing questions, had been unblemished.

So not Trevor, then.

Cole let that thought settle in for a few seconds.

If Trevor wasn't the bad guy here, could he have been a victim?

What if Trev too had been drugged and used? What if he too remembered answering traitorous questions? Cole stifled a groan at the implications of his trail of thoughts. What if Trev hadn't committed suicide? What if the traitor had killed Trev?

Trev had been planning that barn . . .

Cole sent his CO a text. Think we got the wrong guy. It's not Trevor. Then he added, I'm at the airport. Heading back to Hope Hill.

His CO would get in touch with him as soon as he got the messages. He could be anywhere. He could be over in Yemen with a team right now, rounding up the recipients of the coded Hope Hill information. Cole was on his own.

He grabbed his bag and walked out of the terminal, straight to car rental.

He reached the desk just in time. The parking lot was flooding. He got the last car they signed out before piling the rest on trailers to move to higher ground.

He drove through Philly in driving rain, going at half the speed he could have if the road wasn't slick, visibility crap, and his mobility limited by his injured shoulder. The trip to Hope Hill took twice as long as it should have, and he found himself grinding his teeth at the delay.

He was soaked to the skin by the time he ran from the parking lot into the building.

He checked Annie's room first. Still not there. She'd probably decided to stay at her house to make sure her animals were OK during the storm. He wanted to text her, dammit, wanted to make sure she was safe. Instead, he grabbed his phone and started typing messages to his CO. He began with the flashbacks and listed the questions he remembered having been asked.

He was typing out the fifth question, focused on the mouth forming the words, when the full face flashed into his mind at last.

Son of a bitch.

Cole hurried down the hallway as he sent the last message.

Dan Ambrose. It's the staff psychiatrist.

The door to the hallway with the staff offices hadn't been locked yet for the night, so Cole simply walked through. Ambrose's office stood empty.

Right. The guy would have no reason to be here at eight o'clock at night.

Murphy Dolan's office was empty too. Cole couldn't see any other staff. Only two offices had the lights on, but nobody sat behind the desks.

Cole ran to the staff break room down the hall. Since the facility was inpatient, they had staff on duty around the clock. Somebody had to be here who could tell him where to find Ambrose.

Cole burst into the break room. The three women sitting at the round table in the corner looked up from chatting over coffee: Libby the reflexologist, Kate the touch therapist, and Margie from the cleaning crew.

"Does anyone know where Ambrose lives? It's an emergency."

"Everything OK?" Libby came to her feet.

Kate, too, immediately moved toward Cole. "What can we help with?"

"I need Ambrose's address. I need to talk to him."

Kate stopped. "I'm sorry, but we can't disclose personal information to a patient. I'm sure that whatever is wrong, we can help."

As the floor vibrated behind him with footsteps, Cole turned in time to see Murphy Dolan stride up to him.

"Where's Ambrose?" Cole grabbed Dolan by the arm and turned him so when he responded, Cole would be able to read his lips.

"He didn't show for your session either?" Dolan glanced down at the hand, then over at the women who looked uncertain, clearly worried about Cole's brusque manner and demands. "Dan didn't show for any of his afternoon patients. I left him two messages earlier, but he never called me back."

Dolan ushered Cole out of the break room. The guy sensed a threat, and his first move was to protect the women. Cole could respect that. He meant no harm. Not to them.

He closed the door behind him.

"I came to Hope Hill undercover," he told Dolan. Cole needed his cooperation to find the psychiatrist. "I think Ambrose has been drugging patients. He's been getting confidential military information out of them, then passing it on to a connection in the Middle East."

As Dolan's eyes narrowed, the phone vibrated in Cole's pocket.

His CO with a text. **Organizing Backup.** Cole clicked to call, and when the display showed that the other end picked up, he said, "I'm going to give the phone to Murphy Dolan. You need to tell him I check out. You need to tell him to give us assistance."

He handed the phone over.

As Dolan listened, the man's jaw went from tense to tenser. Within five seconds, his eyes glinted with murder.

Then things went from bad to worse.

Cole remembered another question Ambrose had asked.

What's your relationship with Annie Murray?

Why was Ambrose interested in Annie?

Cole thought of her stalker, her intruder, the hit-and-run that almost pushed her into the reservoir. And so far the police couldn't pin any of that on her ex. Last Cole had heard, they were still pushing for a confession from Joey and Big Jim.

Cole held his hand out for the phone. "Find and detain Ambrose," he told Dolan. "The police can help. I need to find Annie."

Then Cole was running.

Chapter Twenty-Six

THE MAN WALKED DOWN INTO HIS BASEMENT, HOLDING AN EMPTY JAR IN ONE hand, a sippy cup in the other.

"Hello, Mother."

The woman who had abandoned him in his childhood lay on the bed in a short, sleeveless nightgown. He kept the basement warm so she wouldn't catch a chill.

"Do you know who I am?" he asked, setting the sippy cup on the bedside table.

She shook her head, her blue eyes widening with fear.

"Don't worry. I'll help you remember."

He picked the leeches off her one by one as she shuddered with revulsion, tears leaking out of her eyes.

"Are you feeling better?"

She nodded. He'd trained her to do that, but sometimes she forgot. The curse of Alzheimer's.

He set aside the jar of leeches, then treated the wounds on her thighs. He'd thought if he re-created the pain of childbirth, maybe she'd remember giving birth to him. She hadn't. He'd have to try something else in a few weeks, when she fully healed.

Her wounds taken care of, he helped her sit and lifted the sippy cup—a strawberry-flavored protein shake—to her lips. He smiled as she drank.

"Aren't you glad I found you in that home? It's so much nicer for family to live together, isn't it?"

Her straight, patrician nose—which he'd inherited from her—ran. He wiped it.

"I was going to bring someone home to meet you." He sighed. "But she disappointed me. I'm afraid she won't be able to join our family after all. Isn't that a shame?"

Teary-eyed, his mother nodded.

Annie huddled in the garage with her animals while Rupert pounded on the roof. She didn't want to leave them alone in the storm. Her garage was pretty sturdy, and she felt safe. Right now, the house was more vulnerable since the wind could tear the plywood patch off the back, leaving the inside open to the elements.

The storm raged outside, but Annie was too numb to care. Her heart had been broken into a million pieces that had fallen away like dead leaves from a tree. There was nothing inside her. She was empty.

She was so empty it hurt, with a sharp, pulsating pain.

She moved between the separate animal enclosures in her garage. She petted the llamas, scratched the pig behind the ears, gave the donkey a treat. She thought about opening the gates and bedding down with them, but Dorothy, the pig, had no respect for personal space. And if Dorothy was too aggressive, pushing her snout into the skunks, one might spray.

The garage had a metal roof, and the rain was insanely loud as the fat drops hit. The wind bent the locust tree next to the garage, the branches scraping over the siding. The noise was so bad, she almost didn't hear when someone knocked on the door.

She could barely make out the dark shape of a man through the glass. Only one person ever came with her to take care of her animals. She hurried to let him in. "Cole."

But the man who pushed inside wasn't the man she'd expected.

"Dan?" She shut the door quickly before more wind and cold rain could rush through the gap. "What are you doing here?"

"You have to come with me."

"Did your car break down?" Did he slide into a ditch and need a push? Pushing wouldn't work in all this mud. "Stay here until the weather blows over."

He grabbed her. His eyes usually conveyed care and concern. Right now, as he held on to her arm, Annie thought he looked determined and almost angry.

"Things could have been different," he said, and his words had a bite to them.

"What are you talking about?"

"I chose you."

For a second, she didn't understand. Then . . . this was about refusing to go out with him? She blinked. He was still angry about that? "You know we can't—"

As if her words flipped a switch, Dan's hand jumped from her arm to her neck in an instant, and he held tight. She was so startled she froze.

"Stop your fucking lies. You're fucking a patient. You've disgraced your license. I wanted to mentor you! You could have been worthy of me, if you only tried. You, among all the others." He spit the words into her face, his hard, ruthless gaze making it clear that he meant to hurt her.

She fought to catch her breath as she desperately tried to make sense of him.

They were coworkers. Friends. Bitter betrayal flooded through her again, for the second time in as many days. Was nobody what they seemed? Was everybody lying to her?

Dan shook her, his voice filled with a level of hate impossible to comprehend. "Your whoring days are over."

Cold fear spread through Annie. This was a Dan she didn't know—utterly unstable. *A madman.*

She didn't understand much, but she understood that she was in serious danger.

"Let me go. Please." She struggled, her fighting instinct kicking in at last, but his grip on her neck only tightened.

And then she caught a flash of plastic in his hand. He slammed it into her arm. She felt a pinch. Her brain came to a screeching halt. *What's happening?*

The world went black.

Annie's loaner Toyota stood in her driveway. The house was empty. So was the garage. No sign of struggle in either place, although her animals were agitated, the donkey doing her best to kick her way out of her enclosure.

Cole texted Murphy Dolan: You got Ambrose?

Not at home, Dolan responded. Neighbors haven't seen him. Got APB out on him.

Good, then the cops were looking for both Ambrose and his car. He wouldn't get far in this weather. Few people were out on the roads. The police would have no trouble spotting Ambrose if he was driving.

Cole texted his CO next. Backup?

The response was less than encouraging. Chopper grounded due to weather. Make do with local cops?

Cole was about to text Murphy Dolan for Annie's new phone number when a text popped up on his screen. From Ambrose. Deer blind. Come alone.

A picture came next: Annie, soaked through and lifeless, lying on wet boards somewhere.

You touch her, you die. Cole sent the text, then jumped into his car, cursing Hurricane Rupert.

Water covered the road. He had to be careful if he didn't want to go hydroplaning. The wind grew so strong that it blew the car sideways at times. Cole navigated the hazards with care, one-handed, while his mind went to the deer blind.

He'd only been there once. The blind wasn't far from the walking path, but where exactly did he have to go off the path? *Damn drugs.* A year ago, he wouldn't have had any trouble remembering. He was a freaking Navy SEAL. He *owned* his environment.

He drove to Hope Hill and ran across campus to the woods. He ran down the muddy footpath, most of it underwater. He couldn't see footprints, dammit.

Fear and fury drummed in his head, pounding in his brain.

How bad was Annie hurt?

Was she even really here, or was this a trap?

Annie came to slowly, her head buzzing, her limbs heavy. Several seconds passed before she figured out where she was: in the deer blind, in the woods, in the middle of a hurricane. A squall pounded on the roof, making her head hurt. She couldn't remember how she got here.

Her mouth felt dry.

In another few seconds, her brain began working better. Clearly, she'd been drugged, but the sedative was wearing off, thank God.

The burly shape of a man stood across the small room from her, looking out, into the woods.

Dan. Dan had come for her, drugged her, then brought her here. *Why?*

She didn't move, tried not to make any noise, closed her eyes again. If Dan turned around, she didn't want him to know that she had regained consciousness.

Whatever his goal was and whatever his reasons were for kidnapping her, she was pretty sure the adventure wasn't going to have a good ending.

He *had* drugged her and kidnapped her. He hadn't bothered covering his face. Because he was counting on her being unable to tell the police what he'd done?

Because she'd be dead?

Her mind still addled, she couldn't come up with another reason. She couldn't see how Dan's plans—no matter what they were—would end well for her.

She eased one eye open to a narrow crack. Dan still had his back to her, peering into the rain as if waiting for something. Lightning flashed, and for a second she could see better—see the gun he held by his side, a glint of black metal.

A shiver ran down her spine, and not just from the sight of the weapon. She was freezing. He had on his big puffy coat. His tendency to overdress for cold because of his poor circulation was paying off.

The coat . . .

He looked so much bigger in that coat than he really was.

Suspicion dawned. Bundled up, he could have been the man in her kitchen. *And* the man in the SUV that had run her off the road. Dan drove a deep-green 4Runner. His car could definitely look black in the dark.

Why hadn't she thought of that before?

Because in a million years, she would not have suspected Dan. He was supposed to be a healer, like her!

And yet . . . he'd asked her out, and she'd rejected him. She wouldn't be the first woman to be killed for saying no.

Despair clawed at her. God, this was so insane.

OK, no. No despair. No panic. She couldn't let him win. She was in her woods. This was her turf.

Think! Rush him and ram him over the side?

Under different circumstances, she probably could have. But her legs were still half-numb. The drug wasn't fully out of her system yet.

She shifted to test just how wobbly she was.

He caught the small movement and spun toward her to watch her with disdain, a sneer on his thin lips. "You shouldn't get involved with patients," he said, as if they'd been in the middle of a conversation. "It's a breach of ethics."

Because kidnapping wasn't? She didn't ask him that. But she did ask, "Why did you bring me here?"

"To draw out your boyfriend. I sent him a text to let him know where to find us."

"I don't have a boyfriend."

He stepped over, crouched down in front of her, and slapped her so hard, her ears rang. "No lying."

His voice was as calm as if they were having a professional discussion in his office.

OK. She didn't want to be hit again. She didn't want to be hurt. She needed to be as whole as possible to make her escape.

"Why do you want Cole?"

"He's starting to remember. When they start to remember, the game has to end. Most don't. Ninety percent." He sounded as thoughtful and caring as ever. "But one in ten aren't as susceptible to the drug as the rest. I've had a pretty long run of good luck. Hard to believe now I have three failures back-to-back."

She stared at him.

Three failures back-to-back. Was he talking about patients? Her mind jumped to a horrific possibility. "Trev?" And then, "Mitch?"

"Can't predict these things."

Her mind swirled. "What did Cole remember?"

"Giving me confidential information during a session, under some medical influence. As it turns out, US military information is a hot commodity in the international market."

So that had been Cole's investigation. Dan had turned traitor, and Cole had been sent to root him out. But then why was he leaving? A ruse?

She shrugged off the dozen questions that crowded into her brain. She'd ponder those later.

"I drug them, they blab, they don't remember," Dan went on, sounding pleased, as if he considered himself a genius.

"Except one in ten," she said, so stunned she could barely think.

"No plan is ever perfect. But I'm in the right position for damage control. I can take care of the exceptions."

Cole wasn't an *exception*, she wanted to scream; he wasn't an aberration that needed to be fixed. "Why? You're not political. You're not—"

"For the money. In another few months, I can retire. I'm tired of the same old shit. New day, new people, but always the same problems. I want to focus full-time on taking care of my mother."

"You did this because you were bored?"

"You're in no condition to judge me," he snapped. "Did you spread your legs for a patient because you were bored?" Contempt dripped from every word. "Too good for me, but not too good for him?"

Dan seemed to have no regrets, no scruples. *A sociopath?*

How had she not noticed? But they hadn't been close friends, hadn't spent much time together outside her weekly sessions with him. And in those there had always been a certain professional distance between them.

Until that dinner when he'd kissed her.

Had she become some kind of obsession for him without even knowing it?

"I'm sorry." She did her best to sound contrite. She would say anything that might help. "I didn't understand how you felt."

He stood. "Too late." Anger hardened his voice as he said, "We could have been family. You have no idea of all the wonderful plans I had for us. I was going to introduce you to my mother."

This was the second time he referred to his mother. "I don't understand. I thought she skipped out when you were a kid. I thought you barely even remembered her."

"I found her in Alzheimer's care a couple of months ago. I've been searching for a while. I brought her home." He shot Annie a cold look of hate. "I don't want to talk about her. You don't deserve to know her."

He walked to the other end of the space and looked out, toward the path.

Waiting for Cole.

Annie's heart raced. "You can't shoot him. You'll be caught."

He turned. "Murder-suicide. Nobody will be surprised, considering his family history. Everybody will think Trevor's death pushed him over the edge. If anything, it'll be blamed on you for having an affair with a patient. Cole snapped, he killed you, then he killed himself." Disappointment crept into his voice, as if she were a slow student.

He added, "Technically, I'll shoot him first. Then we're going to finish our date. No more teasing. You are going to give me everything you've given to him. Then I'm going to take whatever else I need."

Fear roiled in Annie's stomach. She needed to get away from here. If she ran, Dan would come after her. He wouldn't be here to kill Cole when Cole arrived. And she might be able to get away from Dan. She knew these woods.

She considered the sheets of rain outside—limited visibility. That was in her favor, if she ran. But to run, she'd have to reach the ground first. If she was too slow on the ladder, Dan would catch her before she was halfway down the tree.

Could she jump? The blind was fifteen feet or so up.

The ground below is soft mud.

Her choices were either to jump out of the blind and maybe break something, or stay and face certain death. And if she didn't do anything, Cole would be killed too.

Annie went for it, pushing herself up then over the half wall in one uncoordinated vault.

She slammed into a puddle, the air knocked out of her, rain beating on her face.

"Annie!" Dan roared above.

She didn't stay down long enough to determine if she'd broken anything. She pushed to her shaking hands and knees and scrambled toward the nearest stand of bushes, then through them, ignoring the skin she scraped off in the process.

She tripped. She sprang up and ran bent over for another few feet before she straightened. When she glanced back, she could barely make out the blind. She didn't see Dan.

She ran in lurching, sliding strides toward Hope Hill.

"Annie!"

If she wasn't so scared, she would have smiled. Dan was still behind her.

Good.

She wanted him to think that he could catch her. She didn't want him to give up and go back to lie in wait for Cole.

She ran, but not too fast, to lure Dan farther away.

Cole spent way too much time locating the deer blind. *Empty.*

Somebody *had* been here, though—muddy footprints covered the floorboards, and there were more footprints at the base of the tree.

He pulled out his LED light and examined the prints close-up, squatting down and dragging his fingers in the indentations. The churned-up mud betrayed a lot of slipping and sliding. Had they been struggling? Had Annie escaped Ambrose?

Cole took off, following the prints.

He couldn't hear the rain, but he could hear some of the thunder when lightning crackled across the sky. He used every second of that light to scan the forest in front of him. How far ahead of him were they?

Where Cole saw prints, he followed them, and where puddles covered the tracks, he chose the easiest path. Annie would want to get away from Ambrose as fast as she could. She'd be running for the openings in the vegetation, probably back toward the main track, back toward Hope Hill.

When he wasn't scanning the ground, he was scanning the bushes for a scrap of fabric, hair, blood—any indication that he was on the right path.

A full ten minutes passed before he finally had to admit that he'd lost their track.

He roared his frustration into the storm.

Then he backtracked and tried again.

Annie ran forward in the dark, so wet and cold her teeth chattered. She'd run far enough now, she thought, so that Dan wouldn't be able to find his way back to the blind if he gave up and turned around. Cole was safe.

Time to get away from the madman before he caught up with her.

"Annie!" The call came out of the darkness from way too near. And, before she could turn around, Dan barreled into her.

They crashed to the muddy ground. She had the presence of mind to roll away. A second later they were both on their feet again.

In a flash of lightning, she could see the gun in Dan's hand. *Now or never.* She flowed into the one good self-defense move she knew, her one kick.

Pain shot up her leg, but Dan went down again, sprawled at her feet.

She kicked his hand with everything she had. He lost hold of the gun, but the weapon didn't slide away nearly far enough. And he was scrambling up. Annie ran.

Her body hurt from the fall from the deer blind, and from Dan's tackle. Branches smacked her face. She slipped and, once again, nearly twisted her ankle. She didn't stop. She didn't slow.

"Annie!"

She hoped the storm helped her blend in. Dan couldn't just look for movement. Everything moved in the gale-force winds.

In the end, that became Annie's downfall.

She knew the woods. She navigated by landmarks—a fallen log, an odd-shaped tree. But all the trees were twisting, presenting different shapes. She could barely see shapes. She could barely see anything.

She thought she'd been cutting back to the walking path, but the walking path was nowhere to be seen. Not daring to stop, in case Dan was close behind, she kept moving in the general direction she thought the buildings should be.

Soon she was gasping for air from the effort, not sure how much farther she'd be able to run, but she still hadn't reached Hope Hill.

"Annie!"

She shuddered at the shout. She was lost in the woods. And the madman chasing her was closing in.

Could she find cover? Could she shelter in place until morning? Hide?

Except, she could only see for seconds at a time when lightning crackled across the sky. She hadn't seen any suitable shelter so far. At least running kept her warm. Temperatures were steadily dropping. If she stopped, she'd be exposed to hypothermia.

She stumbled, ignored the pain in her ankle, and kept going. Who was she kidding? She couldn't stop moving if she wanted. Nerves and fear pushed her forward. Panic was making her decisions.

She cut through some bushes and realized the ground was tilting slightly downhill. Did that mean she was heading toward the facilities at last?

She slipped, tried to catch herself, and failed. *Don't break anything.* But instead of hard ground, she hit water and immediately went under.

She touched bottom pretty fast, then kicked herself back up to the surface. No way she was at the pond. A natural pond stood at the northern edge of the Hope Hill property, but she knew she hadn't been moving in that direction.

She gasped for air, the water too cold. Then lightning flashed, showing her where she was. A giant tree, blown over by the storm, had twisted out of the ground. An enormous root ball towered above her, a huge, thick spiderweb. She was trapped in the rain-filled root-ball crater. The hole was no more than six feet in diameter and probably not much deeper than that. Just enough to drown in.

In the dark again, Annie reached blindly for the edge.

The muddy bank crumbled under her panicked fingers.

She was chilled through to the bone. Even her insides shivered as she tried to claw herself out. She was *not* going to drown in what amounted to an oversize puddle.

Except that, try as she might, she couldn't get a firm grasp. Every time she grabbed for a handhold, she came away with a handful of mud and slipped back into the cold water.

Cole had his eyes on a stand of yews when Ambrose stepped out from behind them with his gun aimed at Cole's head.

Cole dove to the side, hit the ground, and rolled in mud until he was behind the cover of a log large enough to hide him. He regretted few things as much as he regretted not being able to bring a gun to Hope Hill, although he understood their strict no-weapons policy.

He heard a shot, but so muted, as if through a silencer. It missed him. If Ambrose was moving around to get a better angle, Cole heard none of that.

He rolled to the left into an indentation in the ground deep enough to hide him, hoping he was rolling away from the man instead of toward him. The hole was filling with water. The muck helped cover him.

He peeked out into the darkness, everything wild and violent movement around him, yet the storm, silent. He stayed still and looked for other still forms. Tree, tree, tree . . . *there*. Ambrose huddled behind a stand of bushes, sticking his head out to see better.

Several seconds passed before the man edged to the right. He was going toward better cover too, an old maple. He'd be out in the open for six feet or so, looking away from Cole.

Cole would have to cross twelve feet to bring down Ambrose. It would all come down to how fast Ambrose could bring his gun around.

Ambrose pushed forward.

Cole lunged.

He missed his mark by an inch.

Ambrose didn't.

Blood pulsed from Cole's right shoulder, running into the mud under him. Freaking Ambrose had winged him.

The man stood over Cole, gun pointed at Cole's head, from a lot closer this time. He might have been talking, but Cole couldn't make anything out in the dark. His shoulder pulsed with pain.

The guy wasn't a half-bad shot. A hunter?

But good shot or not, he knew nothing about close combat.

"You never stand this close to the enemy unless you're sure they're dead," Cole said as he swept the man's legs from under him.

He heard the faint pop of the shot Ambrose squeezed off before he hit the mud. This bullet missed. Then Cole was on top of the man, wrestling for the weapon.

Under better circumstances, disarming the bastard would have taken seconds. But Cole didn't have use of his right arm. And he was leaking too much blood.

He wasn't sure how much time he had before his blood pressure would drop so low he'd lose consciousness. He knocked out Ambrose by driving the man's nose into his face. Ambrose didn't move again.

Then Cole rolled away, pulled off his belt with his left hand, and made a tourniquet for his shoulder. That'd slow the blood loss. His head swam as he pushed himself to his knees. He'd bled too much already.

He tugged off Ambrose's belt next. After considerable struggle, he managed to tie the man to a thick branch above his head, both arms looped high, only the toes of Ambrose's shoes touching the ground.

The pain in his contorted shoulders brought Ambrose around, and he groaned, spitting out some of the blood that had run from his nose into his mouth.

Cole had some serious questions for the guy, but not now. He had to find Annie. Even if Ambrose decided to talk, Cole couldn't read his lips in the dark and the driving rain.

He took the gun and counted the bullets. Only two were missing—the two Ambrose had fired at him. Some of the tension eased in Cole's chest at the thought that Ambrose hadn't shot Annie.

Had he hurt her in other ways?

Cole stumbled forward to find her, ignoring the buzzing in his head, the pain in his shoulder, and the weakness in his knees.

"Annie!" he roared at the top of his lungs.

He wouldn't be able to hear her if she answered, but she would hear him and know that he was coming.

He refused to think that he might be too late.

Chapter Twenty-Seven

ANNIE SWALLOWED ANOTHER MOUTHFUL OF MUDDY WATER AND CHOKED. She'd slipped under again, dammit. The side of the hole was too slippery, too crumbly for her to climb out.

Thunder shook the ground, and then a different kind of clap sounded. *A gunshot?*

Then shortly, another one.

Was Dan shooting at Cole? Had Cole caught up with him?

Or did Dan think that Annie was holed up somewhere nearby and he wanted to flush her out?

The second shot sounded louder than the first. He was coming in her direction. And she was trapped, unable to get away from him. When he got here, it'd be—literally—like shooting fish in a barrel.

She switched tactics and tried to pull herself up by the fallen tree's roots, but she couldn't hold on. Everything was way too slippery with mud and rain.

"Annie!"

Cole?

"I'm here!" He wouldn't hear her, but she couldn't stop screaming. "Cole! I'm here!"

She ripped off her sweatshirt. White. Maybe Cole would see it. The wet fabric wasn't keeping her warm anyway. She tossed the shirt on the root ball then spread it out as much as she could, like a white flag. She would have taken off her flannel shirt too, but it was dark green.

She slipped back in, slipped under. God, she was cold. And so incredibly tired. She clawed her way to the surface anyway. This time, it took forever. She kept slipping back.

Then Cole was there, barreling forward.

"I'm here." He fell to his knees next to the hole and grabbed her with his left hand, yanked her out like a kid yanking a frog from a puddle. He didn't let her go, his arms tightening around her. His voice was rough and gravelly in her ear. "Taking the tree-root meditation a little too far, aren't you?"

She was gasping for air, her whole body trembling.

"Are you all right?" He lay her gently on the ground to examine her and brushed her soggy, matted hair out of her face. "Nod your head."

She nodded, but she stayed flat on her back. She didn't think she could get up if the fate of all the rain forests in the world depended on it.

Until lightning lit up the sky, and she saw the blood on Cole's shoulder.

She sat up and reached out. How bad was the injury? No way for her to ask in the sudden dark. But she'd seen enough to know that he needed immediate help. She struggled to her feet and reached for him.

She glanced in the direction of the earlier gunshots. Where was Ambrose? He had to be incapacitated, or Cole wouldn't have shouted for her. He wouldn't have risked drawing Ambrose's attention.

Then Cole turned, and Annie saw Ambrose's gun tucked into the back of his waistband. So Ambrose and Cole had had a confrontation, and Cole had won. For now, Annie didn't need to know more than that. She'd worry about the details later.

Now her only goal was to get Cole to help before he collapsed.

Which way?

As if he heard her silent question, he grabbed her hand and pulled her forward without hesitation. She went with him.

A whole hour passed before they reached the edge of the woods.

Annie couldn't believe Cole was still upright. He simply kept going, refusing to let her wedge herself into his armpit and take some of his weight. He just kept asking if she was all right.

The lights from the facilities lit up the night. Annie and Cole staggered in through the back door.

Libby was the first person Annie saw, at the end of the long hallway.

The reflexologist ran toward them. "Are you all right? What happened?"

"We need a first-aid kit and 911."

Libby was dialing her phone even as she spun around and took off running for the kit.

Cole leaned against the wall, his face pale.

He had a belt cinched around his shoulder. She hadn't seen that before. She tested it. Tight, although blood was still seeping out. The question was, how much blood had he lost before he'd gotten that belt in place?

"Sit," she told him. "Help is almost here."

Blood covered his entire side. He had to be standing through sheer will.

"I'm sorry I couldn't tell you why I was here." He held her gaze, his voice weak. "That's the way undercover ops go."

She wanted to cry. Instead, she snapped at him. "That's what you're worried about right now? You're *shot*, dammit."

Bleeding. He could die. The thought cracked her heart in half. "I forgive you. But I reserve the right to still yell at you later when you're fully recovered."

"Deal."

Annie tugged on his left arm. "Sit down."

He slid to the floor, leaving a wide smear of crimson on the white wall behind him.

Her stomach tumbled at the sight. She shook off the nausea and pressed her hand against the still-bleeding wound. She refused to pass out. Cole needed her.

People came running, Libby first, then Kate.

Libby was carrying a first-aid kit and set it on the ground next to Cole. "An ambulance is on its way."

Kate dropped onto the floor next to Cole. "Holy mocha brownies. Don't worry. I have this." She began administering first aid with the confident efficiency of a woman who knew that every second counted.

Annie removed her hand from the wound and leaned against Cole. She wouldn't look at her fingers that dripped with red. She hadn't lost any blood, but she felt as if she might pass out before Cole did.

Libby ran off again, then returned a few minutes later with blankets and wrapped them both up, careful not to get into Kate's way.

"Bullet didn't come out on the other side," Kate told them. "It's still in there."

"I can feel it." Cole rasped the words.

Under the blankets, he took Annie's hand and squeezed. He let his head drop against the wall and closed his eyes, drawing slow and measured breaths against the pain.

"What happened?" Libby couldn't hold her curiosity back any longer. "Murph is out with the police looking for Dr. Ambrose. Did Ambrose have anything to do with this?"

"Dan kidnapped me," Annie said, the words beyond surreal. "He was my stalker."

She couldn't tell them about Cole's mission, so she fell silent.

"Why? Where is he?"

"The police found an old woman in Dan's basement," Kate put in without looking up from her task. "Murph texted. She was in bad shape. She had to be taken to the hospital."

Annie's thoughts were a hopeless jumble. "She's his mother."

The two women stared at her. Kate said, "I thought—"

"He found her."

"Where is Ambrose?" Libby asked.

Cole, because his eyes were closed, didn't see the question and remained silent.

Annie closed her eyes too. "I don't know."

She just needed to breathe there for a minute. If Dan was out there in the storm, frankly, she didn't care, as long as he couldn't hurt them.

She leaned her head on Cole's shoulder, wrapped her arms around his torso, and refused to worry about what anyone might think.

The ambulance came first, then Harper Finnegan arrived while the medics were loading Cole in the back.

"Ambrose is tied to a tree, five hundred feet east of the deer blind," Cole told the detective before his eyes rolled back in his head.

The medics started an IV. They wanted Annie in the second ambulance pulling into the yard, but she wouldn't let go of Cole's hand.

Cole was no longer unconscious but still close to it. Blood loss was a bitch. It got you, no matter how tough you were.

He kept his eyes closed. He didn't want to deal with the hundred questions the medics would throw at him if they knew he was awake. He had Annie's hand. Annie was all he needed. Annie was safe. He could relax.

When the ambulance stopped at the hospital and he opened his eyes, Annie had an IV too and was wrapped in enough blankets to look like a mummy.

The back of the ambulance opened. Four men unloaded Cole's stretcher. Another tried to walk Annie away. She resisted.

Cole couldn't see their lips, but he had an idea what they were arguing about. *Family members only.*

He rumbled, "She's family."

Then she was back at his side and holding his hand again. Not for long, though. As soon as his injuries were assessed, two orderlies were pushing him into emergency surgery.

He felt the blackness close in on him before they administered anything. He was passing out again. He didn't care at this point. Annie was safe. And she was his.

Annie was dry, in a hospital gown, wrapped in a blanket, holding Cole's hand. She'd been by his side since they'd rolled him out of surgery.

She wasn't a fan of macho posturing, but she couldn't stand seeing him weak like this. She'd rather have him strutting around, going on about how SEALs were invincible. "If you die, Cole Makani Hunter, I'm going to kill you."

She ignored the chuckle from a nurse walking by the open door.

"In what kind of combat?" Cole asked in a rusty voice, his dark eyes open to a crack at long last.

She dropped her head onto his chest and said a prayer of gratitude.

"Naked wrestling?" he suggested, his chest rumbling under her forehead.

She pulled back. Something wet tracked down her face. *Ah, dammit.* Now she was crying?

She sniffed. "I told you we won't be doing anything naked together. Therapist-patient relationship."

"I told you I'm not your patient."

"Then what are you?" She wiped her eyes with the back of her hand.

This time, his voice was stronger. "I'm the man you're going to marry."

Her heart squeezed. "Are all Navy SEALs this bossy?"

"Pretty much." He offered a faint smile. "But you don't have to worry about any of the others."

She sniffed again. "You don't even know me."

"I knew everything I needed to know when I walked into your garage and saw those stupid skunks."

"Don't call my skunks stupid."

"Exactly. You're the kind of person who stands up for a skunk." He paused. Smiled. "I've been falling in love with you since you ordered me into that gas-station bathroom to wash my bloody knuckles."

Her breath caught. *I've been falling in love with you . . .* Her heart broke into a mad rhythm. "We barely know each other."

"You can get to know me during our long engagement. I'm reenrolling at Hope Hill. I'm going to get my act together."

When she smiled, he added, "Except for ecotherapy. I can't do that. I'm planning on seducing the ecotherapist at the first opportunity. I'm planning on doing things to the ecotherapist that would make Freud faint."

She felt the smile taking over her face.

"Say, do you know what that deer blind needs?" he asked. And when she didn't respond, he told her. "A good mattress."

He shifted over in the bed and opened his good arm. "Climb in."

When she didn't move, he added quietly, "I need to hold you, Annie."

Annie climbed onto the bed and lay on her side next to him, putting her head on his shoulder as his left arm came around her. She gave silent thanks for having each other to hold. They could have died tonight in the woods, in the storm.

Heat rolled off his large body. She relaxed against that warmth, tilting her head to his so he could read her lips. "I feel like I'm snuggled against a grizzly bear," she said. "Minus the fur."

He wasn't wearing anything on top except for the bandages over his right shoulder, so she had a lovely view.

"You have a chest-hair fetish?"

She didn't think she could laugh today, but she did. "Not really."

"Good. Because what you see is all you're going to get."

Was she? Was she really going to get him?

She tucked in her chin and snuggled deeper into the crook of his arm.

He pressed a kiss on the top of her head. "We are both too smart to let go of what we have between us, aren't we?"

Since he couldn't see her mouth, she simply nodded.

She stayed with him all day while he slept.

He woke as the sun was going down outside.

When a nurse came in to check his vitals and bring him food, Annie went to use the bathroom, then left to find her own meal in the cafeteria. While she was eating her soup, Kelly called to let Annie know that she was feeding the animals. She was coming to the hospital later and bringing clean clothes for both of them.

Annie thanked her, then went back upstairs. She climbed right back into bed with Cole.

"You haven't said it yet," he whispered against her lips.

"What?"

"That you love me."

"I thought snipers were patient."

"I'm a former sniper. Also, Navy SEALs want what they want, and they always get it. Very stubborn."

"I haven't noticed."

His dark gaze held her captive. "The words, Annie."

"I love you, Cole Makani Hunter."

His kiss was as thorough as a military campaign.

Saturday

When Annie woke, the hospital outside the door was buzzing with morning activity. The sun was shining through the window. The storm had moved on.

Cole was awake already. When he realized that her eyes were open, he pulled her closer and brushed a kiss over her lips.

A cart rattled in the hallway.

Annie jumped from the bed and had barely settled into the chair next to it when a nurse shuffled in. The older woman checked Cole's vitals and removed the IV, praising him for his speedy recovery.

"I want to take a shower," Cole said after the woman left. He reached for Annie. "I'm going to need your help."

He was using his I'm-a-Navy-SEAL-and-what-I-think-should-happen-will-happen voice. He was barely twenty-four hours out of surgery, and still he was as imposing as he'd ever been. How was that even possible?

But she let him pull her up.

They began by brushing their teeth together, like an old married couple. The warm intimacy of that small, insignificant act made her smile.

"You look sexy in scrubs," he said as he put his toothbrush into the glass. Then he stepped behind her and began easing up her green top.

"They're going to kick us out of here, I hope you know that."

He reached around her and locked the door. "I'm ready to get out of here anyway."

He tugged off her top. Since he only had on pants to start with, now they were even.

His gaze dropped to her chest and heated. He pressed her back against his front and lifted his left hand, watching in the mirror as he ran his thumb over one nipple first, then the other.

Her nipples tightened. The self-satisfaction on his face was something to see.

"It's from the cold," she said.

"Then let's get you under some warm water." He reached to her waist and pulled down her pants.

There was nothing for her to do but step out of them. She didn't have underwear on. The ones she'd come in with had been soaked from her midnight swim, along with the rest of her clothes.

Cole turned on the water, then chucked off his own pants. Annie just tried to keep from fainting. Because—Holy Mother of Skunks— Cole Makani Hunter was completely naked. With her. *With her!*

She stepped into the water for some breathing space, not that it worked. Because Cole was not only completely naked, he was completely hard. Everywhere.

She closed her eyes. "How is this even possible? You lost a ton of blood. Do the laws of hydraulics not apply to Navy SEALs?"

His laugh was a low rumble near her ear. "I'd say it's the miracle of IV fluids, but I'm pretty sure it's the miracle of Annie Murray."

His warm lips brushed over hers just as she was opening her eyes. She closed them again on a helpless groan. No feeling on earth compared to Cole kissing her, the hot steam rising around them.

He kept a careful couple of inches between them, but she stepped forward, into his arms. One strong arm went around her, naked skin pressed against naked skin, soft parts pressed against parts extremely firm. Hard. Steel.

"We can't," she groaned against his lips.

"I could."

"I won't be responsible for a relapse."

He kissed her again and again, owning her mouth. He grew harder, if possible. When he broke away, it was on a strangled groan, as if he was stopping himself at the last second.

His voice was hoarse, his gaze all consuming, as he said the single word. "Turn."

She obeyed.

His hand left her for only a few seconds before returning to the middle of her back, soapy and slippery. He gently scrubbed her back, her bottom, her legs, the outside on the way down, the inside on the way up. Then he slid his hand to the front of her body.

He got lost on her breasts for a while. He pressed himself against her back, his erection pressing against her. "Lean back against me, and loop your arms around my neck."

She did, and he moved his head over her shoulder to better see what he was doing.

He tortured her breasts until her knees trembled, then his hand slid down her belly and his palm covered her sex. His breathing became more ragged, rasping in her ear.

"Annie?"

She tilted her head back so he could read her lips. "Yes."

His mouth descended on hers at the same time as his fingers slipped inside her.

He . . .

He . . .

She pulled away from the kiss and bit her lip, hard, because she didn't think hospital rooms were soundproof enough to handle the sounds she needed to make.

Then she came in a warm rush of tingling sensation, a melting warmth of pleasure and well-being that didn't want to stop.

Cole kissed her again, and he kept kissing her long after her orgasm had faded.

He shut off the water and dried her while she stood there, stunned and limp. That last part was pretty much the opposite of Cole. But he didn't push for more. He toweled himself off too—his shoulder dressings miraculously still dry—then he grabbed two clean hospital gowns from the bench next to the shower.

"Let's go back to bed." He pressed a kiss to the middle of her forehead.

She was still barely conscious, the only thought in her head: *What just happened?*

Chapter Twenty-Eight

Eight months later

ANNIE WAS WATCHING THE LLAMAS IN THE EAST PADDOCK WHILE THE PONIES and Esmeralda chased one another in the west field. Esmeralda had matured, given up butt nipping, and become the ponies' nanny over the past couple of weeks.

Dorothy lay on her side in the sun, enormous. She was going to have her piglets any day now—the result of a brief affair with another rescue pig that had only stayed for three days.

Annie sat on the deck with a glass of lemonade as Cole rounded the corner of the farmhouse. When he wasn't working on his business, providing security consulting for places that worked with vets, he was helping out with the animal sanctuary.

Since the sanctuary was growing by the day—they were big enough to take horses now—Annie had withdrawn her request to go full-time at Hope Hill. She had plenty to do right around the house.

"I see nobody's here yet." Cole walked over and kissed her breathless.

She floated on a sea of joy and bliss. "Kelly's running late."

"Want me to drive around and get your grandfather?" He nibbled her bottom lip.

She ran her fingers through his short, dark hair, which now covered the barbed-wire tattoos on the sides of his head. "Kelly and David have the new bed that tilts up. They have to go there anyway to drop it off. They'll bring Gramps over."

Switching houses had been Gramps's idea. He couldn't get up the stairs anymore. When Annie finally renovated her little rancher, she updated it with a wheelchair ramp, wide doorways, a handicap shower, and level floors throughout. In exchange, Gramps donated the farmhouse and land to her animal sanctuary, with Kelly's enthusiastic approval.

Both renovations had been done live, on local TV, with Kelly as the show host. Her business was booming.

Cole pressed one last kiss on Annie's lips, then looked over at the table, set for six. "What can I do to help?"

His right arm was steadily improving. She'd talked him into going back to acupuncture, and that made a difference, as nothing else had. He saw an old Chinese woman in West Chester. He refused to go to Milo at Hope Hill, and he wouldn't tell Annie why.

"Fire up the grill." She hooked her arms around his neck. They had time for one more peck. "So are you going to reveal your secret sauce recipe?"

"Not even under bloody torture."

"Fine. Then I'm not going to tell you about my secret sauce."

A low growl escaped his throat as he pulled her onto his lap. "I know all about your secret sauce." He moved her legs until she straddled him, and then he pulled her against his massive, hard body—as much as her growing belly allowed. "Your secret sauce is mine, all mine. And don't you forget it. I'm planning a leisurely sampling later."

Heat spread through her body. "They probably won't be here for another twenty minutes," she said, because she was weak.

Cole nibbled his way down her neck. "You can't rush anything that has to do with secret sauce."

Damn Navy SEAL self-control and mastery over one's body and discipline and all that crap. She wriggled against him, rubbing her center against the hardness between his legs. She might have succeeded in swaying him, but the sound of a truck in the driveway interrupted them.

She slid off Cole's lap and patted down her hair. "I guess they're not as late as Kelly thought they would be."

Cole adjusted himself. "I'll go in and grab the burgers and the ribs."

She smirked. "You're going in to stand in front of the fridge."

"That too." He fixed her with a pointed look. "Do not say *secret sauce* while they're here or I'm going to pop up all over again. The word is off-limits until we're alone."

"You're not above me in the chain of command."

"But I can wrestle you into submission."

Before she could argue, he disappeared into the house. Not a moment too soon.

Their guests were coming around the corner of the house, Kelly balancing Gramps's birthday cake.

David—Kelly's brand-new husband and Broslin's star TV producer—carried two bottles of wine: one red, one white. Beyond them, Tyler, David's six-year-old, walked in, holding Gramps's hand.

Tyler had probably been told to secretly help Gramps navigate the uneven path. While Gramps had probably been told he was keeping track of Tyler. The two were generally inseparable.

The grumpy old man had accepted Tyler from the second Kelly had brought David and his son for dinner that first time. And the kid dove into the family as if into a pool. As if all his short life, he'd been dying to be in all that water, dying to be part of a family.

His mom had died when he was two. All Tyler remembered was a series of babysitters. He wanted family with an endearing greediness that melted everybody's heart every time he walked through the door.

Tyler escorted Gramps to the nearest chair at the edge of the large patio. Gramps glanced toward the table on the other end, then back at Tyler. "Go grab me a cookie."

The kid cast a longing look at the bakery box. "Kelly said no cookies before dinner."

The old man harrumphed. "If I want a cookie, I'll have a cookie, boy. Don't make me put on my butt-kicking boots."

Tyler's eyes went wide, his gaze snapping to his father. "Gramps said butt-kicking boots."

David shook his head, but he was clearly fighting a smile. Which his son didn't miss. Tyler giggled.

"Gramps." Kelly tried to look disapproving, but failed, so she went for distracting Tyler. "Hey, let's go inside and wash hands."

Tyler wasn't ready to be distracted. "Can I see your butt-kicking boots? What color are they?"

Annie shook her head. Now would probably be a good time to interfere. "We have the baby's room ready, Tyler. Want to go and see?"

They had the guest room ready too. Cole's mom was coming up from Chicago to help, and she was going to stay through the baby's birth.

Annie's mother was gone. Annie had contacted her father and told him about the baby, leaving it up to him if he wanted contact with his grandchild once the baby was born. He didn't.

You win some; you lose some.

Annie was happy with her winnings.

Tyler ran to Annie and threw his arms around her growing belly. "I can't wait to meet my new brother."

"He'll be your cousin, honey," Kelly said, and exchanged a look of pure love with David, who put his arms around her from behind. "Talking about your brother or sister . . ."

Kelly flashed a smile and pressed her palm to her belly.

Wait a minute . . .

"When did you find out?" Annie jumped up. OK, she intended to jump. Point was, eventually she made it to her feet. "I'm so happy for you."

Then they were hugging and crying—all happy tears. Ecstatic.

"What are we having a feminine drama fest over now?" Cole came from the house with a tray of ribs.

"Kelly is going to have a baby." Annie's eyes were leaking.

"Another boy? A few more and we're going to have a decent team to play football in the backyard after Thanksgiving dinner."

He shook Tyler's hand first, then David's, then Gramps's, then finally threw his arms around Kelly and Annie, who were still embracing.

Annie elbowed him in the side. "We're both going to have girls just to spite you."

Cole pulled her back and turned her in his arms. "Then David and I will keep going until we get a full football team. We'll be the Testosterone . . ." He paused and glanced at Tyler. "What else starts with a T?"

"Taters!"

Gramps snorted. Kelly was shaking her head.

Cole never gave it another thought. "Good job, buddy." He ruffled Tyler's flyaway brown hair. "We'll be the Testosterone Taters."

"Can I be the captain?" Tyler wanted to know immediately. "I want to be the captain of the Toasted Taters!"

Cole winked at him. "That's a given."

With a big smacking kiss on Annie's cheek, he let her go and went to put the ribs on the grill.

David chased Tyler and demanded that at the very least, they arm-wrestle for the captain position.

Annie caught Kelly's eyes. Kelly had tears too.

"I'm just stupid happy," Kelly said. "You know what I mean?"

Annie glanced at Cole. "I think I might."

"I think the Murray Love Curse is officially broken."

"I'll drink to that. When we can drink."

Kelly followed her gaze and lowered her voice. "I love David to pieces, but I think Navy SEALs in aprons should be a thing. A new trend."

Annie sighed, her heart more full of love and gratitude than she could ever have imagined. "At the very least, there should be a calendar."

"Talking about printed materials." Kelly pulled a flyer from her purse and handed it to Annie.

Concert promo for Hershey Park. "Thanks, but I think I'm out of the rock-concert scene until after the baby comes." She'd never been into the rock-concert/groupie thing to start with.

"Look at the guy in the middle."

She did. Then she choked. *Xane?*

"Xane is in Men on the Moon?" She'd heard the band on the radio, but she hadn't really paid attention to them in particular, couldn't have named any of the members if someone had bet her solar panels for her roof.

She read the flyer. "They're the main act. They have a cover band."

"They're supposed to be the next big thing."

"Oh my God." Annie collapsed into a chair next to Kelly.

"Are you OK?" Kelly sat with her and took her hand. "Is it the baby?"

"It's a hundred grand."

"The what now?"

"You know my website for the animal rescue? I have a tip jar on it. People can donate a dollar or two. When I started putting up regular pictures and stories, people started asking me if they could help. Anyway, I had a hundred-thousand-dollar donation this morning from Moon Productions. I figured someone got a couple of zeros wrong. Or a kid signed in with her parents' account or something. I was going to contact them tonight to figure out how I could send the money back."

Kelly's eyes were comically wide. "You think it's Xane?"

"He said he'd pay me back when he made it big."

Kelly squeezed Annie's hand. "If I wasn't such a lady, I'd say *holy shit*."

Cole called over, "What is it?"

Annie told him.

He frowned. "I don't like another guy giving my wife money."

"It's for the animals."

"We're doing fine by the animals. If Mr. Rock Star thinks he's going to come around—"

"Are those ribs almost done?" Annie pushed to her feet. She was keeping the money. Cole needed distracting. "I think I'll go and see if I can find more of my *secret sauce* in the pantry."

Cole's gaze heated. He put the spatula down. "I'd better come with you, sweetheart. I think it's on the top shelf."

His look promised he'd kiss her senseless.

She lost her breath.

"Are you sure you're OK?" Kelly asked behind her.

"I just need a cold glass of water."

Then Cole was next to her, his arm around her waist as he steered her toward the sliding glass doors. "No worries. I'll make sure she gets what she needs."

When Annie glanced back, Kelly was fanning herself with her hand and grinning her full endorsement.

Cole took Annie into his arms and twirled her into the pantry. She laughed.

He couldn't hear the sound, but he could see the way her eyes crinkled, the way her lush mouth turned up at the corners, the way everything about her softened. *When I'm in your arms, I'm home,* her body said.

If he could hear, he might never have noticed all that. He was beginning to learn the advantages of always keeping his eyes open.

Some things might have been taken away from him, but he'd definitely received a tremendous number of blessings.

He didn't feel deaf. Or crippled. He just was. Was a pine tree better than an oak? Who could tell? Who cared?

Ambrose was in prison. He'd confessed to the stalking, the dead animals, even Trevor's and Mitch's murders, as well as the transfer of military information. The other end of his operation in Yemen had been rolled up.

He'd gone to grad school in England. Some Yemeni bigwig's son had been his roommate. They'd been friends. And when the guy had turned radical and reached out, offering a fortune, Ambrose hadn't resisted. He wanted enough money to never have to work again. He wanted to stay home to take care of his mother.

Lilly Ambrose had passed on the day after her son's arrest. According to Murph, Ambrose was inconsolable. The psychiatrist wasn't going to see the outside of a prison cell ever again.

Hope Hill had survived the scandal—better than survived it. The media attention focused not just on Ambrose but also on the amazing results Hope Hill was producing with alternative therapies. They gained a couple of new donors, along with a growing reputation for helping vets.

They were going to add another building.

Joey was cleared of the grand theft auto charges and had joined the navy.

Cole had Annie.

All was well with the world.

"I love you," he said against her lips.

"I love you," she said back.

He didn't hear it with his ears.

He heard it with his heart.

Acknowledgments

With my most heartfelt gratitude to Diane Flindt for her brilliant insights, Sarah Jordan for making this book (and many others) possible, and the wonderful team at Montlake, including Sarah Engel and Jill Kramer, and especially my editors: Alison Dasho and Selina McLemore. Thank you!

About the Author

Photo © 2011 Tunde Tucsek

Dana Marton is the *New York Times* best-selling author of the Agents Under Fire series, the Hardstorm Saga, and the Broslin Creek novels. She is the winner of the Daphne du Maurier Award for Excellence in Mystery/Suspense, the Readers' Choice Award, and the RITA Award. For more information about Marton and her work, please visit her at www.danamarton.com or on Facebook at www.facebook.com/danamarton.